THE
BEAUTIFUL DEAD

BELINDA BAUER

ISIS
LARGE
PRINT

First published in Great Britain 2016
by
Bantam Press
an imprint of Transworld Publishers

First Isis Edition
published 2017
by arrangement with
Transworld Publishers
Penguin Random House

The moral right of the author has been asserted

This book is a work of fiction and any resemblance to actual persons, living or dead, is purely coincidental.

A catalogue record for this book is available from the British Library.

ISBN 978–1–78541–452–7 (hb)
ISBN 978–1–78541–458–9 (pb)

Published by
F. A. Thorpe (Publishing)
Anstey, Leicestershire

Set by Words & Graphics Ltd.
Anstey, Leicestershire
Printed and bound in Great Britain by
T. J. International Ltd., Padstow, Cornwall

This book is printed on acid-free paper

THE BEAUTIFUL DEAD

Crime reporter Eve Singer's career is in a slump when a spate of bizarre murders, each carefully orchestrated and advertised like performance art, occurs in her territory. Covering these very public crimes revives her byline; and when the killer contacts her himself, she is suddenly on the inside of the biggest murder investigation of the decade. Eve welcomes the chance to tantalize her ghoulish audience with the news from every gory scene. But as the killer becomes increasingly obsessed with her, she realizes there's a thin line between inside information and becoming an accomplice to murder — possibly her own . . .

SPECIAL MESSAGE TO READERS

THE ULVERSCROFT FOUNDATION
(registered UK charity number 264873)

was established in 1972 to provide funds for research, diagnosis and treatment of eye diseases. Examples of major projects funded by the Ulverscroft Foundation are:-

- The Children's Eye Unit at Moorfields Eye Hospital, London
- The Ulverscroft Children's Eye Unit at Great Ormond Street Hospital for Sick Children
- Funding research into eye diseases and treatment at the Department of Ophthalmology, University of Leicester
- The Ulverscroft Vision Research Group, Institute of Child Health
- Twin operating theatres at the Western Ophthalmic Hospital, London
- The Chair of Ophthalmology at the Royal Australian College of Ophthalmologists

You can help further the work of the Foundation by making a donation or leaving a legacy. Every contribution is gratefully received. If you would like to help support the Foundation or require further information, please contact:

THE ULVERSCROFT FOUNDATION
The Green, Bradgate Road, Anstey
Leicester LE7 7FU, England
Tel: (0116) 236 4325

website: www.foundation.ulverscroft.com

Thanks to the Cardiff Poker Tour for all
the laughs and free money . . .

Look at the beauty that only death can bring.

See Medusa's raft, where the waxen corpses recline careless on the splintered timbers, fists unclenched and eyes closed on the horrors of the world. At peace at last, their faces are serene, while those of the luckless survivors twist in shipwrecked shock.

See Death claim his Maiden, his flesh still rotting on his bones. See her turn her head away in modest horror — while one sly arm embraces him . . .

See the two martyrs in the arena as the snarling tiger reaches them. They, too, are beautiful. Calm — even as the first claw punctures the flesh. Their hands are linked in the certain knowledge that the agony of existence will pass and that they will be together on the other side . . .

A great artist knows how to lead us uncomplaining out of this life and into the next. The Old Masters did it with china-white and elegant hands, with lashes closed on pale cheeks — with stoic mourners and tragic heroes.

Who wouldn't want to be remembered thus? Who wouldn't relish everlasting life in a world that's kinder than this one? Who wouldn't want to be so beautiful?

Be honest, dear reader.

Who wouldn't rather be dead?

PART ONE

CHAPTER
ONE

1 December

Layla Martin's shoes were killing her.

She had bought them on Thursday even though they rubbed her little toes.

A hundred and thirty pounds. A third of her weekly wage.

She'd worn them on Thursday night and again on Friday night while making cheese on toast for tea. And she had worn them to work on a Saturday even though she knew she'd be the only person on the eighth floor — quite possibly in the whole building. She'd wanted to break them in for Monday, when she was planning to walk past the glass-walled office of the new accounts manager at least twenty times, because he had a sports car and a great bum, and the ridiculously high heels made her calves look fabulous.

But now it was those very same heels that she was running in.

Running for her life, she had to assume.

And, as the machine-gun clatter of her brand-new heels rang through the empty stairwell, any conscious-ness Layla Martin could spare from the terror of being chased by a madman was consumed by the desperate wish that she'd come to work in her usual weekend garb of jeans, jumper and Reeboks.

Because right here, right now, her shoes might mean the difference between life and death . . .

The man had appeared across the wide open-plan office. She had looked up from the ToppFlyte file and seen him standing at the lift. It had given her a little jolt of surprise and fear. Silly, really — in broad daylight in the middle of London. But she was alone on the eighth floor, and that made all the difference.

Still, he was an ordinary-looking man. Not weird. A delivery guy, most likely — or lost.

"Hi," she'd said. "Can I help you?"

"I am a friend," he'd said. "I am not fierce."

She'd frowned. "Say again?"

By way of an answer, the ordinary man had put his gloved hand inside his coat and drawn out a knife.

Layla Martin had never been in danger before, but she'd hesitated for only a second before leaping to her feet, grabbing her bag and running.

Because he'd been blocking her way to the lift, she'd headed for the stairs . . .

Layla didn't scream. The thought of the sound bouncing endlessly up and down the stairwell only frightened her more — and she was trying not to panic, trying to *think*. She ran as fast as she dared in those *bloody shoes*, clutching the black-plastic-covered handrail in case she lost her footing, watching the stairs

4

blur underfoot with eyes that bulged in concentration, desperate not to fall, her long blonde hair swinging into her mouth, her bag bumping her ribs.

There would be someone on the fourth floor. She had once come halfway up in the lift with a woman who'd bitched about working at weekends.

Layla stopped above the fourth-floor landing, panting, gasping. She forced herself to be quiet so she could listen.

She heard nothing. No one.

Maybe he wasn't coming after her. Maybe he'd never planned to. Maybe he hadn't even had a knife.

He had though . . .

She started downstairs again — slowly this time — her knees like jelly and her toes on fire.

She pulled open the fire-escape door marked with a giant 4 and took a tentative step on to the carpet.

"Hello!"

The lift door slid open. The man was inside. Calm and still, and with the knife — it *was* a knife! — held casually by his side.

He smiled.

Layla gave a shriek of shock, fear and disbelief. She swung her bag at his head, hitting him a glancing blow, showering him with assorted bag-junk, seeing him flinch and duck. Then she turned back into the stairwell and ran downstairs again.

At the next landing she kicked off her heels and left them there.

This was better.

Layla was not that fit, but she was young and slim and — without the killer heels — she was nimble. She started to get into a rhythm. She barely touched the stairs now, leaping from five or six treads up on to each landing, grabbing the rail as it turned, using it to slingshot around the blind concrete corners. Somewhere behind her she heard a door slam shut. But it was a long way back.

He wasn't catching her. *He wasn't catching her.* She was going to make it!

The sobs that had choked her became hysterical glee in her throat. Her stockinged feet skidded and slid but she *used* that. She worked it, baby! She had it all under control.

Run jump grab skid turn . . . Run jump grab skid turn . . .

It was a helter-skelter without the mats, but with added terror. But that was *good*, because it was all going to be OK in the end.

With manic laughter bubbling inside her, Layla burst through the door marked G and into the vast, bright lobby with its shiny polished floor. She turned towards the exit so fast that she skidded over on to her right side with a bang, but was on her feet again before the fall even registered.

The door was right there.

Escape was in sight. More than in sight . . .

Escape was panoramic.

Coldharbour was a new building and the lobby was a sleek and shiny glass-walled, marble-floored expanse that still smelled of stone dust, and not yet of people.

The front wall was entirely glass — smoked grey and impenetrable from outside; but from inside Layla could see that, just thirty yards away, Oxford Street was teeming with Christmas shoppers beating a path through dirty snow.

She ran to the door, fumbling under her armpit and into her bag, her fingers spreading panic among the random objects, clutching and sifting with unaccustomed urgency.

The keys. The *keys!*

At weekends they had to let themselves in and keep the doors locked. Something about cutting security costs. The cheap bastards. She'd like to see what they thought about cutting costs after *this* little episode . . .

A door clicked behind her and she turned and saw the man standing at the entrance to the stairwell.

Not coming for her, not running; just standing, watching her escape.

She cackled at him like a witch.

"*FUCK* you!" she shrilled. "Fuck *YOU!*"

She turned back to the door. Mentally she was already outside. Already safe.

Where were the *keys?*

Then she heard them — that wonderful chink of familiar metal — and for a glorious split second Layla was *on* Oxford Street in all its slushy glory. She was stepping out on to the crowded pavement alongside that bottle-blonde woman and her Goth daughter. She was brushing past that young man with the cheap bouquet, who had his back to the glass wall and who was looking up and down the road, waiting for someone special. She could already feel the wet city snowflakes melting on her hot cheeks . . .

And then she realized that her keys were jangling *behind* her.

With one clutching hand still in her bag, Layla looked around slowly.

The man had her keys.

Maybe they'd hit him in the head when she'd swung her bag; maybe she'd never put them *in* her bag and he'd picked them up off her desk.

It didn't matter how he had them.

He had them.

And she didn't.

He gave a half-smile and tossed the keys a few inches into the air again. They settled in his palm with a sound like money. From here Layla could see the key ring that her flatmate, Dougie, had bought her at the petrol station they used on the Old Kent Road. Lisa Simpson nestled snugly between the black-leather fingers of the man with the knife.

He had driven her down here.

Layla realized that now. Now that it was too late.

He could have killed her on the eighth floor; he could have killed her on the fourth. He could probably have caught her in the stairwell and killed her there. But instead he'd herded her to this very place — like a dumb sheep on that TV show with farmers and collies.

She could see it in his forgettable face: he had her right where he wanted her. Right here in this bright open space with people passing by.

"Be of good cheer," he said. "I am not fierce." And although he did not speak loudly, his voice swelled to fill the marble lobby so that it came at her gently from all sides.

The man put her keys in his pocket and started to walk towards her, almost casually, the hand with the knife in it swinging gently by his side and his murmur caressing her like a breeze.

"I do not come to punish."

She turned and beat the door with her fists. The building was new; nothing rattled, nothing budged, and the heartless glass swallowed the sound smoothly and burped nothing back.

Layla took the deepest breath since her very first, twenty-four years earlier, and screamed.

Nothing came out but a strangled squeak that scurried about the echoing lobby like a silly white mouse. She tried again, but her throat was so tight that air could barely get through in either direction.

Suddenly drowning in fear, Layla pressed her back against the cold glass — an infinite half-inch from where people were safe — and waited for the man to reach her.

He did.

"Softly shall you sleep in my arms," he murmured kindly.

Right up until the very last second, Layla Martin didn't believe that she would — or could — be murdered. She knew that *something* would save her.

It didn't.

The knife had gone in; the blood had come out, warming the killer's hands with the joy of creation.

At first the girl had flip-flopped like a fish on the floor. But once she'd understood, she'd calmed down, and died as she should.

Beautifully.

Searching his face with her grateful eyes until they'd faded to ash.

And as she had emptied, so he had filled up.

For the first time in a long time, his heart had started to beat, and he had cried with relief.

Thank you, he'd sobbed against her clotted ear. *Thank you.*

And knew he would do this again.

Wanted to. *Needed* to.

Looked forward to it.

CHAPTER
TWO

Eve Singer threw up her breakfast into the shiny white toilet.

Toast and Marmite.

She knelt on the glittery black floor and rested her cheek against the bowl — her straight dark hair bunched in her fist at the nape of her neck — waiting to see if she was going to throw up last night's Chinese takeaway too. While her stomach thought about it, Eve stared dully at the words under the rim: Armitage Shanks.

Quality.

She had thrown up into many toilet bowls since starting work at iWitness News and thought of Armitage Shanks as an old friend — a comforter who supported her head with a cool porcelain palm while she retched and groaned. There was Mrs Twyfords and Dr Imperial too, and any number of lesser manufacturers whose names she'd registered vaguely over the years, but she always felt most at home vomiting into a Shanks bowl.

Being a TV crime reporter was thrilling, but the sight of blood made Eve sick. And after three years of gory murder scenes she'd had plenty of opportunities to perfect her emetic technique.

Today's was a belter.

She hadn't been able to see a thing from Oxford Street because of the one-way glass, so after doing her piece to camera she had sneaked in through a side door manned by a newbie copper, who had been no match for her combination of threats and wheedling — a technique her cameraman, Joe Ward, called "threedling".

The cop had let her in, and Eve almost wished he hadn't.

The body had been removed, but the blood alone had been enough.

Before her stomach had twisted over on itself, Eve had registered the sheer shocking *quantity* of it. Splatters up the glass walls, and a wide, calm, maroon lake, as if someone had gripped the young woman in giant hands and squeezed her like toothpaste until she was empty. And from one edge, a trail of red footprints, where the killer had climbed out of the lake on to dry marble land and walked out of the front door.

Eve dry-heaved into the bowl again at the memory and then laid her forehead on the rim, gasping and trying to think about starlight and ponies. That wasn't easy when she worked on what everybody but Human Resources called "the meat beat". An endless round of bodies, black bags and bloodstains.

She was twenty-nine years old, but on days like this she felt forty. Already she had an ulcer that flared at moments of tension. Probably an ulcer. She hoped it was an ulcer, because she didn't have the time to let a doctor find out for sure.

"You OK?"

A man's voice outside the door.

Eve lifted her head only long enough and high enough to give her the strength to sound pissed off.

"Do I *sound* OK?"

She laid her face down again and felt the cold sweat drying on the back of her neck.

Bloody Guy Smith.

She hated people knowing she was squeamish. You had to be tough in this business. If you weren't tough you were picked off and brought down like a wounded wildebeest.

Especially if you were a wounded female wildebeest.

Eve spat and grimaced into the porcelain bowl. Her stomach had apparently decided to call it quits, so she got slowly to her feet and flushed, then opened the cubicle door.

Guy Smith from News 24/7 was checking his eyebrows in a mirror ringed by showbizzy light bulbs.

Eve rinsed her mouth and washed her face, then pulled a paper towel from the dispenser.

"Sick, eh?" said Guy.

Eve gave her reflection a cursory glance, then said sharply, "Dodgy curry last night, that's all."

He grinned slyly and jerked his thumb at the door. "No. I mean, whoever did this. Sick."

Eve eyed him suspiciously. She didn't trust Guy Smith any further than she could throw him. He was as vain as a teenage girl and lied like one too. Plus he routinely spoke to her breasts, as if tits were the windows to the soul. She balled up the used towel and tossed it into the bin.

"What are you doing in here, Guy?"

He shrugged. "Free world, last time I looked."

"This is the Ladies, you know."

Guy licked his thumb and pushed an errant brow back into place. "Are you always this tetchy?"

"Yes."

She brushed down the knees of her good black slacks and walked out, hoping to leave him behind.

But Guy followed her through the rear of the vast lobby, peopled by police and forensic teams. It was late now, and the Oxford Street Christmas lights glittered beyond the windowed walls.

Two policemen stood deep in conversation, reflected in the dark-red puddle where the victim had bled out. One of them was Detective Superintendent Huw Rees. He had no love for reporters, so they stayed close to the wall and left in practised silence.

Once outside, Guy walked on, but Eve stopped to smile at the young officer who'd let her in. "Thanks," she said. "I owe you a drink." She dug about in her bag. "I'm Eve," she said, although he probably knew that already. "Here's my card."

It was a good card. She had designed it herself. Black, with white type and a single blood spatter in one corner.

EVE SINGER
iWITNESS NEWS
CRIME CORRESPONDENT

"Thanks," he said.

"My mobile number's on the back," Eve pointed out. "So keep it just in case you ever come across anything interesting."

"OK," he said enthusiastically. "I will."

She knew he would. They always did. They always called her and she always took them for a drink to let them know they were all on the same side in the war on crime — and that was usually enough to make her the first civilian they called when something bloody happened. She couldn't have done her job without this network of insiders she cultivated. Police and paramedics and firemen and coroners' officers and court ushers. She thought of them as her safety net for all those times when she needed a free pass, a blind eye, a nod and a wink. Those times when she needed an *edge*. Last Christmas she'd bought an ambulance driver named Mandy Flynn a bottle of pink champagne, and today Mandy had told her the dead girl's name. By tonight, iWitness News would have a photo of Layla Martin, while News 24/7 would still be calling her "a twenty-four-year-old woman", and Eve's job would be safe.

For another few days, at least.

Mentally, Eve flipped through the next few hours. What needed to be done, who needed to be called. Mrs Solomon was always first on the list. Eve wouldn't be home before midnight and that meant paying the sitter double time.

Couldn't be helped. Murder was murder.

Guy Smith fell into step beside her. "Do we know who she is yet?" he asked, then corrected himself. "*Was*."

15

Eve only shrugged. For her to succeed, Guy Smith must fail. It wasn't her nature, but it was the way her world worked, and they all understood.

It was five thirty and already dark, and the Christmas lights that spanned Oxford Street made everything look like a film set. A carefully lit thriller, with crowds of curious shoppers and office-party drinkers craning for a glimpse of something they didn't really want to see.

"Want to share a cab?" said Guy, waving his arm. "My bloody monkey's buggered off."

He meant that his cameraman had left without him. Joe had left too, but that was fine. Eve always did her report *before* throwing up.

"I'm not going your way," she said. It was true. She wanted to go back to the office to recut another Layla Martin package so it looked fresh for the breakfast bulletins.

"Well, maybe I'm going yours," he said with a suggestive wink.

Eve wasn't flattered. Guy Smith's flirting was indiscriminate. She wasn't even his type. She'd seen him with his type at last year's NTS awards — a giggling teenager who had left the after-party falling-down drunk and carrying her shoes.

A black cab stopped and Guy held open the door invitingly.

"Night," she said, and walked away under the lights of the Christmas-card street.

CHAPTER
THREE

The twenty-minute walk home from Osterley station led Eve down quiet streets hemmed by middle-class, semi-detached houses. It was the kind of place where the residents banded together to save their old red phone box but never went into each other's homes. The pavements had been cleared of snow and salted. The front windows of the houses were framed by blinking fairy lights, and there were pinecone wreaths on the doors and signs on the gates that demanded "Santa Stop Here!" At Easter there'd be bunnies and eggs; at Halloween, pumpkins.

Half an hour on the Tube and she was in Narnia.

Except for one thing. Every two minutes between dawn and eleven p.m. the Isleworth sky was ripped apart by the deafening roar of an airliner coming in to land at Heathrow — so low and so slow that Eve could see the tread on the landing-gear tyres. Between each plane, the silence healed itself so completely that the next flight was always a fresh shock to the senses. People who bought homes here got used to it fast, or moved on. Those who stayed learned to live to a rolling rhythm, like sailors at sea. They slept soundly through every shuddering fly-by, but would wake for a snuffling baby. They spoke in casual two-minute loops, not bothering to raise their voices to shout over the noise, but stopping mid-sentence, then picking up where they'd left off with perfect timing, or completing through mime and smiles. They no longer noticed the jumbo jets sailing calmly over their rooftops, barely higher than the trees and with their wings spanning three streets. If the planes had all fallen out of the sky miles short of their destination, the residents of Isleworth and Hounslow would have sensed that something fundamental was missing from their world — although it would probably have taken them a little while to identify just what that might be.

But the Layla Martin murder had sucked up the rest of a long day, and now it was well after the Heathrow cut-off.

Without the planes passing overhead it was eerily quiet. Eve found it a little disconcerting.

Unnerving.

Her ears, grown used to abuse in short, sharp bursts, twitched nervously in the silence.

Which is why she heard the footsteps from a long way off.

They were behind her, but not close, so she didn't turn to see who was there. She was less than five minutes from home. She'd made this walk a thousand times. This was *her* street; these were *her* neighbours; not far up ahead would be *her* street lamp, *her* red phone box.

Eve felt safe.

Ish.

She picked up her pace a bit, telling herself it was only because she wanted to be home and warm and out of the bitter night. That it was only the recent proximity of violent death that was making her jumpy.

The footsteps behind her speeded up too.

Louder. Grittier.

Closer.

Much closer.

Too close for Eve to turn and look at the man (it *had* to be a man; it was *always* a man) without appearing to be afraid. She didn't know why she didn't want to look as nervous as she felt, but she didn't. She wanted to seem as confident as she would if it were one o'clock in the afternoon, with traffic passing and young mums with buggies making their way to school to pick up their children ... Not one in the morning, with everyone asleep and the street lamps casting strange shadows between the parked cars and behind the trees.

She speeded up a bit more.

And so did he.

Eve's heart bobbed at the base of her throat.

If the man meant no harm then he wouldn't do this, surely? Wouldn't follow so closely behind a lone woman in the early hours unless he wanted to scare her, at the very least. Nobody could be that stupid, could they? That unaware.

He knew what he was doing.

A hundred yards away, illuminated by a street lamp, Eve could see her hedge. Unkempt, it bulged between its neat neighbours.

She should get an electric trimmer. Or a *man* with an electric trimmer.

She fixated on the rough privet. Mentally *reached* for it as her pounding heart swelled into her throat and her head.

The footsteps were right behind her. He was closer than even a fool would be. Close enough to reach out and clutch the trailing ends of her woollen scarf and pull her backwards off her feet . . .

Close enough to kill her.

She wasn't going to make it!

In a horrible split second, the last shred of Eve's rational mind worked out the angles and the distances and told her she wasn't going to reach her hedge, her gate, her home, her *future*.

She almost cried out with the terror of that certainty.

But instead she turned to face her killer.

"Excuse me," she said.

The man stopped dead — otherwise they would have bumped. He wore a black jacket over a hoodie and a dark scarf. The scarf was wrapped around the lower half of his face, while the hood cast a shadow across his eyes.

"Can I ask you a favour?" said Eve.

She hadn't even known she was going to speak. Yet here were words! Coming out of her mouth! She was shocked by how calm they sounded. Inside she vibrated with fear, but her voice didn't waver, didn't crack. It was an afternoon voice, filled with passing mums and broad daylight.

Somehow her mouth even smiled.

20

"There are so many weirdos about . . ." she said.

The words hung there in the cold night air.

A normal person would say something. Would smile or nod and agree with her: yes, there *were* so many weirdos . . .

This man said nothing.

It made Eve's brain feel like lead, but her mouth was still thinking.

"So," it went on, "would you mind walking me home?"

The man flinched. And the light of the street lamp caught a glimmer in his eyes.

"It's only just up the road," she hurried on, "and I'd feel so much safer if I had you with me." She didn't know where she'd got this stupid idea, but it was out there now and she couldn't take it back.

For a moment the man seemed to sway — first backward, and then forward — as if he might run away.

Or launch an attack.

Then he spoke, low and muffled by his scarf. "OK," he said.

"Thank you," said Eve.

Every fibre in her body was screaming at her to kick him in the balls and *run* . . . But instead she turned sideways and inclined her head a little to invite him to fall into step beside her.

And, after a moment's hesitation, he did.

They walked together in silence. Past her phone box, to her street lamp, to her unruly hedge, and — finally — to her little wooden gate. As if by magic.

Eve opened the gate and slipped inside and pivoted to close it, all in one rapid movement.

She clicked the latch shut and turned to face him, breathless with fear.

He was just . . . *there*. Not moving at all.

"Thank you," she said. "You're very kind."

He hesitated. And then he gave a small nod and said, "Yes."

"Good night then," she said.

He said nothing.

"Happy Christmas," she said.

He said nothing.

Eve took a deep breath and forced herself to turn her back on the man like a normal, un-scared person.

Her skin crawled as she hurried up the path to the aeroplane roar of her own fear, and she made a fist around the keys in her pocket — the Yale protruding from between her first two knuckles, ready to puncture and rip.

She heard the gate squeal, sensed him barge through it, braced for the shove and the fall to the concrete path. She could already feel the crack of her forehead on the ground, the weight of a killer on her back, the smell of the hard earth and cold weeds under her cheek . . .

She spun, key fixed in her fist.

Terrified and murderous.

The man was gone.

CHAPTER
FOUR

Eve slid into the house and turned and pressed herself against the front door like a gecko, as if the key and the deadbolt were not enough to keep it closed. Her breath came in short, shaky bursts against the wood, and she couldn't feel her legs.

From the front room came the sound of the television. Goofy music that encouraged a sitcom laugh.

For a long minute she just listened to her heart bumping in her chest. Then, slowly, she pushed herself away from the door. She was home. She was safe.

And *there* were her legs . . .

Now that it was over, she felt pretty silly.

She giggled.

That poor man! She must have scared the shit out of him, turning on him and demanding that he walk her home! No wonder he'd taken off so fast. She was a crazy person!

Eve giggled again — still shaky, but recovering.

She took off her scarf, gloves and coat, while the terror dissipated slowly into the recesses of her being, then she went into the front room.

Mrs Solomon was on the sofa, knitting something blue and shapeless. She was a large woman with the beginnings of a Fu Manchu and big arms covered in soft white skin, as if she were made of raw dough and ready to roll.

"Hi," said Eve quietly. "Is he asleep?"

"He is *now*," said Mrs Solomon with meaning. That meaning being that she'd earned *every penny* of her money and so Eve mustn't quibble about paying for the whole hour after midnight — even though it was only five past now.

Eve didn't quibble. She was far too tired to quibble. She just thanked Mrs Solomon and paid her — and opened the door for her. She took a cautious step back as she did, but there was nobody there. No mad axeman waiting to cleave Mrs Solomon in two and then rampage through the house.

Of course there wasn't. The man who'd walked her home had been perfectly innocent. Perfectly ordinary. *She* was the one who'd behaved like a nut!

The Layla Martin murder had really shaken her.

Still, she deadbolted the door behind Mrs Solomon. Then she turned down the thermostat, and drank a glass of water so cold that it made her fingers tingle.

She lifted her hamster, Munchkin, out of his cage in the front room to say goodnight. His whiskers quivered against her cheek, and as soon as she put him back he rushed into his wheel as if it were a getaway car. Eve switched off the lights and went upstairs to the tiny squeak of frantic non-escape.

She went into her father's room and looked down at him.

He was getting so *small*.

24

Duncan Singer had been a big man. Not fat, but *full*. Full of life and generosity and funny stories.

But now he was shrinking. His old clothes swamped him, and his new ones were boys' Large.

He lay on his back with his mouth a little open, although he did not snore.

Just breathed deeply in.

And deeply out.

Wrinkles were cutting vertical paths down his face, slowly usurping the happy crows' feet around his eyes. His hair was thinning and greying, along with his skin.

He was fifty-five and looked seventy.

The rails on his bed were up. He'd never fallen out, but he had started to wander at night. The raised sides were a discouragement, no more, but so far they had proved effective.

Eve sat.

Although she didn't want to wake her father, she took his hand.

His hands hadn't shrunk. They felt as they always had — big and rough and workmanlike. They were hands that had rewired houses and dabbed bloody knees and lifted pints and thrown sticks for dogs. Now they were hands that dropped spoons, and couldn't button trousers.

Eve could never look at his hands without thinking of them pushing her hair from her eyes when she was seven years old and *so worried* about the bean-bag race on school sports day. Worried about running too slowly and coming last; about running too fast and falling; about missing the bucket with the bean bag; worried

25

about everything, but especially about dying, because that's what her mother had done just a few months before, leaving all of them shell-shocked by sudden mortality . . .

By the time the bean-bag race had been announced over the windy PA system, Eve had worked herself up to tense tears.

Her father's hands had cleared her vision and wiped her nose and then he'd said, *You don't have to win, Evie. Just keep going all the way to the end.*

It was a revelation. He wasn't expecting her to win, and he didn't care if she lost. For the first time Eve had understood that the outcome couldn't change his love for her, or her fundamental worth. And she had nodded — calmed by the simplicity of the task at hand.

Anyone could *just keep going* — even her!

Then she'd run *so fast* and hadn't tripped, and the blue bean bag had dropped *perfectly* into the red bucket, and she'd turned on a sixpence and headed for home, and had been running in silence, with only her ragged breath to keep her company.

She dared not look behind — afraid she'd see the other kids closing her down.

Instead she'd kept going — kept heading straight for her father's open arms — until she had won, and Duncan Singer had lifted her into the sunshine above the daisies in the grass and the straight white lines of chalk. Lifted her in these same big, rough hands.

It had become their family motto.

Just keep going.

That's what they had all done in the months after Maggie Singer had died. And for all the years after that. Not because they knew *where* they were going or *why*, but because the only alternative was to —

Stop.

Duncan had kept working, kept providing, kept making a home and a life for them. Her younger brother, Stuart, had just kept going so well that Eve hadn't seen him for two years. He lived in Aberdeen and worked on the rigs and had a girlfriend she'd never met. Rachel or Ruby or something else with an R.

Eve had just kept going until she'd landed the iWitness News job, when most of her contemporaries were still toiling in local radio. When she'd told her father, he had picked her up in a bear hug, just like he had on that long-ago sports day, and said, "Noddy and Big Ears!"

Eve had laughed and asked what he meant. When he'd only looked blank, she'd repeated what he'd said, and he'd laughed too and said, "No bloody idea!"

Back then it had seemed funny.

Back then was another country . . .

Within the year she'd given up her flat in Camden, with its canal views and ironic décor, to return to the family home she thought she'd left for ever. At first she'd been resentful, but now — three years on — she was resigned to it. Occasionally even comforted. Sometimes, when she woke to pop stars and teddy bears, she was fourteen again.

But by the time she went to bed she was always old.

Eve got up, unfolded the old tartan rug from the foot of the bed and pulled it up so that her father's arms were not cold.

The rug was a family heirloom. They'd had it for years. Just the smell of it recalled sunny childhood.

They'd had a very old Triumph with tan leather seats that sloped gently backwards so that she felt safe and comfortable laid out under the rug, while her father sang "their" song. She remembered it only vaguely:

There were birds in the sky . . .

Eve wished she were a child again, asleep on the back seat, with the cracked leather against her cheek, her mother's hand on her shoulder, and her father driving *where*? Who knew? It didn't matter. He was in charge and would keep them all safe until they got there.

She hadn't felt safe since he'd got sick, and she missed it like a limb.

"Love you, Dad," she whispered.

Her father's eyes flickered and opened and, just for a moment, he smiled at her.

As if he knew who she was.

CHAPTER
FIVE

The killer reeled away from the bulging hedge on College Road.

What was he doing?

He almost went back. Almost turned around and opened her gate and followed her up the icy path and finished the job.

But he didn't.

Why?

Instead he walked on, not seeing where he was or where he might be going. Not caring. Confused and bemused.

What had just happened? He didn't know. He didn't know!

He had seen her in Oxford Street, as he stood with the throng of shoppers and gawpers, rubbing shoulders with their awe, revelling in their hushed tones, adoring their shock.

But there was something about *her* — the reporter. Some connection. He did not know what it was — only that it gave him a frisson of pleasure.

And anticipation.

So he had followed her to an office block.

Then he had waited and waited, the knife sticky in his pocket.

Then he had followed her again, nearly all the way home. Nearly all the way! Until she had turned —

Can I ask you a favour?

As if she knew him! As if he were an ordinary man! As if she *trusted him*.

The killer stopped dead in his snowy tracks under a street light and panted surprised fog into the air.

She'd *trusted* him.

She'd trusted *him*!

In the cone of white light, the killer put a hand to his numb heart, as snow crystals, too tiny to fall, spun around him like stardust.

Nobody had *ever* trusted him — not even his mother. But this woman had trusted him with all that she had — with her very *life*. One moment it had been his for the taking, and the next it was in his gift to bestow.

She had placed her life in his hands.

And instead of taking it, he had given it back to her!

He had shown mercy that he'd never known he possessed.

The only question was *why*?

CHAPTER
SIX

2 December

"I heard you pebble-dashed the porcelain."

Ross Tobin leaned against the door of Edit 1 and grinned, showing teeth that were browned by the forty cigarettes he insisted on smoking every day. He was militant about it, and had upped his daily consumption from thirty in defiance of the ban on smoking in the workplace. Because he could no longer smoke in the office, Ross spent about nine hours of every ten-hour day going up or down the four flights of stairs from the newsroom to the street and back. That and the smoking kept him thin, despite his diet of Big Macs and late-night kebabs. Eve liked to imagine that his body was planning a sneak heart attack, and evidently she wasn't the only one. Felt-tipped graffiti in the ladies' loo said *Ross Tobin = Rottin Boss* — and not even the cleaners had erased it.

"Who told you?" she said. She doubted it was Joe, but if it was, she'd make him pay.

"Guy Smith told his cameraman and he told Gareth in Sports and Gareth told Terry downstairs."

Radio Terry. Eve sighed. That was the trouble with working in a newsroom. Even the men were gossips.

"This the Oxford Street stuff?" said Ross, nodding at the screen.

"Yep," she said. "Just brushing it up and then we'll go back." Her initial report had gone out live, but they needed a fresh report they could play until the next live.

"*Police have not released the name of the victim, but iWitness News can reveal that she was twenty-four-year-old Layla Martin, who worked for Launchtime Advertising on the eighth floor of the brand-new Coldharbour building here in Oxford Street.*"

The festive lights twinkled behind Eve; with the sound down she might have been doing a piece on Christmas shopping.

It reminded her that she needed to do her Christmas shopping.

"Get some blood this time, will you?" said Ross. "That's what people want to see. Not this snow-globe fairy-light Santa's-grotto *bollocks.*"

She snorted. "You know what tight-arses the Met are. No cameras at the scene."

"So what? You've got a phone, haven't you?"

Eve sighed. They couldn't have broadcast bloody footage of the murder scene and they both knew it.

"Tired?" he said.

She smiled at his kindness and shrugged. "I'm fine."

"Katie can always take over if you're not up to it."

Ross wasn't being kind: he was poking the bear.

Katie Merino had arrived eight months ago — five years Eve's junior, smart and hard-working . . . and

32

blonde. Hers was the kind of foot Eve didn't need in the door of her career.

"Piss off."

Ross laughed and they watched the package play out.

"Miss Martin went into work to do some overtime. Overtime that cost her her life."

Right on cue, the body bag was wheeled out of the doors behind Eve and into a waiting ambulance.

"You always had good timing," said Ross grudgingly. Then, as the ambulance doors closed, he added, "You get any shots of the body before the bag?"

"No, Ross," she explained patiently, "because we're not in Mexico."

"You're going soft in your old age," he said. And when she looked at him, expecting a grin or a wink, he gave her neither.

She pursed her lips.

"Oh, get off your high horse," he said, rolling a cigarette as he headed off for a smoke. "Our job is to give the public what they want."

It wasn't clear whether he meant more gore, or younger, prettier reporters.

Either way, Eve knew he was probably right.

"Do a vox pop today," he told her, turning in the doorway. "Girls saying how scared they are. Murder in the city. The London Ripper."

"Right." Eve nodded, and mentally rolled her eyes.

"Pretty girls," Ross went on.

Then — in case she didn't understand English words — he explained, "No dogs."

So here she was, waiting for Joe to set up the shot in front of the glass-walled office block, blowing into her cupped hands and stamping her feet to keep them from freezing clean off her legs, now unable to glance at passing women without an automatic, albeit shameful, evaluation of their dogginess.

"How much longer?"

"Ju-u-u-ust a second."

The exchange was meaningless. Eve asked him the same question half a dozen times on every job — and got the same answer every time.

"I can't feel my feet," she stated.

Joe glanced at her. "I told you to wear those yeti boots."

"With this coat?" She pulled a face and he smiled without looking up. Joe was cute when he smiled, in a *National Geographic* kind of way. In a six-three, bearded, chunky-jumper kind of way. He had very white teeth, serious eyes, and the tattoo of a vine on his shoulder that sometimes peeked out of his T-shirt in summer. She'd never seen all of it, of course, because Joe was far too young for her. She liked mature men, although when she'd told her best friend that, Charlotte had rolled her eyes and said that "mature men" was an oxymoron.

Eve thought she might have a point. Her last boyfriend had been thirty-four, but he'd still thought a bottle of red and an Xbox was an acceptable date. He'd drifted away after she'd moved back to Isleworth, vaguely citing work commitments, but Eve guessed that it was *her* commitments that had been too much for him.

She couldn't blame him, she supposed; sometimes they felt like becoming too much for *her*.

"How old are you, Joe?"

"Twenty-six," he said. "Why? How old are you?"

"Today?" she sighed. "A hundred and three."

Joe searched her face carefully, then shrugged as if it really might be so.

Eve laughed. "Bastard!"

He smiled and fiddled with his light meter some more.

As he did, Eve wondered what it would be like to be thirty, which she would be in July. In principle, she didn't mind thirty. She and Charlotte laughed in the face of thirty. Laughed at the inevitability of it, and laughed at the women who were pumped so full of Botox by the time they hit that mark that, if they ever stopped, they'd look like disappointed scrotums.

But if she didn't care about thirty, then why not just tell Joe she was twenty-nine?

Eve knew she'd got the iWitness job partly because she'd been young and reasonably attractive. That didn't mean she didn't have talent — just that she'd leap-frogged over older, plainer journalists who might have had more. When she'd been at college there'd still been a few women on camera in their forties and even well-preserved fifties.

No longer.

Apparently, men grew wiser with every grey hair, while women just grew invisible.

Eve was good at her job, but she knew she needed to get the hell off the meat beat — or to make such a blistering mark on it that she was headhunted by *Newsnight*.

She'd once had such ambitions . . .

But when she'd moved back in with her father, Eve had clung to her job like a child to a sucky blanket, suddenly nervous of upping the pressure at work while she was adjusting to a whole new pressure at home. So she'd missed her chance to jump. And now she had the uneasy sense that it was only a matter of time before she was pushed.

So every time some fresh ingénue appeared at a crime scene on the coat-tails of a cameraman from another channel, Eve redoubled her efforts to make the best of her job — even as she worked to escape its brutal confines.

Soon, she used to tell herself. *Soon*.

But soon had become sometime, and sometime had become never.

And she just kept going.

Every day she pushed the envelope, but had never opened an invitation to another life . . .

"It gives me the creeps," Joe said out of nowhere.

Eve blinked back to Oxford Street.

"What?"

"This murder," said Joe.

"Gives *you* the creeps?" Eve snorted. "Look at you! You're built like a brick shithouse."

"Seriously," he said while he checked the light. "Imagine all those people right there, half an inch away through a pane of glass, Christmas shopping. While some sicko is gutting you like a fish."

Eve *had* imagined it. How could anyone not? It made her feel . . . like not imagining it. She shivered, but not from the cold, and changed the subject. "Have you done your Christmas shopping?"

Joe checked the light for the millionth time. "Yep."

"Everything?"

"Yep. You?"

"No," she said. "Not all of it."

She hadn't even started. She had to buy for her father and her brother — even though she probably wouldn't see him until July — and for Charlotte and for Joe, of course. Joe always bought her something thoughtful.

"What have you got me?" she asked, although she knew he wouldn't tell her.

"Nothing," he said without looking up.

"Liar."

He looked up and cocked an eyebrow at her. "Then why'd you ask?"

Eve didn't know when she was going to have time to go shopping. She thought she might have to buy everyone a charity goat. She'd got a charity goat from Charlotte a few years back, in the form of a thank-you email from Oxfam and a photo of a goat that looked like a piebald sock puppet. They'd both agreed it was a fine and altruistic idea, and never to do it again.

She couldn't get Joe a goat. Or anyone a goat, really.

"Shit," she said under her breath.

Joe looked up at her, then realized what she meant as Guy Smith appeared at his shoulder.

Guy frowned in fake puzzlement and pointed a finger at Eve. "Hey! Didn't I see you in *The Exorcist*?"

"Hilarious, Guy. And topical, too. Oh, and by the way, thanks for your professional discretion."

"Remarkable," he snorted. "You *are* always this tetchy. Can't you take a joke?"

She ignored him. "How much longer, Joe?"

"Ju-u-u-ust a second."

"I've done my bit already," Guy went on. "And got some great follow-up stuff on the dead girl. Neighbours, friends."

Eve doubted whether that was true. Guy Smith wasn't the world's brightest or most hard-working reporter. If he really did have anything good, she imagined it must have fallen into his lap. Some Facebook so-called friend calling the newsroom, selling pictures under the guise of a tribute.

The jammy bastard.

"Do you have her address?" Guy said. He was fishing. But he wasn't reeling *her* in.

"Yes, thanks."

"Oh. Good." He looked confused, then disappointed. Then he said, "There's a nice little café a few doors up. Fancy a coffee when you're finished? By way of an apology?"

"Whose apology?" she said suspiciously.

"Mine, of course."

"OK. Thanks. I'll have an Americano."

"Great," said Guy cheerfully.

"And Joe will have a hot chocolate."

"Right," said Guy, less cheerfully, and trudged off.

Joe showed Eve all his teeth in a dazzling display. "You're mean."

She grinned back. "I'm mean, he's sneaky, and so the world turns."

He shook his head and said, "Ready?"

But suddenly Eve wasn't, quite . . .

"Hey, Guy!" Her rival turned to look at her over the heads of passers-by. "Did you mention the boyfriend?"

A quick cloud crossed Guy's face and he took a few faltering steps back towards her so they were close enough not to shout.

"The boyfriend?"

"Yeah. I don't want our reports to sound the same. I mean, it's a cliché, isn't it? But I suppose the cops have to go through the motions on these things — examine every possible suspect."

"Oh yeah," said Guy, closing the distance between them all the time. "What was his name again?" He snapped his fingers as if he could pluck it out of thin air.

"Mark Franco."

"Of course," said Guy. "One of her friends gave me his name. He comes from . . . Ealing, right?"

Eve pulled out her notebook and flicked through the pages. "A flat near Blackfriars Bridge, apparently. He's not listed, but two of us working together could find him in half the time. What do you think?"

"Good idea," said Guy.

"After our coffee?" said Eve, and he raised a hand in acknowledgement before hurrying through the snow in the direction of the café.

Joe put his eye to the viewfinder and Eve cleared her throat and glanced behind her. "I'm not blocking the shot of the door, am I?"

"No, you're good right there," said Joe. "Ready when you are."

She did her piece to camera in one perfect take.

Then they did another take, out of habit, for insurance.

Then they vox-popped some young women who were not dogs, who said how frightened they all were.

Then she helped Joe with his gear and they kicked through the greying sludge to the warm and cosy café.

Guy Smith was nowhere to be seen.

They looked all the way to the back. Joe even went into the Gents to check he wasn't there.

He snapped his fingers. "Shit," he said. "I bet that bastard's gone to Blackfriars by himself to beat us to the boyfriend! You shouldn't have told him, Eve. I *knew* he'd screw us over."

"I told you he was sneaky," said Eve. "Don't worry, Joe. I'll get your hot chocolate to go and then we'll doorstep Layla Martin's parents again."

But Joe was still fuming. "That lying, cheating little shit."

"You left out *predictable*," she said.

"Maybe we could —"

Joe stopped with a frown and gave Eve a quizzical look. "You never mentioned the boyfriend to me."

She turned to him in wide-eyed innocence. "Didn't I?"

"Hang on a minute," he said. "Who *is* Mark Franco?"

Eve winked at him. "First boy I ever kissed."

Guy Smith didn't make it back from Blackfriars in time for that afternoon's press conference, where Layla Martin's mother cried so hard that her younger daughter had to interpret for her. The whole time, Mrs Martin wrung a soft grey toy rabbit between her hands without ever referring to it, which made asking its name and provenance so awkward that nobody did.

Detective Superintendent Huw Rees presided. He was a lilting Welshman, whose soft voice belied his hard nose.

He sang all the usual songs — the tragedy, the brutality, the appeal for witnesses — none of which could hide the fact that he had no idea who the hell had killed Layla Martin.

Eve stifled a yawn and gazed around the room.

Today it was Layla Martin. Tomorrow it would be another corpse, another weeping family, another helpless police officer.

The names changed, but the appetite of the audience never wavered.

And Eve was grateful.

Nothing sold like murder, and death was how she paid the mortgage.

CHAPTER
SEVEN

The killer watched Eve Singer on a loop.

His chair was old and French and covered in gold brocade that was silken against his naked thighs, and with castors made of bone.

It was the only chair in the house, and the fire and the television were the only illumination.

The big, dim room was lined with paintings — stacked three deep around the walls. The batons burned well, and the oil in the paint helped things along, although over time it had left a brown slick in the fireplace, and a thick smell in the house that the killer didn't notice any more. Some pictures had been in frames, but they had been the first thing to go — even before the books — and had kept him warm through two winters.

The killer sipped his tea from a cup so fine that the firelight glowed orange through its porcelain sides. It was Flora Danica, decorated with a crest and a V entwined by ornate brambles, and the family motto *For every flower a thorn*.

It had once been part of a huge service.

Vast.

Tureens and gravy boats and platters and chargers. Twenty place settings, with three different sizes of pudding bowl alone.

He had sold it all. Along with the rest of the fixtures and fittings.

Slowly.

Never thinking he would run out of heirlooms or equity before he ran out of life.

Irony, at least, was not dead.

But really, what did one need?

One cup, one chair.

One knife, one fork, one spoon.

Sometimes he stole. Not because he was a thief, but because there were things that he could no longer afford. Things that he couldn't do without. He had made a hole through the wall of the rat-shitty attic to harness himself to the neighbour's electricity supply.

And beyond that? He needed so little!

One notebook, one pen.

Bananas and chocolate.

A television . . .

He watched Eve Singer, and the body bag that cradled his work. They moved in perfect harmony — Eve moving aside as the bag appeared. Stepping to the left as the bag rolled to the right. Glancing over her shoulder at the camera, her dark hair swinging gently across her pale cheek . . .

Why had he not killed her? He watched the review again, wondering, as he imagined the dark, rubbery folds of the bag kissing the skin within. Skin he had pressed under his very own hands, as he'd moulded the girl into something beautiful — something immortal.

As he watched, his fingers picked at the edges of the thick scar that wormed down his chest.

Eve stepped to the left as the bag rolled to the right.

Step.

Roll.

Whoever the cameraman was, he had a good eye for composition, while Eve Singer had a delicious flair for language. She used words like "terrifying" and "bloodbath" and "gruesome". Some other words he didn't approve of, like "senseless" and "maniac", but he forgave her. He was a realist. He knew they had to say those things on the news. If they didn't, then it might seem that murder was committed not only by the deranged and the drug addicted, but that *just anyone* might be a killer. A neighbour. The milkman. Your *babysitter* . . .

They couldn't tell the truth on the news, or people would panic.

Ordinary people.

Again . . . Step to the left; roll to the right. The living and the dead, performing together as if choreographed. Eve Singer glancing at the body bag. Then turning to look coyly into his eyes . . .

His heart thudded in his chest and, with an echoing shout, the killer dropped to his knees, spread his arms, and gripped the corners of the TV like an angular lover.

He knew that look! Eve Singer had looked at him the same way under the silvery lights of College Road. The same tilt of the head, the same sway of the hair. The

44

same invitation to fall into step beside her so that they could walk on . . .

Together.

This was why!

He stumbled to his feet, naked and shaking, heart drumming so fast he felt faint, as life spurted through his sinewy soul and out like sparks through the tips of his tingling fingers.

It smelled like infinity and fireworks!

A jagged pain shot through his chest and he clutched at his heart and cried, *"NO!"*

He could feel the stitching of his own fabric give way, like a teddy bear's arm. He looked down in terror to watch the scar that sealed him unzip from gullet to belly, to see an alien heart pump a stranger's blood on to the cherry-wood floor, until all that was left was an empty him, standing in a puddle of his own entrails.

Not me! Not yet! Not me!

Nothing happened.

He collapsed whimpering into his chair, trembling and foetal with fear.

Slowly the pain faded. The heart became numb once again.

The infinite luxury of time was returned to him . . .

He watched the report throughout the night. He wanted every detail of it imprinted on his brain. He wanted to dream of it when he slept his deep and untroubled sleep.

The killer watched until the light around him cooled to electric and his genitals were puckered blue berries.

Just before dawn, he shivered and rose, and put another painting on the fire.

CHAPTER
EIGHT

4 December

It was bitterly cold, and the bags from the one-stop shop at the station bit into Eve's fingers despite her woollen gloves.

Under the silver glow of the street light, Mr Elias was shovelling snow off the pavement outside his house, and Eve slowed to a slippery dawdle.

Eve didn't dislike Mr Elias, but she didn't exactly like him either. He had a fishing gnome in his garden, but no pond, and a twenty-five-year-old Ford Mondeo. And he'd had a wife once, but she had died some time while Eve was in Camden. Eve couldn't remember her name, but she'd never looked happy and barely ever spoke, which made Eve think that Mr Elias had probably bullied her — or had disappointed her in some way, at the very least.

Sometimes, when she and Stuart were kids, Mr Elias hadn't thrown their ball back for days. He'd ranted out of all proportion when a model plane had accidentally dive-bombed his greenhouse. He'd told them to keep the noise down at completely reasonable teenage parties, and had once called the police, who had stood at the door while her school friends trooped out, which had been *so* embarrassing.

After that incident, she'd tried to avoid Mr Elias.

When she'd come back to live with her father, Eve had started new, more formal, more grown-up relations, and kept them to a minimum. She didn't see him often, but when she did see him, Mr Elias usually looked at her with an odd intensity. *Stared* at her, really . . . Eve didn't like to imagine that her lifelong neighbour was a dirty old man but she feared that might be true. Or might *become* true, if she were too friendly to him.

She hadn't seen him to speak to for a couple of months — had only spotted him from the window, going out every day to clean the red phone box — but she didn't want to get caught up in conversation now. Partly because she felt guilty that she wasn't clearing her own bit of pavement, the way her father always used to, but mostly because she knew exactly what they'd both say.

Hello, Eve.

Hello, Mr Elias.

Cold enough for you?

Haha, yes, thank you.

She'd have to fake the laugh because it wouldn't be funny, of course.

They say we'll have a white Christmas.

That would be nice.

No it wouldn't. Or it would. Eve didn't give a shit one way or the other. The only thing she cared about was not having to make mind-numbing *small talk* about a white bloody Christmas.

Mr Elias straightened up and leaned on his shovel, his breath enveloping his balding head in a series of little white clouds.

He'd finished.

Eve dawdled, willing him to open his gate and disappear. Instead he bent over again and started to shovel salt out of a white plastic sack, sprinkling it on to the pavement so that ice wouldn't form.

She thought about stopping to wait for the next plane and then hurrying past, miming *hello*, but before she could, Mr Elias looked up and saw her and raised a hand in greeting, so she walked on.

"Hello, Eve."

She took a deep breath. "Hello, Mr Elias."

"Cold enough for you?"

"Haha, yes, thank you." She faked the laugh, hating her own hypocrisy.

"They said on the radio it's going to be a white Christmas."

"That would be nice."

She felt his salt crunch under her boots, then was back on the compacted snow alongside her overbearing hedge. She slipped a little and adrenaline spurted through her like electricity.

"Watch yourself," he warned. "It's lethal."

Oh shut up! she thought. But she said, "I will, thanks," and shoved her gate open, annoyed that she'd slipped and proved that he was right for clearing the pavement and she was wrong for not. Just like her hedge was a bulbous disaster, and her grass was unmown, and her flowerbeds were overgrown. She couldn't keep on top of *everything*! Bloody hell, it was hard enough just paying the mortgage, and Mrs Solomon's fees and the bills and looking after Duncan. Mr Elias didn't have a bloody *clue* —

She skidded again on the dirty-iced garden path. It really *was* lethal.

"Where *are* you?"

Eve sighed. She hadn't even closed the door behind her and her father was off.

Like Dr Jekyll waking up after a night as Mr Hyde, she could feel herself struggling to adjust. Leaving herself at the front door and becoming another person whose only purpose was keeping her father from escaping, falling, or burning down the house.

From the front room came the beat of what sounded like a porn film. Eve knew it wasn't porn; it was *How It's Made* — a low-budget, low-key programme that showed the throbbing manufacture of a bizarrely random selection of everyday items — egg whisks and gloves and rattan stools — all accompanied by the formless beats of a Bontempi organ. She recorded every episode, and Duncan Singer never watched anything else.

"Where *are* you?" He was a broken record.

"Here, Dad! Just hanging up my coat."

"Hello, dear." Mrs Solomon bustled into the hallway from the front room, stuffing her blue shapeless knitting into a large flabby bag.

50

As Eve pulled off her hat and gloves and scarf and coat, so Mrs Solomon put hers on — like a panto act changing in the wings. As she got ready, Mrs Solomon gave a monotonous commentary on the night's highlights.

"He wanted porridge for lunch, but I gave him cornflakes, I hope that's OK."

It was. Eve nodded, but didn't answer. She'd learned that answering only prolonged the departure.

"He took the books off the shelf, but I let him get on with that."

He did that all the time.

Mrs Solomon sat down to pull on her boots, puffing with effort. "He broke the remote control."

Shit. Duncan often broke things while he thought he was fixing them.

"He didn't want to go to bed."

You had to con him. Mrs Solomon knew that but was sometimes too lazy to make the effort.

"He likes that programme, doesn't he? All those machines and gizmos."

GO GO GO!

She finally went.

"Where *are* you?" said Duncan Singer.

Eve hurried into the front room. "Hi, Dad."

Her father scowled at her and said, "Not *you*."

It never failed to hurt.

"Where's Maggie?" he went on.

Eve hesitated. The GP always said it was best to be honest — to keep her father grounded in reality by telling him the truth. But there were only so many times you could watch someone learn that their wife was dead before the truth lost its sheen.

"Having a bath," she lied. "She asked me to make supper."

They ate off cushioned trays on their laps. Fish fingers and baked beans, and canned fruit salad for pudding.

On the TV, waffle cones, shoelaces and tents all chuntered out of various machines.

"Finished Mrs Cole's wiring," Duncan said suddenly.

"Finally!" she said, because if she didn't, he would.

The actual date of Mrs Cole's rewiring was lost in the mists of time, but the job must have been epic and completing it was noteworthy.

On a regular basis.

He nodded. "Finally what?"

"Mrs Cole's wiring."

"Oh yes. Got that finished. Finally!"

Eve sighed. Duncan never showed any interest in her life any more. He had been a courteous, sociable man, but no longer had the capacity to care about others.

She was used to it.

No, that wasn't right. She'd never get used to it.

They ate to the musical click of tent pegs.

"Where are my —?" Duncan stopped, then started again. "Where are my —?" He wiggled his fingers at his feet, as if something were missing.

"Slippers?" she suggested.

"No."

"Socks?" He often took his socks off during the day. Eve had found them in the rubbish bin before now and once in the freezer, like argyle veal.

"No." Her father glared at his shoes. "Things. Strings. Long strings of things in the rings." Her father loved words. He'd been an electrician, but had always read a lot and had a personal best at Scrabble of 576 — a Singer family record.

On TV somebody said *shoelaces*.

"Shoelaces!" he said, and pointed at his feet again. "Where are my *shoelaces*?"

Eve looked down at his feet. "They're not the kind of shoes that have laces, Dad. They're slip-ons."

"Slip-on. Nippon. Ripon," he agreed. "Lots of Japs up north," he went on. "And Chinese ones in Morecambe Bay."

"Chinese shoes?"

"Cockle-pickers."

Eve was confused. "Do you mean winkle-pickers?"

"Not *winkle-pickers. Cockle*-pickers! I *told* you!"

"Oh, *cockle-pickers*!" Eve stood. "You can see them from the bedroom window."

"Really?" he said. "Can I see?"

"Of course."

By the time they got all the way up the stairs, he'd have forgotten.

They went up together, he one step ahead, her one behind, with one hand in the small of his back, in case he toppled backwards. His balance was so-so but his concentration was scattergun, and they'd had several near-misses. And one complete miss about a year ago, when he had turned unexpectedly and slid downstairs using Eve as a luge.

"Are we going to pick cockles?" he said.

"You don't like cockles."

"Don't I?" He frowned. "I thought I did. Do I like eels?"

"No."

"Really?" he said. "How strange!"

Halfway up, he stopped. He said nothing, but bowed his head a little.

"Taking a breather, Dad?" Eve said cheerfully, and called over her shoulder, "Everybody take five!"

Duncan didn't laugh, but she hadn't expected him to.

Then a shuddering breath told her he was crying.

"Dad?"

He wiped his eyes on his sleeve and shook his head again. Eve was stuck. She wanted to step up alongside him and comfort him. But sod's law said he'd forget where he was and fall if she abandoned her post, so instead she stood there, one hand on the bannister, the other braced upwards against her father's back, feeling his ribs heave through his old grey cardigan.

"Dad? What's wrong?"

"I'm sorry," he wept. "I don't want to be a burden."

"You're not a burden!" she told him. "Don't be silly."

"You're so good to me," he said. "And I'm nothing but trouble."

He took his other hand off the bannister to wipe his eyes again, and Eve grunted as his weight shifted so that she had to strain to keep him upright, even with two hands against his back.

"You're no trouble, Dad. I love you and I love being here with you —"

She repositioned her feet to keep her own balance as he swayed above her. She glanced over her shoulder as if someone might help her, but of course, there was nobody there.

"Can you hold the bannister, Dad?"

"Who's Dad?"

"Can you hold the bannister?"

"Eh?"

"*Can you hold on to the bannister rail?* And keep going up the stairs? I can't hold you much longer."

"Eh?"

"Just keep going!" she said forcefully. "Keep going!" And Duncan finally located the bannister with his hand and started a shaky new step.

Eve puffed out her cheeks in relief as they resumed their perilous ascent.

Almost at the top, he stopped again.

"What's up now?" said Eve.

"Why have we stopped?" he said.

"You stopped," said Eve, "not me."

Then Duncan pointed at his feet and said, "Where are my shoelaces?"

CHAPTER
NINE

Stan Reddy hunched his shoulders against the flurries of snow whipping around the corner of the Everyman Cinema and hugged the wall to keep away from the sprays of dirty slush thrown up by passing cars.

He hoped the movie would be worth the queue, but he wasn't sure, because he was going to see the new Liam Neeson film.

Stan was a big Liam Neeson fan, but his patience was wearing thin.

It happened to the best of actors. They burst on to the scene full of talent and balls and were hailed as the new Brando or the new De Niro. They made a handful of films that made you proud to be a man. Films where they honed their bodies, bloodied their knuckles, defended the good and sacrificed all in the pursuit of a noble ideal. Films that got you all riled up and passionate and ready to follow them into battle or anywhere else they cared to take you.

And then they got lazy.

Sooner or later all actors lost their hunger and their passion and their raw honesty, and started to do it just for the money.

56

Badly written blockbusters and ill-advised romances, or those movies where they made *one more* bid for an Oscar by playing a lunatic or a cripple, or a bloke with no skin.

Or cartoons.

That was Stan's pet hate: grown men he'd once hero-worshipped being animated ostriches and cartoon fish.

Even De Niro wasn't De Niro any more, with all those comedies and mugging cameos chipping away at his legacy, dismantling his own myth, role by role. And Brando hadn't even *pretended* to be hungry after *The Godfather*. He'd just sat on his island, surrounded by dusky girls, and grown fatter and fatter and fatter . . .

Corrupted by money and fame and ego, they all lost sight of what they were meant to be doing and the reason they'd started doing it in the first place.

And now Stan feared it might be happening to Liam too. The Big Man. The brooding, quiet Irishman, whose intellect had always wrestled with his physique, was making the same movie over and over again, but worse each time, in a depressing inverse of the creative progress.

Stan thought it was a terrible shame.

Whatever happened to retiring gracefully and playing golf?

Or dying of cancer?

Time was, *all* the greats died of cancer — Bogie and Gary Cooper and Steve McQueen. Maybe that was what was wrong with Hollywood now — no bastard died of cancer any more.

Stan sighed. He'd depressed himself now. He really should go home. What was the point of queuing in the snow to see a movie he'd probably hate? He glanced at his watch. If he left now he could still have a pint or two at the Archers before they shut up shop. Maybe find someone who fancied a game of backgammon. Stan played in a league and could usually win enough in casual pub games to cover his drinks for the night.

Sometimes even a pie.

Just as he'd almost made up his mind to do just that, the queue started to move, so he moved with it, but had to stop almost immediately because the man in front of him was playing Candy Crush on his phone and hadn't noticed.

"'Scuse me," said Stan, and when there was no response, he tapped the fellow on the shoulder.

"What?" The man glared round at him in crew-cut aggression.

"The queue's moving," said Stan.

"Keep your fucking hair on, mate."

Stan was taken aback. "No need to be rude," he said.

"Well, keep your hands to yourself, wanker!"

Stan was stunned. He glanced over his shoulder but the couple behind him looked straight through him, while the people behind them were pretending they hadn't even noticed that the line was moving up ahead. They weren't going to be any help if anything kicked off. And there wasn't much more Stan could do alone. He had dodgy knees, which was why he was a paramedic and not a fireman. And although this man was much shorter than he was, he also looked fitter, twenty years younger and, most dangerously, as if he were spoiling for a fight.

Which Stan definitely was not.

It was only Stan's fond memories of Liam Neeson's noble early work that gave him the courage to say anything at all.

"Some of us are here to see a film," he said — reaching for superior but achieving only prissy.

"So who's stopping you?" said the man. "Hey? Who's fucking stopping you?"

"Well," said Stan, and then chickened out of saying *you are*, and instead finished weakly, "Everyone's going in."

"*I'm* going in," said the man. "We're *all* going in. Jesus Christ. Don't fucking panic."

"I'm not panicking," said Stan and the man feinted at him, making him recoil, blinking, across the pavement to the kerb.

"Yeah you are," sneered the man, and addressed the remainder of the queue. "Look at him fucking panicking!" Then he laughed and sauntered to the box office. The rest of the line followed him meekly, passing Stan without looking at him.

A car sped by and a bow-wave of slush shot up the back of Stan's legs. He sighed. He should just go straight home. Forget the Archers. Forget the backgammon. Just hang his trousers over the gas fire and watch that thing he'd recorded about classic British cars, back when the British knew how to make cars. Bristols and Jags and all the Triumphs before the TR7. At least the past couldn't disappoint him.

But why *should* he go home?

The thought brought a frown to Stan's brow.

Would Liam Neeson go home just because some idiot — some knuckle-dragging, mouth-breathing *punk* — had been rude to him?

No, thought Stan, Liam Neeson certainly would *not*.

So, although his trousers were wet and cold against his backside, Stan bought his ticket on principle and then spent ten minutes trying to dry his arse in a Dyson Airblade, before taking his seat in the sparsely populated auditorium.

He wished he hadn't bothered. The film was over-loud and filled with brute violence and what-the-hell plot holes. As if that wasn't bad enough, two idiots in hoodies across the aisle laughed loudly at every gory death, and somebody kicked Stan's seat — twice and hard — which made him tense, waiting for a third time.

The final straw was the tell-tale glow of a mobile phone being used by an idiot behind him, whose attention span was apparently so short that it couldn't even be held by mass murder.

Under normal circumstances, Stan would have turned round and given the perpetrator a hard stare, at the very least. Maybe even said something.

But not tonight.

Tonight he'd made his stand just by sitting down.

So Stan continued to sit, and stared straight ahead, and watched the film — nagged by cowardice and a damp backside.

And behind him sat the killer . . .

Kevin Barr had never got over being five foot five.

Similarly short on good nature and wit, he made up for it by getting his defence in first.

Barr had become so practised at defence that his whole life had become a litany of angry attacks. He couldn't buy a newspaper without haranguing the seller over a disagreeable headline, or order a McBurger without challenging a teenage chip-seller to "take it outside".

Consequently, he rarely had to fight. Most people were so taken aback by his groundless fury that few but the very drunk ever took up his challenge, and the very drunk were easy to beat.

Barr drew his confidence from the baffled fear in the eyes of the remainder.

Like the old git in the queue. You couldn't just let people put their hands on you like they had a fucking *right*. You had to let them know you weren't going to be pushed around, right from the off. Nip it in the fucking *bud*.

He'd come in late, the git, stumbling along the row in front of him in the dark, a big fat silhouette on the screen like a shooting-range target, with a Ben & Jerry's tub in one hand and his torn ticket in the other.

Fucking twat.

Barr hoped the man would want to carry on the argument, because being behind him in the tiered auditorium would give him an extra six inches in height . . .

But the twat didn't turn around. He just sat there and watched Liam Neeson kick arse, eating his fucking Phish Food, too scared to say a *fucking thing*.

61

Stan got up as soon as the credits started to roll on
what he reckoned must be the worst cinema-going
experience anyone had ever had. His bum was still
damp but it was warm now, which made it feel as if
he'd peed himself. He sighed and picked up his
ice-cream tub and turned to go.

He flinched.

The moron from the queue was in the row behind,
arms outstretched, one dirty boot hooked rudely over
the back of the seat in front of him — his eyes
half-closed, regarding him with a fixed grin.

Stan looked quickly away.

If the man said anything, Stan was going to pretend
he hadn't heard him. The last thing he wanted to do
was start things up again.

But the man didn't start things up. He didn't move
at all. Stan risked another glance as he passed. He
looked to be asleep.

Exhausted from being an arsehole.

But there was something not quite right about him,
and Stan slowed and took a longer look.

The man's splayed posture was almost *too* casual,
too abandoned, and the blurred light of the credits
rolling up his form made the pugnacious little shit into
something more compelling, and Stan paused, oddly
arrested by the image.

The eyes between the narrowed lids were dull, and
the grin was fixed and gap-toothed — and Stan felt his
stomach flutter a warning.

Cautiously, he nudged the man's boot with his knuckles and said, "Hey, film's over."

The boot rolled sideways off the back of the seat and the leg dropped heavily to the floor.

The man was unconscious.

Stan was instantly in work mode. He clambered awkwardly over the seats, shouting for help even as he checked the carotid pulse.

Nothing.

Shit!

This was *wrong*. The man's head did not loll properly on the seat back. It seemed somehow *stiff*. His chin was on his chest, as if forced there. And now Stan could see that the gap in the teeth was not a gap but rather a *thing* — some black *thing* protruding from the man's mouth, clamped between his teeth. Had he choked? But on what?

Stan touched the black thing and winced.

Sharp!

Steel.

"What the *hell* —"

He reached gingerly around the man's head and found that the only thing holding him upright was the butt of a knife that had been driven into the back of his neck.

And suddenly Stan was clammy with sweat, because he understood what had happened. Not *how* it had happened or *why*, but he understood the mechanics: the route that the knife must have taken through the man on its way to murder. He knew that the knife must be *very* sharp, and with a narrow, double-edged blade.

He knew it had been inserted at the base of the skull with great force and great precision, into the narrowest of gaps between the occipital condyles. On its way it would have sliced through the spinal cord, and then punched *so fast* through the back of the throat and out of the mouth that it got there before the teeth had snapped together in death.

Around Stan, people were gathering — a few patrons and ushers. He was dimly aware that someone was filming on a phone. He used to go ballistic at that; now it happened all the time, sick clips popping up on YouTube. He had other stuff to think about.

He pressed the butt of the knife with a single finger. It was jammed solid within its human sheath, and when he took his finger away it was slick with cerebrospinal fluid.

The arsehole was irreversibly dead.

Stan couldn't pretend he was sorry. If anything, it gave him a guilty little lift. He was only human, after all.

He wiped his hand on the dead man's jeans.

"He's been murdered," he announced solemnly to a wide-eyed usherette who was holding a black bin liner and a litter grabber.

"Murdered?" she said.

"That's right," said Stan. "He's been stabbed."

"Stabbed?" said the girl.

"Yes," said Stan patiently. "Somebody needs to call the police."

The girl didn't move. She'd come for tubs and Pepsi cups, and couldn't adjust to a corpse.

64

So half a dozen other gawpers rushed to be the first to make the call, while Stan took out his own phone and walked up the dark carpeted steps to the fancy seats he couldn't afford.

Then he sat down and called Eve Singer.

Duncan picked up the phone.

"Hello?" he said.

It rang again, deep in his ear. He frowned at the screen, then, in the space between rings, put it to his ear again.

"Hello?"

It rang once more, making him wince, so he switched it off and put it under the sofa cushion. Then he picked up the remote control and went on watching *How It's Made*. This episode was bentwood chairs, crisps and baseball mitts — all burping from a range of chutes and lathes and belts and spindles that chuntered and hammered and rolled.

There was a lot of work in a bentwood chair.

"For something so *shit*," he scoffed, then laughed at himself.

"Who was on the phone?"

Duncan lifted the remote to his ear. "Hello?"

But nobody answered. He glared at it. "Someone playing silly buggers!" He hung up and *How It's Made* changed to *The Great British Bake Off*.

"Dad, it's me. I'm right here. Who was on the phone?"

He looked up. There was a young woman standing in the doorway. Not the fat woman, but a slim woman in a bathrobe.

"Someone was on the phone," he told her.

"I know," she said. "What did they say?"

"They said each piece of wood is steamed and bent at a hundred and seventy degrees for twenty-four hours. Have you had a bath?"

"Yes. Where's the phone?"

"Did you pay the bill?"

"The phone bill?"

"The water bill."

"Yes," she said. "I paid the water bill."

Duncan was stumped. It was his house and his bath and he didn't want any old Tom, Dick or Harry just waltzing in and thinking they could jump in whenever they felt like it, even if they *did* pay the bill.

"Where's the phone, Dad?"

"Why are you paying my bills?" he said. "Why don't you go home and pay your own bills? And who's this *Dad* person?"

She sighed again. "You are. You're Dad and I'm Eve, your daughter."

"Oh," he said, affronted. "I didn't know I had a *daughter*."

"A daughter *and* a son. Eve and Stuart."

"Oh," he said again. "Well, it's nice to meet you."

"Nice to meet you too," she said. "Where did you put the phone?"

"Here." He handed her the remote. "Call the BBC," he said, gesturing at the TV. "And let's have no more lesbians."

CHAPTER
TEN

5 December

Eve didn't find her phone until the next morning, and by the time she did, and heard Stan's message, their edge on the story had gone.

By the time she and Joe finally made it to the cinema on Baker Street, three other news crews were already there.

"*Shit,*" said Eve as they pulled up. "Shit and bollocks."

Joe said nothing. He wasn't the type to rub it in. But Eve wasn't the type who needed to have it rubbed in. She knew that they should have been way out in front on this story, instead of running to catch up.

Still, Stan Reddy gave them an exclusive interview that was so good they wouldn't be able to use half of it because it was just too graphic — even after Eve had asked him to rephrase certain bits for public consumption.

Bits like "cerebrospinal fluid leaking on to my fingers".

Yum.

But there were other details, like the kicking of the seats and the light of a mobile phone, that painted a vivid picture of the life-and-death struggle that had unfolded behind the paramedic's right shoulder as mock violence played out on the screen.

When they didn't *have* pictures, it was Eve's job to create one in the minds of her audience, and she did it with practised ghoulishness.

Had the kicking been the death throes of the victim?

Had the killer *filmed* his own macabre handiwork?

And, best of all, *Do you know who's sitting behind you?*

It was all designed to strike fear into the heart of every viewer, because fear was a sure-fire ratings winner.

Stan assured her he hadn't spoken to any other news outlet — presumably in the expectation of a bigger bottle this Christmas — so they were still ahead of the game. But only just.

They were barred from going into the cinema, even if it was only to film general shots of the lobby and box office. And more and more TV crews arrived while she wasted precious time arguing the toss with the cinema manager — a sapling of a man-child who appeared to have outgrown everything but his own acne.

Eve felt like screaming.

They should have been here *last night*. They could have beaten even the police to the scene. They could have caught the manager or ticket girl so stunned that they'd have been able to gain access. Instead they were left with generic shots of the outside of the building, and a few close-ups of film posters. Stuff *everybody* could get. And now everybody was going to be there for the body bag too. Even Guy Smith, Eve noted with an exasperated puff of her cheeks as the News 24/7 car parked rudely on the pavement.

Guy got out and straightened his tie in the passenger window before joining the media circus on the pavement.

"Been sick yet?" he asked Eve.

"Find Mark Franco yet?" she threw back at him.

"Touché," said Guy. "Although I did find an old boy who claimed to have been Napoleon's food taster in a previous life."

"Oh good," said Eve. "So the day wasn't wasted then."

Joe snorted and Guy shot him a withering look, then he plucked at the fringe of Eve's woollen scarf in that way that he obviously thought of as playful, instead of irritating as hell.

"What were *you* in a previous life, Eve?"

"Still tetchy, Guy." She tugged her scarf away from his hand sharply and tucked the ends into her coat.

"All right," he said. "Calm down."

Eve bridled. She hated being told to calm down when she was already calm. Guy might as well have patted her on the bum and told her not to worry her pretty little head about it.

Joe said suddenly, "Ross called. We've got to go."

Reluctantly, Eve followed him back towards the iWitness Volvo.

For some reason, Guy fell into step beside them, as if he were part of *their* crew, not a rival one. As if he weren't in danger of a thick lip.

"C'mon, Eve," he whined. "Let me take you out for a drink."

She didn't look at him. "Sure. Can my boyfriend come too?"

"You don't have a boyfriend. Everyone knows that."

"Really?" she said, "Mike *will* be disappointed to find out that he's a figment of my imagination."

"Mike *bollocks*," said Guy. "What's his star sign?"

"Capricorn."

"What's his mother's name?"

"Sylvia."

"What did he get you last Christmas?"

Eve fingered the heart-shaped locket on a slim gold chain around her neck. Her father had bought it for her twenty-seventh birthday. The last time he'd remembered a birthday.

Now he couldn't remember a daughter.

Guy was rebuffed.

But only for a second; he caught her up at the car.

Eve was starting to think she'd underestimated Guy Smith. He certainly was persistent and, for a reporter, that was half the battle.

He leaned in close and lowered his voice conspiratorially. "Listen, if you're, y'know, *gay* or something, just let me know. I won't tell."

He locked his lips and threw away the key.

Eve gave him a look that would have withered a sequoia.

70

It barely registered with Guy. "OK, listen," he said, as if they were in the middle of some kind of mutually beneficial negotiation. "Just say this Mike *was* a figment of your imagination. *Then* would you go out with me?"

"No."

"Why not?" he demanded.

Eve almost softened the blow. But there was something about Guy Smith that sucked the milk of human kindness right out of her and spat it on the floor.

So she just tugged open the crew-car door and said, "I *imagine* I could do better."

Eve fumed as they pulled away.

"Did you *hear* that arsehole?"

"I know!" said Joe.

"If I'm *gay*. It's men like him who make me wish I *was* gay!"

"I *know*!" said Joe, and started laughing.

"*I know you know!*" she yelled and then started laughing too.

That was true: Joe knew her better than anyone. They'd spent so many hours together over the past few years. In this car, or outside random buildings or in the edit suite, giggling at gore, cutting careful packages so people *thought* they'd seen blood, and putting aside the outtakes for the office Christmas party. The dismembered leg bobbing about Canary Wharf with a seagull on it; Guy Smith silently moving his lips while reading a press release. And Eve stupidly repeating the word "coroner" to camera until it had been so emptied of meaning that it didn't even sound like English any more.

Now she grinned as the tension of the morning started to dissipate.

"So what did Ross want?"

"Nothing. Ross didn't call. I just thought we should go before you smacked Guy."

"But we can't go, Joe! We haven't got the bag!"

"But we *have* got the name and address of the victim."

Eve was suddenly interested. "Oh yeah?"

He nodded. "Kevin Barr. And it's close by, too, in Paddington."

"How did you get that?"

"Ricky let it slip. The SOCOs have only just started here, so I thought we could go up there, do the family, pick up a picture, and still be back in time for the bag."

"Who's Ricky?" she frowned.

"Guy's cameraman." Joe rolled his eyes. "God, we really are just monkeys to you, aren't we?"

"Yes," said Eve soothingly. "But you're the *king* of the monkeys."

Her phone rang. It was Ross.

"Did you get the bag yet?"

No *Hello*. No *How are you?* No *Thanks for the great eyewitness interview*. Straight to the bag. That was Ross all over.

"Not yet," she said. "But how about that exclusive?"

"Yeah, great," said Ross unenthusiastically — apparently because Stan the paramedic wasn't hot or blonde.

Or dead.

"Where are you now?"

"We've got a tip on the family of the victim. We're going to do them and come back."

"OK," said Ross grudgingly. "But don't miss the bag."

Eve hung up and turned to Joe. "How come Ricky's suddenly sharing info with us?"

Joe shrugged. "I guess we monkeys gotta stick together."

She smiled, then said, "So everyone knows I don't have a boyfriend?"

"Most people," said Joe.

Eve nodded and bit her thumbnail. "You think everyone thinks I'm gay?"

"Of course," he nodded cheerfully. "Everyone but me!"

The address Ricky had given Joe was a flat above a burger bar off Praed Street. The smell took Eve back to her student days, when her diet had seemed to consist almost exclusively of salt and hot grease. Her mouth watered in remembrance.

There was a panel beside the door with six push-button bells on it — each with a corresponding name-tag. The top one said "Barr" in green ink.

Eve took a deep breath. She'd been knocking on doors like this for too long now. Doors belonging to families who had started the day just like other families, but who had ended it as something else entirely. Something fractured and sad and unbearably changed.

The first contact with a bereaved family was never easy, but every reporter just had to get on with it, or get out of the job.

"I hate this," she said.

"Me too," said Joe.

"Yeah, but they don't hate *you*," she said. "For some reason they never hate the camera guy. They only hate the reporter."

Joe nodded solemnly. "That's because they know the monkey only dances to the organ-grinder's tune."

Eve giggled, then glared at him furiously. "Don't make me laugh! I'm *serious*, Joe! These people are grieving and you're making me laugh!"

"Sorry."

Eve rang the bell for the top-floor flat. There was no response.

"Come on, sad people," she said coldly, and rang it again, feeling that icy spike start to work its way between her heart and her head.

There was a crackling sound and then a man's voice said, "What?"

"Hello, is that Mr Barr?"

"Yeah."

"The father of Kevin Barr?"

"Yeah."

"Mr Barr, I'm very sorry to trouble you, sir. This is Eve Singer from iWitness News. I wondered if we might have a word?"

There was a brief buzzing pause and a whispered off-intercom exchange. Then Mr Barr said, "I'm coming down," and cut them off.

Eve and Joe exchanged hopeful looks and waited.

While they did, the snow started again.

Eve loved snow in the suburbs, where it made everything silent and magical, but snow in central

London was never the same. Here it seemed wet and depressed even as it fell — as if it knew what was waiting for it once it hit the ground and so wasn't bothering to make an effort at any stage. Rightly so, as the snow here slowly met its miserable destiny of green plastic recycling bags piled up outside the row of shops.

Footsteps approached beyond the door; the sound of locks and chains.

Eve took a deep breath.

The middle-aged man who opened the door was short, round, and wearing a red onesie that made him look like Yosemite Sam.

"Mr Barr?"

"Yes."

"We're terribly sorry to intrude —"

Without warning, the man threw a bucket of water over them. "Fucking vultures!" he said, then slammed the door.

"*Shit!*" hissed Joe. He turned away and frantically checked his camera, while Eve stood, open-mouthed, looking at the front of her soaked coat, feeling the icy water run between the buttons, under her breasts and down her stomach.

"Camera's screwed," said Joe. He looked at Eve. "You OK?"

She nodded slowly. Then she muttered, "Bastard!" and reached for the bell again.

Joe's hand stopped hers. "Leave it, Eve."

"Fuck that!" She shook him off angrily and punched the bell with her forefinger.

The door opened immediately.

"He said you'd try again," said Mr Barr.

"Who did?"

"That ponce off the news," he said. "So —"

The second bucket of water hit Eve square in the face.

Eve perched on the corner of a desk and tried to dry her hair with an iWitness tea-towel.

"Why don't you just go out with Guy Smith?" said Joe. "It would make life easier for both of us."

"Why don't *you* just go out with him?" she suggested. "That would make life easier for me."

Her clothing hung over several radiators in the bustling newsroom, and she was dressed in the gym gear she always left at work and never used. Lycra leggings and a crop top, under Joe's jumper.

"I'm sorry," said Joe seriously. "I should've smelled a rat."

"That's OK. I *did* smell a rat but I went along with it anyway. So who's more stupid?"

"You?" Joe guessed.

"Exactly," she nodded. "*And* you told me not to ring the bell again."

"I did," said Joe with a dramatic sigh. "Let that be a lesson to you."

"Yep," said Eve ruefully. "Total obedience from now on."

"You missed the *fucking bag*!"

They both looked round. Ross was coming at them across the room, already furious.

"The camera was waterlogged," said Joe.

"Yes," said Eve. "And so were we. I had hypothermia."

"I don't give a shit if you had *Ebola*! You're paid to do a job and I expect that job to be *done*."

"That's not fair!" said Eve. "And we *did* do the job. We did a bloody good job! We got the only eyewitness interview! *Exclusively*."

"The audience wants to see the body. It's all they care about."

"Bullshit," said Eve.

"Oh yeah?" shouted Ross. "We had complaints."

"I don't believe it."

"We had *complaints*," he insisted.

"Who the hell calls up the TV news to complain about not seeing the body bag?"

"*I* would!" They both looked at Ross in surprise and he shrugged. "There's something about a pretty girl and a body bag in the same shot. And obviously I'm not alone."

"I'm sorry," said Eve sarcastically, "I didn't realize I was here to satisfy your perverted needs."

"Well, check your contract," he snapped. "How's the camera?"

"In the air dryer," said Joe. "In bits."

"If it's broken it's coming out of your pay." He stomped away.

Eve called after him, "So what do you want us to do about Kevin Barr's family?"

Ross turned again and kept walking, but backwards. "Fuck the family," he said. "Now I want the X-ray of the guy with the knife in his head. You know, like those ones of puppies that swallow arrows and shit."

He slammed through the double doors, and Eve and Joe exchanged long-suffering looks.

"What a dick," she spat.

"Massive," agreed Joe. "Massive dick on legs."

"What are we going to do about the X-ray then?"

Joe waved a dismissive hand. "Ross is just whistling Dixie. Nobody's going to get that."

Eve ventured, "Maybe Janey in the coroner's office . . .?"

Joe had taken Janey out a couple of times, but now he gave two thumbs-downs. "Not likely."

"No? What happened?"

"Nothing. She's just . . . thicker than she looks."

"I'm sorry," she said, and patted his arm.

"I'm not," he shrugged.

"I got you some soup to warm you both up."

They turned to find Katie Merino holding out two paper cups of coffee-machine soup.

"Thanks," said Eve.

"I have a sweater you can borrow if you like," said Katie sweetly, even though she was plainly two sizes smaller than Eve.

"Thanks," said Joe, "but I don't think it would fit me."

Katie laughed and squeezed his bicep and said, "No, probably not."

She went back to her desk.

"That was nice of her," said Joe.

"Maybe," said Eve darkly.

They turned as the six o'clock bulletins came on across the wall of screens.

"Every other fucker's got the fucking bag!" Ross shouted through the open door of his office.

Eve sighed and felt her clothes. They were still damp. She turned them over to dry the other side. "I hate this bloody job," she said with feeling.

Joe eyed her carefully. "What's up?"

"Nothing," she said.

"No," he said, "really. We've missed shit before. What's wrong?"

Eve shook her head silently. She trusted Joe, but she couldn't tell him all the things that were wrong with her life. It would make her sound pathetic and needy, and there was nothing anyone could do about any of it anyway, so what was the point? Nothing bad lasted for ever, everything would be OK in the end, and other assorted optimistic bullshit.

She'd just keep going.

She put her hand on her damp coat. "This stuff's nearly dry. I'm going home."

"Not in rush hour!" said Joe in mock horror. They rarely went home on time, and rush hour was a joke that they laughed at to keep from feeling gypped about it — a mythical thing that they'd heard tell of, but never seen with their own eyes.

Eve gave a wan smile.

"Don't go home," Joe went on. "Come out to dinner with me."

"Dinner?" She was surprised. She and Joe ate together all the time — street-corner sandwiches and crew-car takeaways — but they'd never deliberately *gone out* to eat together.

"Why not?" said Joe. "We've had a crap day and I feel like a nice meal and a bottle of wine, don't you?"

"I can't," she said. "Thanks, but I —"

— have to wash my hair.

"— I have to start my Christmas shopping."

She didn't know why she was lying to Joe. He had no idea about her father's illness. Nobody did, apart from the doctor and Mrs Solomon. It was stupid, really, but telling people that Duncan Singer was losing his mind would have felt like a throwaway excuse, when the truth was so complex and horribly real.

So real she might cry.

"But thanks," she went on hurriedly. "Can I take a raincheck?"

"Sure," he said. "And, you know, we don't have to have dinner. We can talk any time."

She smiled and shrugged on her coat. "Thanks, Joe. See you tomorrow."

"Night," he said, and leaned down and kissed her.

Only on the cheek, but it was a surprise, nonetheless.

On the swaying Tube to Isleworth, Eve turned the kiss over and over in her mind. It was a peck on the cheek, and Joe was a friend, and far too young for her. But she hadn't been kissed by a man for years — even on the cheek — and that friendly peck allowed her to imagine asking Joe — or *anyone* — back to hers for a nightcap for the first time in a long, long time.

She was so out of practice! Where would she start? Alcohol would probably be a sensible place. A nice bottle of wine to complement . . . What? Her default aphrodisiac of baked beans on toast? Then after dinner, she and her date could push her father up the stairs together, before relaxing in front of the TV to watch how to make oven gloves, all to music left over from *Debbie Does Dallas*.

Eve smiled wryly at her reflection in the tunnel-black window and decided not to overthink the kiss.

Then she overthought it all the way home.

CHAPTER
ELEVEN

7 December

"We're going Christmas shopping!"

Duncan Singer frowned up at her from the sofa. "I'm busy," he said, pointing at the TV, where *How It's Made* was on. "Have you watched this?"

"Yes," she said.

"I haven't," he said. "It's very good. They make all kinds of things."

Today they were making umbrellas, pocket knives and cowboy saddles. Eve had seen this episode at least ten times just in passing, and knew there was a lot of work in a cowboy saddle. Tinplate and rivets and each layer of thick leather had to be shaved cleverly around the edges to make sure everything was smooth. *In a process known as skiving,* she thought, in time to the voiceover.

"Come on, Dad," she said. "It'll be fun."

Duncan looked up at her as if for the first time.

"What will be fun?"

"Christmas shopping."

"Fun for *you*, maybe," he said. "But what's in it for me?"

"Loads. There'll be lights and presents and we're going to meet Charlotte for a Christmas coffee, like an eggnog latte or something, and a mince pie, and there'll be carols in all the shops. You love carols."

"Who's Carol?" he said suspiciously.

Eve giggled. "Not Carol the person, carol the song," she said, and she started to sing "God Rest Ye Merry Gentlemen".

He joined in and they finished together. He knew all the words, and still had a good baritone.

"So," laughed Eve, "you want to go and hear the carols?"

"Who's Carol?" he said suspiciously.

"I'll get your coat," she said.

She got it from the hall cupboard. It was thick grey wool and very old and weighed a ton. Her father seemed to have had it all her life.

She took it into the front room and held it out for him.

"Is that my coat?"

"Yes," she said. "Put it on."

He did put it on. His shoulders bowed a little under its weight.

"It's very warm."

"I know," she said. "But outside it's really cold."

"Well, we should go outside then," he said, and she laughed again.

"It's not funny," he told her irritably. "It's logical."

"You're right," said Eve. "I'm sorry."

Together they stood behind the front door while Eve put on her own coat and gloves and a woollen hat with matching scarf, then picked up her bag and checked for money and keys and phone. Then she opened the door in a widening slice of dazzling white.

"Snow!" he blinked.

"That's right," said Eve. Another few inches had fallen overnight and everything was smooth and rounded under a bright-blue sky. "Careful on the path."

Gingerly Duncan put one foot on to the path, then quickly withdrew it, leaving a four-inch-deep boot-shaped hole in the white, criss-crossed at the bottom with tread.

"I don't want to lose my foot," he said cautiously.

"Oh you won't," she said. "Here, hold on to my arm."

He held on to her arm and she started up the path, but he didn't budge.

"Come on, Dad . . ."

But Duncan Singer looked around at the perfectly smooth, white garden.

"Dad?"

"What?"

"We're going Christmas shopping."

"Oh yes."

He stepped again into his own print, then carefully placed his other foot down in the fresh snow in front of it and stood there as if stuck. Planted like an Egyptian.

"The taxi's coming."

"I don't think it's safe," he said. "You go on without me."

"Don't you want to go shopping?" she said.

"No," he said. "I'm only outside because I'm wearing this coat."

Eve didn't know whether to laugh or cry. At this rate she'd end up buying Christmas presents from the one-stop shop at the station. Bad wine and Cup-a-Soup and a bumper box of tampons. Woohoo!

She looked at her father teetering nervously in the snow, and sighed. "OK," she said. "Let's go back indoors."

Duncan picked up his front foot and stepped carefully backwards on to the doormat, and from there he reversed into the house.

Eve closed the door and slowly pulled off her hat, gloves and scarf and dropped them on the hall table with a sigh. No shopping, no Charlotte, no eggnog latte, no lights and carols and mince pies.

Shit. *And* she'd have to pay for the taxi . . .

"Have you been Christmas shopping?" Duncan asked brightly.

Eve hesitated and then said, "Yes."

"What did you get me?" he said.

"What did you want?" she said.

"A glass eye," he said.

"Well," said Eve wearily, "that's what I got you."

CHAPTER
TWELVE

All of his life, the killer had been waiting to die.

His earliest memory was of waking in a hospital with a stranger's heart in his chest, and a doctor murmuring nearby, "*He's living on borrowed time . . .*"

The soft, overheard words confused him, and haunted him from that moment on.

How much time had he borrowed? A week? A year? Ten years? From whom had his time been borrowed? Would he have to pay it back? And what would happen when his time ran out?

Could he borrow more?

He fretted constantly about the heart. Sometimes it didn't even work! If he sat very still in a quiet room, he could hear it not beating. He had to press his palm hard against his chest to feel even the faintest flutter. It made him worry that there was nothing inside him but a hole filled with surgical wadding. Only if he ran up and down stairs until he felt light-headed did the sluggish organ bother to stir — and then sometimes it got away from him and beat so hard and so fast that he became all sweaty and panicky. Once he'd fainted and an ambulance had to be called, and a doctor had told him off angrily — as if the heart were not *his*, but only on loan, and to be returned when he'd done with it.

Or when *it* had done with *him* . . .

After that he wasn't allowed to run.

Whenever he dressed for the day or undressed for the bath, the boy fingered the thick red ridge of tissue that ran down the middle of his chest, sometimes picking at its edges until it bled. Nannies slapped him if they caught him. Grabbed his wrist and yanked his arm and shook him like a doll. *Leave it alone! What's wrong with you?* But he didn't *know* what was wrong with him. How could he, when he couldn't trust the heart in his own chest? Was it a shiny pink pump? Or a slack fist of rancid muscle that would soon fail? How could he tell what was true? Doctors said all was well, but doctors were liars. He had only his parents' vague eyes to gauge what was amiss, and they told another — much more frightening — story.

Once when he was six, he'd asked his mother to tell him that story, but she'd become tearful, and his father had told him sharply not to upset her, so he'd never asked again.

His parents had always been distant — as if they knew they would lose him, and didn't want to be too close when it happened.

That distance grew along with him. He never understood them, and they never understood him.

Always wan and weak, he had no friends. He was bullied at school, in the park, and even in his own room on the one occasion another boy came home for tea.

"Cut open a bully and you'll find a coward inside," his father told him afterwards, with the brisk confidence of someone who had never been bullied.

But instead the boy simply stopped going out to play.

At eight he stopped going to school too, and nobody seemed to care. What was the point in preparing him for a future he did not have?

He spent the days reading, or wandering through the echoing house, his only companions the paintings that had been in his family for generations. There was a minor Tintoretto in the opulent hallway, scenes of love and lingering death on every wall, and a crop of delicate miniatures on the piano — all in black velvet frames, so as not to damage the Bechstein's mirrored gleam.

He started to copy the paintings. Idly at first, in biro in schoolbooks, but quickly he developed a young draughtsman's eye, and was soon demanding sketchbooks and charcoal, then canvases, paints, brushes. An easel.

Copying became too small a word. He *ingested* the art. Gulped it through his eyes as he consumed food and water through his mouth, and it nourished him likewise. He gobbled the Masters from walls and from books like a starving man, pursuing the elusive alchemy that turned brute charcoal and oils into divine depictions of death.

So *Death and the Maiden* was his elevenses — the beautiful girl whose modesty could not hide her desire for her skeletal suitor, and *The Martyrdom of St Sebastian* was tea — the beautiful boy bound and pricked like a bun, leaking red rivulets, his eyes turned to heaven where he would dwell for ever . . .

But dinner was the gruesome *Danse Macabre* that wound its wooden way around the walls of his father's study. People going about their everyday lives were waylaid and dragged off by cunning Death in an orgy of mortality. A gambler unwittingly dealt crooked cards to the Grim Reaper, an ignorant knight was impaled on his own lance, a mourner was so distracted by one corpse that he couldn't see he was about to become another.

By day its joyous cruelty excited the boy, but his nightmares were plagued by bony fingers gripping his wrist, or reaching into his chest to take back what rightly belonged to another. Often he was woken, shrieking and sweating, by the tug of veins still attached to his innards . . .

He barely saw his parents. He was supervised by transient nannies, and tutored by a loop of misfitting, misfiring teachers who were either uninterested in life as a whole or uninterested only in him.

Still, better that than the sweaty, grunting Mr Treadwell, who'd been *too* interested in him . . .

The boy had tried cutting Mr Treadwell open to find the promised coward, but there was only blood inside him — and a lot of shouting and threats outside — and his parents decided that their son had had as much schooling as he'd ever need in a world where he already had money and a name, and didn't engage another teacher. They had to sell the Tintoretto to get rid of *that* one, leaving a pale square on the wall as a constant reminder of how much their son had cost them.

But he hadn't cared.

Because while Mr Treadwell had dripped and raged downstairs, the boy's reluctant heart had finally caught up with his daring — and hammered like Thor.

He had sat on his bed of shame and laughed and laughed and *laughed* with the pleasure of knowing that — at last — he was truly alive.

A few months after Mr Treadwell left, a curious thing happened.

The boy's grandmother died.

And then his grandfather died. And then his *other* grandmother died too.

While he outlived them all!

At first he was confused: there was no logic to it. *He* was the one living on borrowed time. But then, slowly, the theory started to grow in his mind that somehow those people were taking his place. That the time he was borrowing could be borrowed from *them*. That they had stepped between him and the Reaper. By the time he entered his teens, he'd begun to anticipate the death of others with something like pleasure.

So he was not sorry to hear that a second cousin once removed had been *permanently* removed by lightning on a Berkshire golf course. And he was also not sorry when a distant aunt was crushed by a taxi near Hyde Park Corner.

90

He was not even sorry when a sudden embolism claimed his own father.

Eventually he was only sorry that he hadn't done a better job with Mr Treadwell . . .

CHAPTER
THIRTEEN

8 December

Joe was sitting on Eve's desk when she got in, and it lifted her spirits to see him there.

More than was usual.

Don't be such a schoolgirl! she told herself firmly. *It was a peck on the cheek.*

"Hi," he said. "Get your shopping done?"

"No," she said. "Got busy with other stuff."

She sat down and while her laptop fired up she sifted through her in-tray. There wasn't much — most communications now came via email.

But there were a few bits of junk and subscriptions, and a small white envelope, addressed in copperplate handwriting.

Joe picked it up. "Fan mail?"

"Probably from Ross," she snorted.

She liked fan mail. There would be a letter inside. Most likely from an old lady, if the writing was anything to go by. Saying how Eve reminded her of her granddaughter, and didn't she have lovely hair? She got at least one of those a month. Most fan mail was sweet.

Letters and teddy bears holding hearts, and the occasional bouquet.

Although once she'd received a doctored photo of herself — naked and spread-eagled — wrapped tightly around a matchbox filled with what looked horribly like semen.

There was no business like show business . . .

Joe ripped open the envelope, unfolded a single sheet of paper and read out loud.

"*Dear Miss Singer. I'm a great admirer of your work —*"

He stopped and raised a mock-petulant eyebrow. "I think he means *our* work."

Eve gave a dismissive flap of her hand. "Well, *I* think he sounds charming and intelligent."

"Yeah, well hold your horses," said Joe. "I haven't got to the bit yet where he wants a photocopy of your nipples."

Eve tapped her watch. "Then get there fast, monkey-boy. You *know* there's always a queue in the copy room."

Joe grinned and read on.

"*But I believe that on this occasion you may have missed something.*"

"*Missed* something?" frowned Eve. "Are you sure it's not addressed to *you*?"

"Ha ha." Joe turned the paper over, but there was nothing on the reverse. "That's all there is."

Eve peered into the envelope, then tipped a little micro-SD memory card into her palm.

"Here," she said. "You missed it."

"Very funny," said Joe.

There was only one file on the card. Eve opened it and a window flickered briefly then consumed the screen in black.

For a single sick second, she thought she'd opened a virus that would bring down the whole channel, but then a video clip started to play. A vertical window of darkness, and the vague shape of a man lounging in a seat.

In a row of seats?

In the background was the sound of shouting and screeching tyres.

And then a flickering light illuminated the scene.

Eve's heart jolted and she slapped her laptop shut with a bang.

"*Shit*," she hissed. "That's Kevin Barr."

They went to Regazzoni's, the little coffee shop they preferred to the big chains. Regazzoni's had chaotic service, bad lighting and hard chairs, but the coffee was great, and the gloom allowed the privacy they needed to watch the clip in full.

Kevin Barr was dead, but he was also strangely beautiful. The flickering light of the movie screen cast him into a startling relief of a human being, floating against the dark velvet seats. With one boot on the seat in front of him, his arms outstretched and his head curiously cocked, he had the bacchanalian air of a man who had died drunk and laughing.

Whatever the truth, the image was compelling.

They watched it again.

"Who the hell sent this?" she whispered. "You think they're trying to sell it?"

"If they are, they have a lot to learn about the art of negotiation," said Joe wryly. He picked up the envelope and examined it closely. "No contact details, no demand for payment. Nothing."

They kept watching — morbidly fascinated.

"Stan said at least one person had their phone out in the cinema," Joe remembered. "It must have been one of them."

Eve shook her head. "But he said he turned and saw the body as he was leaving. So the film was over by then. In this clip, it's still playing. You can hear it."

They watched it again, the teaspoon clatter and steamer hiss of Regazzoni's fading beyond gunfire and the throbbing soundtrack.

"I think the *killer* filmed this," said Eve.

Joe frowned. "If he did, why would he send it to you?"

Eve shrugged. "Why does anyone send anything to a TV reporter?"

"Because they want to see it on TV."

"Exactly."

"Sick," muttered Joe.

"What are we going to do with it?" said Eve carefully.

She didn't *feel* careful; she felt excited. This clip could secure her whole future. She knew that with an unerring instinct that made it a certainty. A cold-blooded killer had reached out to her. Wanted to share his crime with her. Had sent her a *video* of his still-warm victim . . .

This was the break she'd been desperate for. This was her chance to move on to bigger and better things. With more money. More money would mean better care for Duncan, a stair-lift so he didn't fall on top of her, days out in the countryside, respite care so she could go to the spa, or just sit in a coffee shop with a good book and — for once — not worry about Mrs Solomon's overtime . . .

In the split second when all this rushed through her mind, Eve could feel her iron self-control relaxing, could almost smell the salt on the shingle, and turn the rough-smooth pages of a new book —

"We can't use it," said Joe.

It was like a reality slap.

Of course they couldn't. She knew that.

"Shouldn't we let Ross decide?"

Joe shook his head. "We can't give it to him. If he sees it, he'll use it."

Eve knew that too. Because *journalistically* it made perfect sense. But the *moral* buck stopped with her.

"If Ross finds out we're holding out on him, we could both lose our jobs."

"How's he going to find out?" shrugged Joe. "We're the only two people who know about it."

"Not true," she said. "Whoever sent the clip knows it too. And if we don't broadcast the video, what's to stop him sending it to somebody who *will*?"

Joe nodded, then said, "The clip was sent to you, Eve, so the decision is yours. I just don't want to end up doing PR for Jack the Ripper."

He smiled, but his eyes were deadly serious.

Eve knew he was right. She closed her laptop with a soft click that sounded to her like the death knell of all her hopes for a better life.

Stupid moral buck!

CHAPTER
FOURTEEN

Eve was home early and tried to watch every news bulletin on every channel every hour, although her father got crabby every time she switched over from *How It's Made*.

No other channel showed the clip. That didn't mean nobody else had received it — just that, if they had, they'd made the same moral decision as she and Joe had.

The relief was intoxicating, by her pretty low standards, and when the video wasn't on the nine o'clock news, she decided to celebrate by putting up the Christmas tree. She hadn't bothered last year, and had been surprised by how much she'd missed it.

The attic was a minefield of memories and mouse shit. Carefully she picked her way through it, catching torch-lit glimpses of the past. Neddy, her rocking horse, on rusted springs; Stuart's football boots and broken goalposts; a box of her mother's eclectic reading — Collette and Betty MacDonald and Kazuo Ishiguro.

Her father's guitar.

It gave her a pang to see it. Duncan should be strumming old Beatles songs, or out on the lake in his dinghy, or downing a pint in the Black Sheep with his best mate, Colin. The two of them had worked together for years and together they'd been a riot — so sharp and funny that she could have sold tickets. Stories of ceilings collapsing and fingers in sockets and carpets on fire and narrow escapes from randy housewives . . . No story was worth telling unless it was funny at the end — however painful it might be along the way.

Colin had visited for a good while after Duncan got sick, but he didn't come round any more, and Eve didn't blame him. Nobody wanted to be reminded of his own tenuous grasp on sanity. There was no funny ending in that.

The Christmas tree was wedged between a joist and the roughly pointed brickwork that separated their attic from Mr Elias's. There was a separate bag containing the baubles and a bird's nest of fairy lights.

Eve manhandled them to the hatch, then came down the ladder slowly.

In the front room, her father watched her with slit-eyed suspicion as she unpacked the tree from its cardboard box.

"What's that?"

"The Christmas tree, Dad. Remember?"

"No," he snapped. "I don't remember a box of trees. Why don't *you* try remembering some time? See how *you* like it."

Eve ignored him and concentrated on the tree. They'd had it for years and years. Since she was five or six. She used to watch her father do this, thinking it impossibly complicated. It wasn't, of course. The stand, the trunk, the little holders for each of the stiff, prickly branches, each one colour coded and slotting into place. She found a hypnotic rhythm to the resumed drone of *How It's Made* and the roar of unseen jets tearing holes in the sky.

The tree grew in her hands until it was six feet tall, draped with twinkling fairy lights and ripe for baubles and tinsel.

"There!" she said. "Shall we decorate it together?"

She turned around, but Duncan wasn't on the sofa.

"Dad?"

No answer.

"Shit!" Eve's mind reached the kitchen before she did, trying to remember whether she'd turned the stove off at the mains. She had, but it didn't matter. He wasn't frying shoe polish in a pan, or taking the toaster apart.

This time.

"*Shit.*" She hurried to the downstairs loo. Duncan was OK if all he needed was a pee, but if it was anything more, he had to be distracted from the results. He would stare into the bowl for ages, and sometimes reach into the murky water . . .

She rapped on the door.

"Dad?"

No answer.

She cracked it open.

Empty.

She took the stairs two at a time, hoping to head him off in the bathroom.

But he wasn't there either.

"Dad!"

Eve rushed from room to room. She looked in cupboards and under beds. He had never hidden before, but there could easily be a first time.

It was only when she found his wellington boots missing from beside the back door that she knew Duncan Singer had left the building.

Deep footprints in the snow disappeared around the side of the house.

"Shit, shit, SHIT!"

Eve toed off her slippers and shoved her bare feet into her own cold boots, then — without even grabbing a coat — hurried out into the night to find her father.

CHAPTER
FIFTEEN

Abel Elias had lived on College Road for so long that even when he wasn't at home, he stopped talking every thirty seconds to let a plane pass overhead.

It had gained him a reputation for gravitas that had stood him in good stead in the always sombre world of marine insurance. His firm insured big ships for big money. Losses were not only financial, but almost always accompanied by human tragedy.

In such situations, nobody wanted to deal with a gabbler. What they wanted was somebody who took them and their ships and their cargoes and their crews *seriously*, goddammit!

And Mr Elias, who stopped — apparently to think deeply — every few sentences was what they wanted, and business had been good.

At his wife's funeral, Mr Elias had delivered a eulogy so full of heartfelt spaces that it had brought a congregation of death-hardened pensioners almost to their knees with grief.

So he was used to being listened to and being obeyed, and whenever he did the rounds of his neighbours for the purpose of collecting money to maintain the red phone box outside their homes, they were far too intimidated by his silences to refuse.

Of course, Mr Elias didn't need the money. He was rolling in it, truth be told. He could have maintained a thousand red phone boxes all by himself. But he thought it was good for community spirit to give everybody a sense of ownership of the phone box. It ensured that the locals respected it, and the work he put into keeping it nice.

Mr Elias was sixty-six, and missed the office, but keeping on top of things around College Road was his job now, and he put on a collar and tie every morning, even if he was only mowing the lawn, to show he took his work seriously.

That work extended beyond the red phone box to calling the council whenever a street light went out, a pavement cracked or a speed-bump was required — and the police if anyone double-parked or played music that was too loud. Or simply not to his taste.

Things got *done* in College Road, and Mr Elias did most of them.

And his neighbours appreciated it. He knew that, because since his wife had died, several of them — all widows — had started to send him cards, thanking him for his efforts.

Mrs Jamira in number 56 had even baked him flapjacks. They were incompatible with his dentures, but he appreciated the sentiment.

Mr Elias had lived next door to the Singer family for twenty-five years. They had been reasonable enough neighbours, although Duncan was a little *robust* for Mr

Elias's liking. A little too fond of beer, and his children too fond of ball games and loud parties. They didn't really socialize — although Duncan had once fixed his lawn mower — but they exchanged Christmas cards, and Duncan had given him a fiver for the phone box whenever he'd asked.

Then one day three years ago, Eve had opened the door instead of Duncan and dug in her bag for a contribution.

Mr Elias had known Eve since she was five years old. Mostly he knew her from throwing balls and boomerangs and aeroplanes back over the hedge that separated their gardens. But he hadn't seen her for a long while, and when she'd opened the door he'd been a little flustered by the attractive young woman she'd become. She'd told him she was on television now, but Mr Elias only watched the BBC and hadn't seen her. She'd told him that she'd come home because Duncan needed help, and he'd offered any assistance she might require. She'd thanked him, but had never called on him.

He'd been a little disappointed, even as he'd been relieved.

He was rather lonely, and had hoped that Eve's arrival might spark more neighbourly relations.

Oh well.

In the past three years, he had barely seen Duncan, and instead had watched Eve Singer's comings and goings.

Never with a boyfriend, he noted.

Just her — shutting the front door and walking down the lavender path with her dark hair shining like a shampoo ad, and her breasts . . . being breasts.

Abel Elias was not a lech, but he was still a man. Eve Singer had turned from a gawky teenager into a televisual temptress right under his nose, and that would have been as hard to overlook as his own top lip.

Since Jennifer had died four years ago, he had almost forgotten what she had looked like. Even when he was reminded by the picture of his wife on the mantelpiece, he was often surprised by the discrepancy between memory and photographic evidence. Had her eyes really been that close together? Were her teeth a bit buck, and her hair so unflatteringly mumsy?

He'd never noticed before.

Before Eve —

There was a knock on the door and Mr Elias flinched as if the Pervert Police had finally tracked him down.

It was Eve Singer, in just jeans and a thin cardigan, with her arms crossed for warmth across her . . . chest . . . and with two bright circles of red on her pale cheeks from hurrying through the snow.

"Hi, Mr Elias," she said. "Dad's wandered off. It looks as if he's come round here."

She pointed to the snow and he saw large boot prints leading from his gate, up his garden path and around the side of the house. Duncan must have passed his front window, but the curtains were drawn.

"Do you mind if I have a quick look round the back?"

"Of course," said Mr Elias. "Come in for a moment. I'll put my boobs on and help you."

Eve blushed and said she didn't want to be a bother, but it wasn't any bother — he was keen to help his neighbour look for a missing person, even if it were only in his own back garden. It would make him feel useful, and would be the most exciting thing that had happened to him since the flapjacks — and they were in June!

What if Duncan Singer were hiding? What if he'd climbed over the fence at the end of the garden and gone into Mr Speight's garden? That would be dangerous; Mr Speight's garden was an obstacle course of old flower pots and broken cold frames. What if he'd fallen over in the snow and couldn't get up? Mr Elias made a mental note of where his shovel and spare blanket were. Whatever the situation, Mr Elias was ready to leap into action — once his over-socks were on, and his boots were on, and his gloves and scarf and hat and coat were on . . .

He held the door open for Eve, and then she waited for him and followed him around the house and into the back garden by the light of the Maglite torch he rarely got a chance to use.

Mr Elias liked the way she let him lead the way. It was good to be in charge of something again, even if it was only an expedition to the bottom of the garden. It made him feel thirty years younger.

The back gardens here were long and boringly straight, and so Mr Elias had planted evergreen shrubbery in waves down either side, which formed a charming, winding pathway to the invisible shed at the bottom. Duncan Singer's boot prints were clear to see, wending their way between the greenery in the silver snow; all they had to do was follow them.

After the first stand of Red Robin, the house disappeared behind them and it was as if they were completely alone in the heavy, snow-damped air.

"Deep snow," said Mr Elias, and was immediately embarrassed by the dullness of his conversational gambit.

"Yes," said Eve.

He couldn't blame her for the monosyllable. He'd given her nothing to work with. Discussing the weather! It didn't get a lot duller than that.

"They say it'll last till New Year," he said, before he could stop himself.

"Amazing," said Eve, but Mr Elias could tell she wasn't amazed.

By the snow or by him — and deservedly so.

He felt his modest hopes of better neighbourly relations starting to crumble.

Each year since Eve Singer had come home, Mr Elias had bought a ridiculously big turkey and all the trimmings, in the vague hope that he might muster the courage to ask her and Duncan to eat Christmas dinner with him. Each year he had not — and his freezer was always so stuffed with old turkey that by August he had to throw some away to make space for fresh festive failure.

Mr Elias knew what the problem was. He wasn't used to talking to people any more. Not since Jennifer had died. Even before that — not since he'd stopped working. He had nobody to talk *to* any more. These days he was lucky if the postman stopped to chat one morning a week, and then it was always about cars, in which Mr Elias had no interest that wasn't faked. He needed more practice in chit-chat. Then he'd have been prepared. But how was he to know that Eve Singer would suddenly knock on his door and ask him to join her on an important quest down the garden? It was too late now. He would just have to do the best he could in the time remaining.

Which was short, because they were already at the conifer stand.

"Still, we had a good summer."

Mr Elias realized he had totally lost it. While he had been sitting watching TV and defrosting meals for one over the past four years, he'd had no idea that he was losing it. His trademark gaps still came easily, but the talking between the gaps was apparently beyond him now. There was only one more curve in the shrubbery — one more turn before they would reach the shed and find Duncan Singer and then they wouldn't be alone any more, and might never be again, and Mr Elias was seized with a sudden panic. He *had* to say something interesting. *Had* to engage her. Not because of the crush or the dinner, but because of the *humanity*. Had to show her that he was a *person* — not just a boring old fart of a neighbour. Had to make some kind of *connection*. The feeling was overwhelming. Almost *physical* —

It burst out of him.

108

"Would you and your father like to join me for Christmas dinner?"

An Air India 767 yanked the words from Mr Elias, tore them into atoms in the sky, and sprinkled them soundlessly on to the powdery snow.

Mr Elias had said something.

Eve stopped and looked at him. "I'm sorry?"

Mr Elias stared at the jet lumbering away behind the houses.

"Oh nothing," he said with a flap of his hand. "No matter."

Eve gave him an uncertain smile and they set off again, round the rhododendrons — and there was Duncan, trying the door of the garden shed in his trousers and shirtsleeves, his rubber boots his only concession to the weather.

Mission accomplished.

"Dad?" Eve stepped forward and touched her father's arm gently.

And he swung around and punched her straight in the face.

"*PHOEBE!*"

CHAPTER
SIXTEEN

Abel Elias and his wife had not had children.

Not after Phoebe, anyway.

Because Phoebe had been an impossible act to follow. She was as bright as a button, with dark-brown whorls of hair and a ready smile almost from the day she was born. Jennifer's mother — a pessimistic old cow — had insisted it was wind, but Jennifer and Abel had known better. Phoebe was a smiler from the off, and then a laugher, until finally even Granny Bartlett had grudgingly conceded the point.

Phoebe had done everything early. Sat up. Rolled over. Crawled.

She had her own way of crawling. She'd rock along on her belly and elbows, more like a dolphin than a baby, propelled by great scissor kicks of her white towelling legs. By the time she was six months old, she was caterpillaring her way up and down the living room so efficiently that Abel and Jennifer called her The Worm.

Mr Elias hadn't been in marine insurance back then. He'd been doing his teacher training. Geography was his subject. His father had been in the Foreign Service and the family had spent time in the Far East and

Africa. Abel Elias was enthused by the world, and enthusiastic about showing it to the next generation. Teaching geography seemed like a perfect combination.

And it also seemed that The Worm had inherited his curiosity about the world, because *she* couldn't *wait* to go travelling!

Abel and Jennifer would spend the evenings with the television off, proudly watching their daughter wriggle and giggle triumphantly across the carpet, gripping the white hyacinths that Abel grew every year, squealing at her own reflection in the copper fire-dogs, peek-a-booing behind the furniture. Now and then she would stop — but only to brace herself on her chubby arms, as if coming up for air — and stare up at the wall or the ceiling as if she would conquer them *later*. Then she would laugh and turn around and head off in another direction, filled with the joy of motion.

While they watched, they would joke about getting her a little spotted hanky knotted on a stick and sending her out into the world to make it on her own. "I don't know though," Abel would always conclude with faux caution, "let's give her a month or two." And then they would laugh, and kiss each other, and crawl around the floor to head off The Worm at the armchair.

It was forty years since Abel Elias had crawled on a lounge carpet.

Almost to the day.

One evening, just before she reached nine months old, Phoebe had stopped near the fireplace and looked up at them, raising herself on her arms.

"Hello, Worm!" they'd smiled and clapped.

111

But The Worm hadn't smiled. She'd frowned with effort and strained to lift her upper body.

"She's trying to get up!" Jennifer had giggled.

"She *is*!" he'd agreed.

"Shall we help her?"

"She'll make it," he'd said. "Just watch her!"

And she did. Phoebe *did* make it. She went a bit red in the face, and her little arms shook with effort, but suddenly she was on her hands and her feet instead of her belly and elbows, with her bum in the air, and was going to stand up!

They were transfixed. Breathless with anticipation!

Slow to the danger . . .

Phoebe didn't make it.

There was no shame in that. Even a foal, a kid, a fawn, stumbles and falls the first few times it tries out its new legs. And that was what Phoebe did. She didn't have her legs *quite* underneath her when her dimpled little hands let go of the planet.

She wasn't far off, mind. Another few goes and she'd have been standing, they were sure. And soon after that, walking, then running, then they'd have had to buy reins . . .

But instead she'd tilted sideways and toppled over —

"*Oh!*"

Abel Elias had moved fast, but not as fast as Death.

Phoebe banged her head on the corner of the cold stone hearth. And by the time he'd picked her up — already shushing urgently in anticipation of her tears — their Phoebe, their baby, the light of their lives, was gone.

112

And everything had changed.

So much for the worse that Mr Elias tried never to think of it. Never to think of the years that followed, and the years that followed them, and the years that followed *them*. Years of sorrow and blame and self-blame and a dull, aching, burgeoning emptiness. Years when photos were put away and when shared heartbreak and recrimination were separated by a membrane so stretched and patched that all of life was just waiting for the next breach.

Abel and Jennifer didn't talk. Not only about Phoebe. Not only about what they had lost. But about everything that might ever have bound them together.

Abel had moved out of the house with the hearth, and Jennifer had come with him, but only because neither of them knew what else to do or where else to go.

Jennifer had got a job in a shop. She never talked about it.

Abel had got a job in marine insurance. He'd known nothing about it and had to start at the bottom, but no longer wanted to be close to children every day. Or any day. Marine insurance made death a numbers game, and distanced him from its horror.

So when the Singers had moved in next door with a young family, it had been hard.

Every toddler cry, every paddling-pool shriek was a gut-punching reminder of what they had lost.

The only solution was to close the doors and shut the windows; to tend the garden during school hours, and to go away for the summer holidays. Abel and

Jennifer Elias hadn't spoken to each other in the Lake District for twenty solid summers. Nothing more than *Where's the map?* and *It's raining again.*

And when Jennifer's memory had started to fail, Mr Elias had *envied* her. He had wished it were *he* who could forget what they'd lost, and absorb himself for hours with the frayed edge of the tablecloth.

After she'd died, it had become a lot easier not to remember. Easier to forget the people they had been for so long — and why — and to think of himself as another kind of person entirely. A person who got things done in College Road. A person who had a purpose. A person with a future instead of a past.

But he moved so fast that he broke Eve Singer's fall before she hit the snow — thinking of Phoebe with such raw clarity that he shouted her name, then burst into tears.

A plane roared overhead and Eve opened her eyes to see its lights disappear behind Mr Elias's shadowy form.

She sucked in air and choked on it, and he lifted her with an arm that was already under her shoulders, and helped her to sit up.

"Your nose is bleeding," he said.

She nodded stupidly. She could see that now. Dripping down her cardigan and blotting on to the snow around her like black ink.

He gave her a clean white old-man handkerchief and said, "Put your head back."

She did. That was better.

"It might be broken," he said. "You should go to the hospital."

"I'm OK," she said, and looked around her, dazed.

Her father was sitting on the step of the shed now, squeezing snow into ridged lumps of ice and dropping them. Not looking at her.

"Can you get up?"

Eve nodded, although she didn't know whether she could or not, and allowed Mr Elias to help her — first to her knees and then to her feet. When she got there she was dizzy for a moment, and he steadied her.

"Thank you," she said.

"Let's get you both inside," he said kindly.

"Thank you," she said again.

He took her to *her* house, not his, and Duncan followed meekly behind them, like a cow on a rope.

Mr Elias locked the back door behind them and took out the key and put it on the table next to Eve.

"I'll put the kettle on," he said.

So English, thought Eve. *As if tea will make everything better.*

But she was grateful that somebody else was in charge — even if it was Mr Elias.

I'll put my boobs on.

Had he really said that?

Probably not. Eve had known Mr Elias since she was five years old, and had never heard him say anything that was not achingly dull. And the way he had helped her up, and brushed snow off her hair, and steadied her when she swayed — he had touched her only with fatherly concern.

She had been wrong about him being a dirty old man, and felt bad.

She watched him fill the kettle. His eyes were red. He looked the way she felt. He must have a cold coming.

"There's no plug on this," he said, and held up the flex to show her the bare wires.

Eve looked at her father. "Dad, where's the plug for the kettle?"

"I made it safe," said Duncan, then he wandered out of the kitchen, leaving a trail of ice-melt across the floor to the hallway. Drawn by the siren of the television, she guessed.

She sighed and told Mr Elias, "He does that. He thinks he's fixing things. But he just takes them apart."

"I'll warm some milk on the stove," said Mr Elias seamlessly, and found a saucepan.

Eve didn't have the energy to stop him. She stared at her hands and the ruined handkerchief, both grubby with drying blood. Now that the shock of the blow was wearing off, she could feel the pain spreading through her face — her nose, her eyes, her cheeks. Everything there was starting to feel hot and tight.

Mr Elias set down a mug of warm milk.

"Thank you," she whispered, and took a sip. She hadn't had hot milk for years and it was just the way her mother used to make it — with a little spoonful of brown sugar.

Mr Elias sat down with his own mug.

"I didn't realize Duncan had got so bad," he said cautiously.

116

Eve shrugged and opened her mouth to defend her father. To minimize the whole thing; to let Mr Elias know that she was coping just fine.

But instead her mouth lost its shape and she said, "I wish he would just die."

The words said themselves.

"I don't mean that!" she said.

"I'm sure you don't," said Mr Elias kindly. "It's the shock."

"Yes," nodded Eve. "I'm just so ... *tired*. It's unrelenting, you know ...?" A plane passed mercifully overhead so she could stop talking. She couldn't believe she'd said that. Couldn't believe she'd even *thought* it. It *was* the shock. And no wonder. Her father had punched her in the face. Knocked her out cold. She didn't know *what* she was saying.

Thank God she hadn't said it to anyone who mattered!

She didn't want to discuss it. Didn't want to give it any more weight. Just wanted to move on and talk about something else.

Anything else!

Then she frowned, remembering.

"Who's Phoebe?" she said.

Mr Elias paused, then smiled and patted her hand, and asked if she'd like more milk.

CHAPTER
SEVENTEEN

9 December

My head is an apple!

Eve woke with a start in the dark, suffocating, and
with her face feeling as if it might split open down the
bridge of her nose and spill hot fluffy stuffing, like an
over-baked apple.

She waited until her heart slowed to a safe rate, then
rose groggily and with a sense of foreboding.

Her father was still asleep. It would be nice to think
he was tired from his foray into Mr Elias's garden, and
that he could be worn out by a good walk, like a beagle,
but Eve knew the answer was more random: sometimes
he slept, sometimes he didn't.

As she stood over his bed, the events of last night
came back to her with surreal numbness.

She could call Stuart, but what was the point? What
would she say? Stu worked on the rigs, so a punch in
the face was unlikely to ring any alarm bells with him.
And even if it did, and brought him rushing back from
Scotland, what could he do? Nothing. He would come,
and see, and go again, and she would still be here, but

with a new sense of resentment at the fresh abandonment to add to her other woes.

So telling him was pointless.

Telling anyone would be pointless. And embarrassing. She didn't even want Joe knowing what had happened. It would all come out. It was a whole can of worms.

Mr Elias knew, of course. He was not a stranger any more. Just another person to put on her Christmas list.

Another bloody gift to buy . . .

Her father turned over in bed and covered his ear with a cupped hand, like a child.

I wish he would just die.

Eve flushed and grimaced — then winced at the little jag of pain that punished her for her heartlessness.

She was a bad person. A bad, bad person.

She was ashamed.

She went into the bathroom and examined her face. Her nose was twice its normal size across the bridge, and she had dark smudges starting under each eye. She sighed and brushed her teeth with great care, gripped by the weird feeling that at any moment her face might give way under its own weight and drop off into the basin.

Ross was going to be furious.

Mrs Solomon arrived at seven thirty.

At seven thirty-two, Eve's phone rang.

It was Joe. From the way he said *Hi*, Eve knew it was bad news.

"Guy Smith got the X-ray."

★   ★   ★

Guy's report was no good, but it didn't have to be. The X-ray was all anybody cared about — that shadowy skull, punctured by a bright-white blade, and two comedy eyeballs. It was TV gold, and watching it was like rubbernecking at the best kind of car crash, except that the wreck looked to Eve very much like her career, burning up on the hard shoulder.

At morning conference, Ross Tobin yelled at her.

She had been yelled at before — every reporter knew how to take a good bollocking on the chin. Usually Eve fought her corner with flair — accepting blame if it were due, while making a spirited defence of her own actions in order to remind the yeller that there were two sides to every story. She'd always been an expert at talking an angry boss down — even Ross Tobin — and, on occasion, had been known to talk a bollocking down to a boozy lunch, where he'd picked up the bill!

But this time she just sat there and took it. Even though nobody could have been expected to get that X-ray, and Guy Smith wouldn't have got it either, if he hadn't slept with Janey in the coroner's office — which was what Joe had heard from Ricky, and was an edge that was not available to her.

So she *had* a defence. But she was too scared to launch it. Scared of making Ross even more angry. Scared of losing her job and not being able to pay Mrs Solomon. Scared of having to put her father in a care facility, and scared of keeping him at home. Scared of it going on for ever, and scared of it ending.

Just as surely as her father had changed her life on sports day when she was seven years old, so Eve suddenly realized that he had changed it again — more slowly — over the past three years, making her a weaker, more fearful person just when she needed to be at her strongest.

So she just sat there, silent and defenceless, until Ross finally ran out of steam and allocated jobs to everybody.

Except her.

Symbolically, it was damning.

We don't need you, it said, and everybody there knew it. They filed out without making eye contact with Eve.

Ross snapped, "And what the *fuck* happened to your face? How am I supposed to put you on-screen looking like that?"

"I don't know," she said.

"Well, Katie can take over," he said. "You're on the desk until you look like a fucking human being again."

Eve walked back into a newsroom where everybody was apparently too frantically busy to notice her.

Joe touched her arm. "Are you OK?"

"Of course," she said brightly, and sat down.

"You sure?" He perched on the corner of her desk.

"Sure," she nodded. "Massive dick on legs, remember?"

"I'm not talking about that."

She reddened. He meant her face, but she couldn't tell him. She couldn't say it even inside her own head: *My dad punched me in the face*. It was too awful.

Instead she said, "Joe, we have to give him the Kevin Barr video!"

Her words hung in the air between them like a rotting carcass.

Joe didn't look at her. He sat on the corner of her desk and fiddled with a bulldog clip. From his silence, she wondered if he'd been expecting this, and for a moment she hated him for not having more faith in her — however unjustified.

She lifted her chin defiantly, waiting for an argument, *wanting* an argument. Wanting to be argued *out* of it and reassured that everything was going to be OK anyway . . .

But still Joe said nothing. The air creaked under the weight of unspoken judgement.

"It's all right for *you*," she finally snapped.

"What do you mean?"

"You're not on-screen and you're not a woman," she said. "In twenty years' time you'll still be doing your job, but I'll be lucky to have mine a year from now."

She hadn't meant to sound so bitter, or to pit them as adversaries, but the way the words fell out of her mouth, it sounded like *both* those things.

Eve should have just told him how much she needed this job. How she couldn't take the risk of losing it — and why. But she was so scared of looking weak that it had come out all wrong. She wished she could start all over again and say it *right*, except that she didn't know how.

She looked at Joe, hoping that somehow he'd magically see through her clumsy words to the desperation that had spawned them.

And he might have — if he'd looked at her at all.

Instead he said, "OK," and stared into the middle distance for a moment.

Then he got up and walked out of the newsroom.

When she showed Ross the clip, he actually kissed her — wet and smoky on her cheek — and danced an awkward little jig, like a sailor puppet.

"Fuck *me*!" he kept yelling. "Fuck *me*! We got an in with a killer! He sent us a clip like on *You've Been* fucking *Framed!* Manna from heaven! The mountain comes to Mohammed! Eat my shit 24/7! Fuck *me*!"

He used it, just as they'd known he would.

It was a sensation. Just as they'd known it would be.

Before it even went out, the tabloids got wind of what iWitness News had secured and were falling over themselves to buy the rights to the screenshots.

Guy Smith's X-ray was forgotten and consigned to the dustbin of history. It couldn't compete with the clip of a murder victim apparently taken by his actual killer. Nobody gave a shit any more about the white knife and the comedy eyeballs. The world had moved onwards and upwards, and Eve was moving right along with it.

Halfway through the lead story on the prime-time bulletin — against the creepy, flickering image of Kevin Barr — Ross Tobin turned to Eve and gave her a strained grin.

"This is your lucky day," he told her.

But it didn't feel like it.

She called Joe's mobile three times, and it went to voicemail each time.

She finally left a message, but he didn't call her back.

Eve made omelettes for supper. She would have made them Spanish, but Duncan Singer had taken all the knobs off the oven and put them somewhere she couldn't discover and he couldn't remember.

"They're somewhere *safe*," he kept saying. "Somewhere *safe*."

Then he wouldn't eat his omelette — even after making a big fuss about having goat's cheese instead of Cheddar.

"What's wrong with it?" she asked him.

"Everything," he said, and tipped his plate slowly vertical so that the omelette flopped on to the floor with an eggy slap.

"*Shit*."

Eve scooped it off the tiles and into the bin. Some fell on her shoe.

"Don't swear," he said. "I don't like it when you swear."

"Well, I don't like it when you throw food on the floor," she snapped.

"I'm not eating muck."

"Don't eat anything then!" she yelled at him.

"I won't!" he yelled back. "See if I care!"

Eve swabbed furiously at the floor with a dishcloth and wished they had a dog to take care of spillage. They'd had a dog when she was small. Arnie — a giant

Airedale who'd taken up the whole of the sofa and driven them from the room with his farts.

Maybe not a dog.

She tossed the dishcloth in the bin after the omelette.

Her father had days like this. Not often, but often enough now that she never had time to bounce back properly between them any more, never picked herself up so entirely that she could find them funny.

"What do you want to eat then?" she said angrily.

"Peanut brittle."

She gave him granola and honey and he stabbed at it with a spoon with a sour look on his face.

"See?" she pointed out. "Nuts."

"*You're* nuts," he said, "not me!"

Her phone rang from her bag in the front room.

She nearly didn't answer it, because her father was so truculent that she didn't want to leave him alone, even for a moment.

Then she did answer it, because her father was so truculent that she wanted to leave him alone, if only for a moment.

"Hello?"

"Hello, Eve."

A man's voice. Then silence. Already annoying.

Eve went from zero to tetchy in two seconds flat.

"Who is this?"

"Guess."

"No," she said. "I'm very busy."

There was a short laugh. "That's very *you*, Eve."

Was it Guy? It didn't sound like Guy . . .

"Whatever," she snapped. "Tell me who this is or I'm hanging up."

Silence.

She nearly hung up.

"I sent you a video."

Eve stopped breathing. "What?"

She'd heard him. She just needed time to adjust from daughter to reporter — and then to evaluate what he'd said.

"*What?*" she said again.

"I'm so glad you showed it. It looked much better on TV. But then, everything does, doesn't it?"

His voice was smooth and cultured. Calm and confident.

"It's like a tree falling in the forest," he laughed. "If it's not on TV, does it really happen?"

"W-w-where did you get the clip?" Eve stammered — something she hadn't done since she was a child. She'd grown out of it. She *thought* she'd grown out of it.

"I made it," he said calmly.

Eve went cold. Not chilly, but *ice* cold. As if all her blood had been sucked from her skin and rushed to her core, just to keep her heart and lungs going, while her brain was frozen.

She was talking to a killer.

Standing in her front room. With egg on her shoe.

"W-w-what do you want?" she whispered.

"I want to show you something," he said. "Piccadilly Underground. Westbound. Tomorrow at six."

He hung up before she could say *No*.

Or *Yes*.

CHAPTER
EIGHTEEN

10 December

It was a school day, but they weren't at school.

It had been Carla's idea. Most things were.

"We'll bring clothes in our bags instead of books," she'd said. "Nobody will ever know."

Nobody will ever know was Carla's go-to assertion. Nobody would ever know that they stuffed tissue in their bras; nobody would ever know that they drank vodka from her mum's drinks cabinet and filled the bottle with water; nobody would ever know that they'd borrowed money from the electric meter.

The assertion didn't always bear close scrutiny after such events, but *beforehand* it was a persuasion almost impossible to resist.

Zoey had been enthusiastic about Carla's latest plan, Maddie less so. This, too, was the way they usually were. Maddie was the voice of reason — or, at least, as reasonable as a thirteen-year-old girl can be. Maddie had never been drunk; she'd never smoked and she'd never had sex, even though she was constantly assured that nobody would ever know if she did. She'd kissed a boy once — Jez Costa — and had been unimpressed.

His lips had been too dry, and afterwards he'd wiped his mouth with the back of his hand, as if *her* lips had been too wet. So she wasn't eager to try it again any time soon, regardless of Carla and Zoey's nagging. *They'd* both kissed loads of boys. Tons of them. And got risky with some of them too. Carla said she was planning to have proper sex quite soon with Mattie Amir.

"Isn't that, like, *illegal* if you're under sixteen?" Maddie had asked her.

"Only for the boy," Carla had said breezily. "And anyway, *nobody will ever know.*"

So the three of them had carried out the first half of Carla's plan to a T. They'd caught the bus to school, then left school and caught the Tube at Hammersmith, after changing their clothes in the station toilets. They'd shopped all day, which meant a lot of looking and trying on, and minimal actual buying. Carla's stepfather had given her fifty quid for her birthday and so she was flush, but Maddie only had seventeen pounds to spend after her train ticket, and Zoey even less than that. Zoey made up for it by nicking a mascara from Superdrug. Maddie was shocked, but didn't want to show it and ruin things. They'd all tried the mascara, exclaiming how excellent it was and how their lashes looked mega.

Carla had bought a hat she looked cute in, and a dress she did not. Maddie had been pointedly restrained in her admiration of the dress, but her subtlety had been no match for Zoey's OMG-overload. Then Maddie had bought a blue micro skirt with a gold tasselled hem for fifteen pounds, and Zoey had pinched a £7.99 necklace.

Not even a nice one.

Maddie had made up her mind never to go shopping with Zoey again.

Despite that, they'd had a laugh and the hours flew by, so that by the time they got to the Tube station to head home, the entire population of London seemed to be down there with them.

They'd already missed one train in the crush.

"Shit," said Carla. "Why are there so many *people*?"

"Rush hour," shrugged Maddie.

"Gross," said Carla. "It stinks down here. Someone smells like cat pee."

The woman in front of them turned to glare and they all giggled.

"If we don't get the next train we're going to be late and my mum'll have a fit," said Maddie.

"No she won't," scoffed Zoey. "You can just say the bus broke down. I tell my mum that all the time."

"Doesn't she check with the school?" asked Maddie, and Zoey gave her a look so blank that Maddie knew that such a possibility had simply never occurred to her — or, probably, to her mother.

"This is shit," said Carla. "We shouldn't have gone to Superdrug. That queue was, like, a mile long."

"Yeah," said Zoey. "No wonder people have to nick stuff from there."

"Let's get right down the front," said Maddie. "So we definitely get on the next train."

So the three of them did that, squeezing their skinny way between the dark-coated mass of humanity, blithely breaking unspoken commuter rules in their colourful ski jackets and fake-fur hoods, like little fireflies, giggling and making airy, empty apologies as they twisted and flitted through the crowd.

"*Sorry. 'Scuse me. Sorry.*"

If they'd been men, they might have met resistance — if only in the form of muttered tuts. But three pert girls, all bright and happy? The crowd indulged them. When they got to the edge of the platform, grudging would-be passengers made way for them by shuffling backwards and sideways into each other.

Carla and Zoey and Maddie giggled at each other. Their plan was back on track. Now all they had to do was catch the train that would get them home on time, so that *nobody would ever know* . . .

Joe still wasn't answering his phone. Not to *her*, anyway.

Bollocks.

Eve looked at the clock. Five thirty.

Then she looked at her watch: five thirty-one.

She hadn't told anyone else about the call because she didn't know whether she should go to Piccadilly to meet the man or not. They'd played the clip; he'd had his fifteen minutes of fame — what more did he want?

What more did he *have*?

The moral buck had stopped with her, but now she didn't know whether to spend it.

130

She called Joe again. This time she left a message, speaking low and casting furtive glances about her. "Joe, the man who sent the clip called me last night. He wants to meet us at Piccadilly Tube station tonight at six. Please call me."

The man hadn't said he wanted to meet *them*, he'd only said *her*, but it was a very white lie, and designed more to get Joe to call her back than anything else.

He didn't, again.

It made her feel defensive, even though Joe wasn't attacking her, just ignoring her.

She looked at the clock once more.

Should she go?

It would take her fifteen minutes to walk to Piccadilly Circus. At least another five to get to the westbound platform at this time of day.

She'd be safe going alone. She wasn't meeting a contact in some dark alleyway — she'd be in a well-lit Tube station with thousands of fellow travellers. What could go wrong?

Hell, if she *didn't* go, she wouldn't be doing her job. Ross Tobin was as fickle as a bonobo, and she needed to keep producing the goods to cement her position. Another exclusive would certainly help.

If this was an exclusive, of course. Or a story at all. Right now she didn't know this man was the killer; he might be someone who wanted to *turn in* the killer! And he may not even show up — in which case, Piccadilly Circus was her station and she would be delighted to go home *on time*.

One thing was sure: if she didn't go, she'd never know.

She checked her watch again.

Five thirty-eight.

She stood up and pulled on her coat and scarf.

Katie Merino smiled as she passed. "Going home early, Eve? You've certainly earned it."

Oh piss off, thought Eve, and left.

Despite the bitter weather, Eve walked the fifteen minutes to Piccadilly Underground station in a dystopian throng, because taking a cab at this hour in central London was an expensive way to be overtaken by pedestrians.

The snow had stopped, but the wind had picked up with an icy intensity that made her shiver, and she was relieved when they all descended from the biting cold of Piccadilly Circus into the netherworld of the subway system.

There was no wind here, but somewhere a busker on a clarinet played "Smoke Gets In Your Eyes" — which only made her think of the deadly fire at King's Cross station, and feel uncharacteristically claustrophobic.

There was an unholy crush, and Eve joined the human lava flow, funnelling slowly but inexorably towards the turnstiles.

It was a strange feeling, this subjugation of the self. This was no place for the individual, no place for independence or free-thinking, certainly no place for an emergency. If she'd been chasing a pickpocket, or a lover — or if she'd needed to be on the next train to save the world — she would still have had to submerge her identity within this collective colloid, shuffling shoulder to shoulder, hip to hip, toe to heel through the steel bottlenecks.

She suppressed the desire to turn around and get the hell out, and instead braced herself to move down the escalators into the white-tiled intestines of London.

At least it got warmer the deeper she went. Although with the warmth rose the damp-dog smell of other people. It was odd to smell people in the twenty-first century. It made Eve feel medieval.

The damp and the heat brought out the essence of the unwashed, punctured by curry, or fried onions; now and then a fragrant shampoo on sleek hair two inches from her nose brought heady relief, or — if she was lucky — that Lush lemon soap that cut through it all like menthol. More often, any respite from body odour and wet coats came in the form of an eye-watering wince of over-optimistic aftershave.

Down the escalator, and then another bottleneck under the white vaulted ceiling, while she waited her turn to get on to the platform, let alone a train.

Stationary for a moment, and with her view blocked all around by people taller than herself, Eve felt suddenly, completely, *crushingly* alone.

Alone at work, and alone at home.

She had tried so hard for so long to behave as if Duncan Singer was in a state of flux, and at some point would recover and remember who he was, and remember her, and be aghast that he could ever have forgotten someone he loved so much.

But deep down, she knew that wasn't true. There was no going back with this disease. Her father was on a road that led to only one end. There had to *be* an end. But how long would it take to get there? And what sort of shape would they both be in by the time they reached that end?

A year ago, Eve thought she had found the limit of her resilience. She'd teetered on the edge of a breakdown, and simply *could not take* another day of juggling work and Dad and Ross Tobin and the mortgage and all the blood.

Something *must* snap.

And while she'd been expecting to snap, another day had passed.

And another. And another.

Until it turned out that her resilience was a false-bottomed well. There was still water in there — even if it was increasingly distant and muddy and difficult to reach.

But simple logic dictated that one day it must run dry.

Maybe today was that day.

And what would happen to her father if it were? And what would happen to her?

Her new distance from Joe felt like the straw that might break the camel's back and suddenly Eve wished fervently that she hadn't given Ross Tobin the clip. Fuck her journalistic instincts — it wasn't worth it if it meant losing Joe's respect.

Eve's eyes stung and she sniffed soupily. A middle-aged man in front of her turned to look at her with an expression that might have been sympathy, or might have been a warning not to get snot on his coat. The crush was so deep around her now that just getting a tissue out of her pocket to blow her nose made two people glare at her for digging them with her elbow.

She turned round and tried to go back, but quickly gave up. The crowd behind her was a wall hundreds of people thick. There was nothing she could do but allow herself to be carried onward by its relentless shuffle.

Eve sighed and was propelled forward as trains squealed in and out of the station, unseen, ahead of her. Finally she reached the platform, but just failed to get on to the train that was there. The man who'd looked around at her was the last person squeezed into the carriage, so squashed that the belt of his overcoat was trapped between the doors as the train pulled out of the station. If he needed to get out of the opposite door at the next station, he was going to be in trouble.

At least missing that train meant she was in plum position for the next one. She hurried freely down the platform ahead of the mass of people, almost all the way to the end, sticking close to the yellow safety line so she wouldn't be jostled backwards in the surge for the doors.

The platform filled quickly behind her.

The distraction of moving had made her feel marginally better, and she was able to blow her nose without disapproving glares.

The strains of the busker had faded to nothing and the air echoed with the silence of many people not talking.

A bored voice announced that the next train would not be stopping at Barons Court, and shortly after that came the familiar rush of warmth that preceded each train's arrival.

Eve!

Eve looked back down the platform. Had somebody called her name? She couldn't see anyone she recognized. Or anyone who appeared to have recognized her.

It was nothing. Just random tunnel sounds playing into the hands of her ego.

She was about to look away —

"*Oh!*"

Near the far end of the platform a girl in a pink ski jacket suddenly stumbled out of the dark commuter ranks, across the yellow line.

It happened so fast. But Eve had time to think, *Somebody catch her!*

Both arms outstretched, the girl almost fell flat on her face.

If she had, she would have been OK.

But the girl didn't fall. She kept going in rapid slow motion. Feet stuttering, arms reaching, ponytail bouncing.

Gravity calling . . .

Ohmygod! Somebody catch her!

People broke ranks to do just that. But nobody actually *did* . . .

With a shriek, the girl pin-wheeled off the edge of the platform and into thin air.

She never hit the ground.

Her cry was cut brutally short as she exploded on the front of the train like a pink-and-blood bomb.

136

Eve stood on the platform with the clattering noise of the train filling her head in time to her own guilt: *It serves me right I shouldn't have come. It serves me right I shouldn't have come. It serves me right I shouldn't have come . . .*

But the train wasn't moving. It was stationary in front of her.

Vaguely confused, she turned her head slowly to the right.

And the people had gone.

She hadn't noticed them leave. Hadn't noticed the panicky exodus, hadn't noticed the shoving, the crying, the falling down and the helping up.

All she knew was that four hundred would-be Tube passengers had disappeared, seemingly in an instant.

Further down the platform, a small knot of people in Day-Glo and dark green were tending to two brightly dressed teenage girls, maybe thirteen or fourteen years old. Bright leggings and ski jackets. Ear muffs and mittens.

The dead girl's friends. One bent double and clutching her stomach as if in pain, the other on her knees. Faces distorted, mouths agape.

Crying without noise.

Eve turned her head stiffly to the left. Still clattering.

Another group of officials were looking serious, huddled around what she assumed was the train driver — a grey-faced young man who sat cross-legged on the platform next to his cab. He looked as if he had climbed out and sat down, and now might never have the energy to get up again. He had a foil blanket

137

around his shoulders, and two paramedics squatted in front of him, trying to help.

But the time for help had passed, and there was nothing anybody could do now.

The sound of a train was her teeth chattering, she finally realized. She stopped them with difficulty, and the train inside her head gave way to the more terrible sound of uncontrollable howling from the two distraught girls.

She watched them being helped away.

Eve knew it was sad, but she couldn't *feel* it. There was a strange disconnection between her heart and the rest of her, so that she couldn't even be sure her heart was still in her chest.

Her teeth started chattering again and she let them drown out reality.

She looked at the driver tableau. Nobody had moved. Further to the left, close to the wall, a pink woollen glove caught her eye.

Eve frowned. There was something odd about it.

It lay on its back on the smooth pale platform under a red splodge on the tiled wall, like a carefully arranged piece of modern art.

But that wasn't what was so odd about the glove . . .

Eve's mind tried to assemble disparate information into a logical conclusion. And suddenly she wished it hadn't.

"Oh no," she said, and took a step backwards. "Oh no!"

She felt her legs start to give way and sunk ungracefully to her knees. She clapped a hand over her mouth, but the vomit escaped past it and spattered on to the platform.

Another shudder, and acid tears in her eyes and nose.

"Are you OK?"

A woman's hand on her back. Green legs. Black Dr Martens. A paramedic had stopped. Eve didn't look up — just shook her head and then waved her arm to the left and choked, "There's a hand in that glove."

There was a pause, and then the woman said, "Shit," and the green legs hurried away to alert somebody in Day-Glo.

Eve didn't want to see what happened next. She stayed on all fours for a minute, staring down at the sick. Trembling. Then she raised her head and looked straight ahead at the side of the Tube train. Also empty, she now registered, so that she could look through the windows to the curved, poster-covered wall on the opposite side of the tracks.

She stared, seeking the distraction of meaningless commercial enterprise. *Les Misérables* and the British Museum and Vodafone. Each giant poster had at its centre a small white flyer advertising an exhibition. Not allowed, she imagined, defacing the big, expensive hoardings. But there anyway. Artists were rebels. Always. Caravaggio and Van Gogh and Warhol. Going their own way, doing their own thing. Swimming against the tide and — finally — towing the world along with them.

Well, nobody would be going to any exhibition today, Eve thought darkly. Nobody would be switching to

Vodafone or booking *Les Mis* after what had just happened here. Her own mission was a dim memory, slight and meaningless now. She wished she'd stayed in the office.

The office.

Eve sat back on her heels and wiped her mouth on the back of her glove. Then she peeled off her soiled gloves and dropped them beside the vomit. She got slowly to her feet.

She called Joe.

"Joe —"

His voicemail picked up. She couldn't squeeze another word past the lump in her throat, and she hung up. She couldn't sob on the shoulder of his voicemail; she needed the comfort of a human.

Any human would do.

She called Ross Tobin.

"What's up?"

"There's been an accident at Piccadilly." She took a deep breath. "A young girl just fell in front of a train."

"Yeah?" he said. "Is she dead?"

"Yes."

"Got pictures?"

"What?"

"Have you got pictures?"

She was stunned by the question. It wasn't why she'd called. It wasn't what she'd wanted.

"No," she whispered, and explained, "It happened *right in front of me!*"

"We're a TV news show," he snapped. "Get pictures or get a job on the fucking radio."

He hung up and Eve stood on the platform, shaking as if she'd fallen through the ice on a lake.

She looked down at the phone in her hand and heard the Apple Genius's words as clearly as the voice of God.

"*. . . eight megapixels . . .*"

Eve spoke over the pictures — not trying for stylish, only stating the facts. She panned the phone slowly around. The blood-spattered platform, the driver in the silver blanket, the stationary train, *Les Mis* and Vodafone, and the scattering of shoes kicked off in what must have been a stampede off the platform.

At first she was halting, but it got easier. The viewfinder brought welcome detachment. She even remembered to press the selfie icon that enabled her to be in shot — mentally editing as she went. She found the professional presence of mind to wonder how she looked — and then the cynicism not to give a shit. The worse she looked, the better.

On her way up the escalator, she filmed a team of men coming down. They were dressed in orange and carried bin bags and shovels.

Come to clean up the mess.

With shovels.

Eve's stomach clenched again but was mercifully empty.

CHAPTER
NINETEEN

Eve didn't sleep that night. Not even fitfully.

It was shocking how long an hour could be, when your only companion was a young girl pin-wheeling into the path of a train, over and over like a viral GIF. So when her phone rang at two a.m., she grabbed it before the second trill.

"Joe?"

"No."

"Oh."

There was an awkward silence. She checked the number but it was withheld.

Then he spoke. "I'm glad you came today."

A chill passed through her. A goose on her grave. A killer on the line.

"I didn't see you."

"But I saw you. In the flesh." Then he laughed. "Or at least, very near to the flesh."

Eve's mind turned over slowly. Not quite catching, like a cold-morning car.

"W-what do you mean?" *Damn her stammer!*

"Well, I enjoyed your show. Did you enjoy mine?"

"Your what?"

"My show."

"Your *show*?" She wracked her brain. There had been a busker, "Smoke Gets In Your Eyes" . . .

"*Our* show," he said, as if correcting himself.

"I-I-I don't know what you mean."

"The girl in pink," he said impatiently.

"What?"

"You heard me."

Eve blinked. It took a thousand years.

The warm rush of the approaching train . . .

Eve!

Her name in the air. Her mind playing tricks.

His voice. *This* voice. He had called out her name.

"The girl who fell?" she breathed.

He laughed. "Did she fall or was she pushed? What do you think, Eve?"

"I don't . . . I don't know," she said haltingly.

"I didn't want you to miss it. I knew you'd show it to best advantage. And you did. Your review was . . . *visceral* — even better than the Coldharbour girl."

Eve caught her breath. *The Coldharbour girl. Layla Martin.*

Loops of gore . . .

Her mind bubbled and spat like panicky soup. What was he saying? That *he'd* killed Layla Martin? And Kevin Barr? *And* the girl at the station?

"You're lying," she said with a shaking voice. "You're a liar."

"You know that's not true, Eve. We're in the same line of work, you and I. I need people to die in order to live — and so do you. We're the same. We want the same things."

"Don't you *dare* tell me we're the same!" Her voice shook, but her stammer was gone. "I'm not the same as you! You're a fucking *murderer!*"

"I have good reason to do what I do," he said mildly, as if to a child. "You're only in it for the money."

Eve's self-righteous anger caught in her throat.

"Be honest, Eve," he went on. "We both crave death. And an audience."

There was a yawning silence where she almost denied it.

But she couldn't.

Because it was true.

She had cheerfully stoked the fires of fear in the wake of the Coldharbour murder; she'd given Ross the video of Kevin Barr, even though she *knew* he would use it; she had accepted the killer's invitation to his "show", and then — instead of running from the scene the way four hundred ordinary, decent people had — she had taken out her phone and filmed herself reporting on the brutal death. Of a *child* . . .

What was *wrong* with her? Every step of the way she had given him what he wanted.

Not even unwittingly.

Selfishly.

Eve saw it now for the first time. Her whole career was built on the bones of the dead and the tears of the bereaved. Had she encouraged this? Had she enabled him? Had she followed his lead?

Or had *he* followed *hers?*

She couldn't breathe.

She really couldn't breathe.

144

"I give you the art," he said, as if he'd read her mind. "And you put on the exhibition."

"N-no," she whispered. "No."

But his low voice wormed into her ear and wound its thorny way around her guilty heart.

"We're in it *together* now, Eve."

PART TWO

PARADISO

CHAPTER
TWENTY

11 December

Dust to dust.

The killer watched the dust dance in the shards of sunlight that sliced between the heavy velvet curtains. Each speck had once been part of something else. The eye of a woodworm, a shaving off the leg of a Chippendale chest, a flake of his own pale skin. Each fragment was fallen from a whole and reduced and reduced and reduced, until it was anonymous and uniform, and so tiny that it could be supported by the thickness of air, as it sought the light that would lend its existence beauty beyond the darkness.

He moved the curtains a few inches one way, then a few inches the other. The sharper and thinner the beam, the more intensely the swirling motes fought for their moment in the sun — showing off in the spotlight like ballet-school brats. But as the curtain was opened, so the light seemed to weaken as it shared itself around the room, and the dust got sulky and withdrew to the corners and the floor — because how could any individual speck shine among such multitudes?

It was top billing or nothing for dust, and the killer respected that ambition.

Could relate to it.

He drew back the curtain with a flourish and stood for a moment, framed by the window, glorying in the weak warmth of the winter rays that made his pubic hair into whorls of raw gold.

His scar dribbled down the middle of his chest like grease.

In the house across the road, the dumpy woman with the bucket and sprays flapped an angry duster at him, and he tingled as her gaze fell upon him. She shouted something soundless and then hurried into the dark interior of the house.

They'd had people like her when he was a boy. Women who *did* — that's what his mother had called them. Cooked and cleaned and shopped and made the beds.

But *he'd* never had a woman who did. Not personally. He wondered what a woman might *do* for him.

He could only think of one thing.

He turned away from the window and watched his own shadow ripple across the Belgian lace counterpane.

The time he had spent in this room.

The hours. The days.

The *life*.

At this bed he had cared for his mother, even though he barely knew her.

Two years of cold, creeping misery. Hell in a glass of water, purgatory in an egg sandwich. Dirty sheets.

150

That infernal bedpan.

More dirty sheets.

And more.

And more.

Fed repeatedly into the hungry maw of the washing machine he grew to hate. But it was never enough to cover the stench of urine and shit, or that strange, sour *rot* that made him gag every time he'd returned to the house with supplies.

The tyrannical machine had watched and waited, greedy for more filth and fever, not wanting it to end, however bad it got. Until it had seemed to him that his mother only lingered in order to feed it.

And how she had lingered!

Breathing *his air*, while he appraised her with cold, glue-factory eyes.

Finally he had gone downstairs and beaten the washing machine to death with a sledgehammer in the echoing ballroom, watched only by dust and the spidery wires where the crystal chandeliers had once been.

The Hotpoint had been transformed from a squat white cube into a jagged collection of disparate parts that, once separated, could barely be credited with having once belonged to the same cohesive whole.

And never would again.

The killer had started on the machine in a rage, but the smaller it got, the less angry he'd become.

Eventually he had stopped and leaned on the sledgehammer, sweaty and gasping, but with the same joyous pounding in his chest that he hadn't felt for years.

Not since he'd cut Mr Treadwell.

It had taken him days to separate the ugly white outer properly from its internal organs. As each new wonder appeared — the motor, the pump, the fan — he'd taken them apart too, to discover hidden gems of washers and seals and valves and switches and neat bundles of vivid veins.

It was a Russian doll of discovery.

Once the machine's deconstruction was complete, he could hardly believe that he had hated it so much. It had been nothing but a greedy hole demanding to be fed with stinking sheets. Now that it was laid carefully out in a precise twenty-foot square in the middle of the ballroom floor, he could see how well it had been made. How much care and attention had gone into its manufacture. How every tiny component played its clever part in the whole.

There was nothing wasted, nothing left over, nothing to add.

So his final shred of hatred had been snuffed out. It had been replaced by an understanding of the machine's complex new beauty.

It was perfect.

Only then had he gone back upstairs to find that, while he'd been gone, his mother had done the decent thing.

He had sat at her bedside for days — moving only to relieve himself or to drink his neighbour's water from the tap — and thought about his future.

He had never had one before, but his bastard heart had reminded him that he might have one now. Like a

Geiger counter, its crazed ticking had alerted him to new possibilities. The first time, when he'd cut open Mr Treadwell, he had been too young to understand. But its response to the death of the washing machine had been a timely reminder.

So he had mapped out his own future.

And that of others.

His mother's death had filled him to the brim with . . .

Borrowed time.

And he had spent it carefully, that bequest from the final member of his family. But it could not last for ever and the time had inevitably come when he'd needed to borrow from strangers.

Strangers he repaid with the handsome interest of being immortalized by art.

The low morning sun had moved around now, so that his lithe shadow fell across his mother's face.

It had sunk in on itself like a bad cake. The eyes had fallen back into deepening pits. The cheeks were sucked hollows, and the lips were as thin and black as a dog's.

The killer put out a gentle hand and touched his mother's brow.

She had been dead for two years now.

And grew more beautiful every day.

CHAPTER
TWENTY-ONE

Halfway through taking the fairy lights off the Christmas tree, Duncan Singer remembered who he was. It was like a flashbulb going off — a sudden brilliant illumination of everything, so clear and so bright that he gasped.

In an instant he knew he was Duncan Singer, father to Stuart and Eve and husband to Maggie, who had been dead for more than twenty years. The shock of her death, and the shock of having *forgotten* her death, tore at his heart like a double-barbed fishhook.

And then the flash was gone, but while its after-image faded, he stood transfixed in the gloom, beside the dark tree, and with constellations of lights bundled in his arms.

By the time the fat woman came into the room and asked if he was all right, Duncan couldn't remember why his heart ached so badly, or why he was crying.

All he knew now was that it must have been something quite terrible, and that forgetting something that could make him feel so bad was even worse than remembering it.

"No," he said, "I'm not all right."

Then he stared down at the twinkling lights and sobbed, "All my stars fell out of the sky."

On her way to the station, Eve checked her phone. Still no word from Joe.

Good.

She didn't know what to say to him. He'd told her not to give the clip to Ross. Joked about doing PR for Jack the Ripper.

How she wished she'd listened to him.

The man who'd called her might be a liar and a fantasist. But until she knew for sure, a yoke of guilt hung heavy on her shoulders.

The *Metro* she picked up on the train had named the dead girl as thirteen-year-old Maddie Matthews from Hammersmith. The photo they were using was a selfie lifted from Facebook — the face slightly over-exposed, and showing random details of Maddie's bedroom behind her. Posters and teddy bears and hair straighteners. Eve recognized the teenage trappings. Maddie's identity expressed through Beyoncé and BaByliss.

Eve looked up and saw that the Tube was stopped at Hammersmith. Without thinking it through, she got to her feet. The train doors closed buzzingly on her arm but she levered them aside and stepped down on to the platform.

She called in sick to work.

"Sick?" Ross Tobin said. "You're in the middle of the biggest story of your career. Maybe the biggest story of *any* career. And you're fucking *sick*? What's wrong with you?"

"I've got a cold."

She didn't have a cold, but her swollen nose made it easy to fake one.

"A *cold*? Jesus! It's hardly death's door, is it? More like death's catflap."

"I feel like shit," she said, and she did.

"Well, Katie Merino wouldn't feel like shit," said Ross spitefully. "*She*'d do your job with one fucking leg!"

Eve laughed. Ross couldn't scare her with Katie Merino any more. She was so far beyond Katie Merino that it seemed ridiculous that she should ever have cared about anything Katie did, or might do.

Ross snapped, "Just get well fucking soon!" And cut her off.

Eve sat down on a frigid metal bench and scrolled through Facebook.

It only took two minutes of teenage gossip before she found the names of the girls who had been with Maddie the day before — and only another thirty seconds on Google before she had an address for the one with the more unusual name — Zoey Kihn.

Time was, a journalist would have spent a day knocking on doors and making phone calls to arrive at the right address.

Anybody could find anyone now.

It was scary really, if you thought about it.

But mostly it was just useful.

Zoey Kihn's mother's face was swollen from crying at what might have been.

"I just keep thinking," she said for the third time since they'd sat down at the kitchen table, "it could have been Zoey."

Eve nodded.

Again.

She didn't have children, but she guessed that that kind of thinking could ruin your whole life if you weren't careful.

Zoey herself only tutted. "Don't keep *saying* that, Mum. It *wasn't* me. I'm *fine*."

"Thank God," said Mrs Kihn, although Eve had long suspected that God had very little to do with things like this. After all, if it was God's doing that Zoey Kihn was alive, then it must also be God's doing that Maddie Matthews wasn't, which seemed perverse.

She didn't point that out though. It was usually best to let the bereaved and the nearly bereaved lead the way through these difficult conversations.

She blushed hotly at her own guile. All these tricks she'd learned. All the ways she knew to pick and to pry and to peel back the flesh to expose the raw hurt so that her audience could gawp and tut — and then change the channel . . .

But she needed to know. Not for ratings, but for *her*. She needed to know if the man on the phone was a killer or a liar.

Mrs Kihn dabbed her eyes. "You let them go out. They want to go out. They want to be treated like adults, but they're *not* adults, are they?"

"Mmm," said Eve carefully. She didn't want to alienate either Mrs Kihn or her daughter.

"They don't understand, do they?" the woman went on. "They don't know how dangerous things are, how quickly things can go wrong, you see?"

Eve did see. If anyone could, *she* could. After all, if things didn't go wrong so quickly and so often for so many people, she'd be out of a job.

"I mean," said Zoey's mother, "one minute they're messing about on the platform . . ."

"We *weren't* messing about," said Zoey. "I *told* you."

"And the next — *BOOM*. Gone. Just like that. Poor Maddie. Her poor mother . . ." Mrs Kihn pulled a tissue from the box on the table and blew her nose.

Zoey rolled her eyes and looked at Eve. "We weren't messing about. We're not *babies*."

Eve suppressed a smile, because Zoey was wearing Hello Kitty pyjamas and large fluffy slippers with eyes and whiskers on them. She was a pretty girl in the way that all teenage girls seemed to be these days — with clear skin and straight teeth and long glossy brown hair. She was very pale, but Eve couldn't tell whether that was shock or just fashion.

"What *did* happen then?" she asked.

Zoey sighed and flapped a hand. "I don't know." Her lip wobbled for a moment, making her look eight years old. Then she cleared her throat and went on, "We were just standing there, laughing . . ."

"Messing about," said her mother.

Zoey ignored her. "And Maddie kind of shouted . . ."

"What do you mean?"

"I don't know. Not shouted. More like '*Eek!*' Then she sort of *tripped*. Like, stumbled forward."

158

Eve said carefully, "Could she have been pushed?"

"I suppose so." Zoey stared blankly across the kitchen at the white sky beyond the windows. "It was crowded. I wasn't looking at Maddie because I was talking to Carla, but I felt her *bump* my shoulder . . ."

Zoey unconsciously touched her own shoulder at the memory, and her mother took another tissue from the box.

"Did you actually *see* anyone who might have pushed her?"

"I didn't *see* anyone," said Zoey, "but she did *eek*. And she did bump me quite *hard*. So . . ." She tailed off and opened her hands in a gesture of *you decide*.

Frustrating. Not the definitive answer Eve had wanted.

"Did she have a boyfriend?" asked Eve.

"No."

"What about enemies?"

Zoey shook her head.

"Maybe she was having a row with someone at school?"

"No," she said. "She would have told us."

"Was she having any . . . personal problems?" asked Eve hopefully. "Anything that might have been, y'know, getting her down . . .?"

"Yes, maybe she killed herself," said Mrs Kihn, picking up that ball and running with it. "Maddie could be a bit *serious*."

Eve mentally crossed her fingers. She willed Zoey to agree — to nod and say, *Yeah, she was crying in the toilets last week but she wouldn't tell us why.* Or *I*

159

think she broke up with her boyfriend. She said life wasn't worth living . . .

But Zoey looked at her mother, wide-eyed, and insisted, "No *way* would Maddie kill herself. She'd just bought this a-*mazing* skirt from H&M."

CHAPTER
TWENTY-TWO

Eve got home to find that her father had had a bad day.

Quite apart from pulling the lights off the Christmas tree, Mrs Solomon told Eve that he'd refused to take his pills, had had what she called "an accident in his trousers", had broken the kitchen radio, and had then taken all the books off the upstairs shelf and put them in the bath.

After she left, Eve went upstairs and found the books were still there, floating in tepid water.

She didn't wonder why Mrs Solomon hadn't stopped Duncan. She already knew why. Because when her father was obsessed with doing something that was relatively harmless, it was easier just to let him get on with it than to intervene. Leaving him alone meant he was occupied — sometimes for days — while intervention could lead to all sorts of unpleasantness. In the same spirit they had both looked the other way while Duncan Singer had carefully peeled every piece of wallpaper off the spare-room wall, using only his fingernails. That particular endeavour had brought them weeks of silent relief. Eve had even read a book! It had been a fluffy bit of rubbish about some woman who couldn't stop shopping, but it was a *book*! And she'd *read* it!

It had been such a respite that after he'd finished the spare room, she'd encouraged him to strip the paper off his own bedroom walls — even making a start behind the door for him — but he'd become furious at her wanton vandalism and bundled her out on to the landing.

There was no rhyme or reason to his madness.

Eve sighed and pulled the bath plug, and started to shake water off the books and lay them out on towels to dry. They were books that had been on the shelves all her life. She knew their spines like old friends. She'd opened each of them at some point, even if only to see what was inside and then close them again. She saved the hardbacks first — her father's old dictionary and her mother's biographies, scientists and artists and explorers, their pages swollen now and their covers warped. She put them on the towels and dabbed at them pointlessly, then went back in for the soggy holiday pleasures of Wilbur Smith and Stephen King.

Finally, swirling gently around the plughole, she retrieved her own sodden copy of *Winnie-the-Pooh*. Her mother had given it to her when she was five. They'd read it together endlessly.

No, not endlessly.

The end had come shortly before Eve's seventh birthday.

Now she sat on the damp bathmat and leaned against the side of the tub. She peeled the book open and felt herself sucked back through the years.

Those little pen-and-ink drawings. She remembered touching them, could almost see her own dimpled finger pointing at the pages while she could feel her mother over her, under her, all around her, laughing and reading so close to her ear that it tickled.

Pooh eating hunny. Tigger bouncing. Eeyore's gloomy birthday balloon.

Eve ached for the innocence.

She shut the swollen book, then put it on the radiator in the box room to dry out.

All the others she bundled up in her arms, carried dangerously down the stairs and tumbled into the bin. She told herself she would replace them all, but she knew that would never happen.

She switched on the kitchen radio. As advertised, it wasn't working; there was a sticker on the back that had been peeled off one of the bananas in the fruit bowl.

Fyffes.

Eve sighed and dropped the radio into the bin after the books.

She called Joe. She didn't leave a message. *What the hell*.

She needed a drink.

Eve snorted quietly at herself. She'd heard people say that in movies for years, but had never imagined a moment might come when she'd feel the same way.

Needing a drink.

Not fancying a glass of rosé with supper, or getting tipsy fast on party Prosecco, but really feeling the *need* of something to warm her and steady her and take the edge off reality, all at the same time.

She wasn't much of a drinker, but she was sure there was something in the kitchen cupboard.

There was. Half a bottle of Advocaat from a few Christmases back, when Stuart had come to visit and the girl he'd been with had wanted snowballs. *Marcie.* She had brought all the makings with her, which had rung alarm bells with Eve, and she'd been relieved when Stu had broken up with her a few months later.

Eve had never drunk Advocaat and didn't like the look of it, but she poured herself a tumblerful and downed half of it in one go.

Jesus Christ! It was bloody *awful.* Thick and sweet and burning, like whisky custard.

She coughed a bit and drank the other half.

Then she refilled the glass and went into the front room and picked up her phone from her bag, and Munchkin from his cage.

She took all three into the hallway, closed all the doors and put the hamster on the floor for a safe bit of exercise, while she peered at her phone through wincing sips of Advocaat.

She called Stuart. There was no answer.

She sat on the bottom stair in darkness and watched Munchkin waddle purposefully around the skirting.

She started to feel a bit woozy, probably from the trauma.

She hit Redial.

Once again it rang all the way to voicemail.

"Stu," she said. "It's me, Eve."

She stopped talking and frowned.

Meeve.

164

That's what "me, Eve" sounded like to her ears. She'd never noticed before, and dithered about whether to hang up or not.

She took another swig of Advocaat, but it was all gone. Then she realized that she was still connected to the voicemail system but hadn't said anything for what felt like some time. So she hung up, then redialled and started again.

"Stu, it's me. Eve. I just wanted to call you to say hi. I was wondering how you were and how work's going and all that stuff. And also . . ."

Dad punched me in the face.

Eve covered her mouth. She couldn't say it. Couldn't say it out loud. It was too awful.

And what could he do? It would only make him worried and helpless. Or not bother him at all, which would be even worse.

She fought to keep from crying.

Munchkin stopped at her toe and sat up on his haunches and looked at her, whiskers quivering in concern.

Eve wiped her nose on her sleeve and glanced up — and her stomach tensed into a solid knot.

There was somebody at the front door.

No light was on in the hallway and so the silhouette was clearly thrown against the etched glass by the street light outside. Somebody was just standing there, not knocking. Just . . . *standing*.

"Stuart," she hissed, "there's somebody at the door —"

She put the phone down on the stair and rose warily, looking at the door, but not moving towards it.

Was it locked?

165

What if it wasn't? Sometimes it wasn't! What if the handle turned and the door opened and a killer walked into her house?

Don't be silly, she told herself. *He doesn't know where you live.* But there was no logic in her guts.

Eve looked around the hallway for something with which to defend herself. There was the empty vase on the hall table.

And there was a tennis racquet.

She hadn't played since September, but she also hadn't put the racquet away in the cupboard under the stairs because she was lazy with house stuff. At first it had bugged her every time she had looked at it. Then she'd made an effort not to look at it. And now every time she caught a glimpse of it, she thought that it would only be a few months before she and Charlotte started playing again at the courts in the park, so she might as well just leave it there. It was ridiculous really, when all she needed to do was put it in a cupboard, but there it was.

All this passed through her fuzzy brain in a split second as she darted over and picked it up and unzipped the head cover.

Once the tennis racquet was in her hand, Eve felt invincible. She was a strong player with good hand-eye coordination, and the alcohol said she could probably kill a man with a topspin forehand.

In fact, she thought, why the *hell* was she cowering in her hallway waiting for someone to burst into her home and terrify her?

Fuck *that*!

In a stride she was at the door. With her Advocaat heart pumping brave blood through her body, she twisted the Yale knob slowly, raised her racquet and took a deep breath.

Then yanked the door open.

There was nobody there.

But Eve didn't drop her guard. She stepped quickly off the porch and on to the snowy path, swinging the racquet in swift, lethal arcs, first to one side and then the other, like a Wimbledon ninja.

Still nobody.

Had she been mistaken? Had the shadow been that of a person? Or a tree?

Eve turned and nearly skidded over. Then she righted herself and frowned at the porch, trying to work out what she'd seen.

The gate closed quietly behind her.

She spun into a lethal backhand, but only got halfway before somebody grabbed her arm, interrupting the stroke and making her shriek with sudden fear as she struggled to escape a powerful embrace.

"Eve! Eve, it's me!"

She stopped and twisted round furiously. "Jesus, Joe! You scared the *shit* out of me!"

"Sorry."

He let go of her arm and she set about him with the racquet.

"Ow! Don't!" He put up his hands to deflect the blows, then grabbed her again in a bear hug. "Stop!" he yelled. "*Stop!*"

She stopped and glared at him, and he released her.

"What the hell is going on?" he yelled.

"I saw a shadow at the door. I thought it was him."

"Who? Rafa Nadal?" Joe touched his lip. "I think I'm bleeding."

"The killer!" she snapped.

"What killer?"

"Kevin Barr's killer. He called me, Joe! He called me and told me —"

Eve stopped.

Then — finally — she burst into tears.

Joe closed the door and double-locked it behind them.

Then he stood and held Eve for five solid minutes while she cried into his jumper.

When her sobbing subsided he said, "Can we turn on a light? It's like a horror film in here."

"Careful," she hiccuped. "Munchkin's loose."

He looked around nervously. "Who's Munchkin?"

"My hamster."

"OK," said Joe, relieved. He turned on the light and they trod carefully into the kitchen, and Eve sat at the table while Joe made tea in a weird action replay of Mr Elias.

Except that this time it was Joe bleeding down his chin.

Eve's Advocaat-and-adrenaline cocktail was wearing off fast. "I'm so sorry," she said. "I thought you were the killer."

"You thought there was a killer at the door, so you *opened* it?"

"It sounds stupid when you say it like that."

168

He laughed, then winced.

"What are you doing here?" said Eve.

"I was worried about you. I left my phone at work the other day, but when I picked it up tonight there were all these missed calls. I was worried about you . . ."

He glanced at her face and she remembered how swollen and bruised it was.

"Oh," she said with a dismissive wave. "Right now my face is the least of my worries."

He didn't look convinced that that was true, but left it.

"Tell me about this phone call."

She did. And when she had told him everything that had happened since they last saw one another, he was quiet for a very long time.

Eve felt a sudden terrible dread that Joe didn't believe her. She knew it sounded outlandish and unlikely, but Joe had always trusted her before.

Maybe she'd lost the right to his trust when she'd given the Kevin Barr clip to Ross.

"Listen," said Joe. "If the man who called you really did push that poor girl under a train, it's because he's a total fucking *nut-job*, and *nothing* to do with you!"

Relief flooded through Eve like a sugar high.

"But I bet he's just screwing with you," Joe went on. "I bet he saw on TV what happened and has decided to claim responsibility to make himself look more interesting. He probably loves manipulating or scaring you, just because you're a strong, successful woman. Or some such feminist claptrap." He winked at her. "I'm only half kidding though. All I'm saying is: don't feel guilty. Yet."

"Until we *know* I'm to blame?" she asked wryly.

"Exactly," grinned Joe. "Then you're on your own."

"Cheers," she smiled.

"Did you call the police?" said Joe.

"No. I mean, I have no proof that the man who called me is the killer of Layla Martin or Kevin Barr or Maddie Matthews — or even the person who sent the SD card."

Joe nodded. "Perhaps we should see how much we can check out ourselves. Then we can go to them with firm evidence."

"Or none," said Eve. "Preferably."

Joe nodded, and drummed his fingers on the table. "What do we know about him?"

"He's a nut."

"Yeah, but he's a nut who's revealed stuff about himself. Just by calling you. Did he say anything weird that might give us a clue?"

Eve shrugged. "A murderer called me. *All* of it was weird." But she reran the conversation in her head, replaying and reconstructing and reinterpreting the words, the speech patterns, the accent. Sorting the wheat of clue from the chaff of crazy.

We're in it together now, Eve . . .

She shuddered. Remembering was still too close to reliving.

Finally she said, "One thing was odd. No odder than the rest of the stuff, really, but the girl who fell under the train . . . He called it his *show*."

"His *show?*" said Joe. "See? That's pretty weird."

"Yeah," nodded Eve. "He said, *Did you like my show?* — or something like that."

"Sick."

"Yeah," she went on. "And he didn't say he watched my report. He said he'd watched my *review*. As if he was an artist and it was —

"OH!" She gasped.

Joe leaned forward. "What?"

Eve looked at him, wide-eyed with realization.

"*An exhibition!*"

CHAPTER
TWENTY-THREE

12 December

The clean-up crew at Piccadilly had done an amazing job.

Eve couldn't help examining the platform and tiled walls for traces of blood, but they simply weren't there any more.

It was late morning and so the crush of people on the platform was far less than it was during rush hour. Even so, Eve was wary of every wave of humanity, and kept close to the wall and away from the yellow line as they walked to the far end of the platform.

The small white flyers were still there on the big posters for *Les Misérables* and Vodafone. Easier to read without looking through blood-spattered windows . . .

EXHIBITION
Venue: Here
Date: December 10
Time: 18.00

"He told me to be here at six o'clock. Maddie Matthews was killed at six o'clock." Standing on the platform, it all came back to her. "I think he called my name, too."

Joe looked at her quizzically.

"Just once. I thought it was my mind playing tricks on me. Like a weird echo. But I looked down the platform to see who was calling me, and that's how I saw it happen."

"Bloody hell," Joe said quietly.

"You think he did?" she said anxiously.

"I don't know," he said grimly. "But if you're putting on a show, it stands to reason you want people to see it."

"If I hadn't looked," said Eve, "maybe he wouldn't —"

"You don't know that," he said quickly. "You can't second-guess him, Eve, because you're not like him."

She said nothing.

We're the same, you and me.

The one thing the killer had said that Eve would never tell anyone.

Joe looked around and pointed to the other end of the platform, where a camera was positioned in a discreet corner.

"CCTV."

He hoisted his camera on to his shoulder. "I'll get a few shots of the flyers and then we'll go and see if we can view the video from that."

"OK." Eve nodded, but her stomach quivered at the thought.

The Security Data Manager was called Craig Banks, and he wore a carefully tended moustache, a starched

173

shirt, a cricket-bat pin on his London Underground tie, and black shoes so polished that they would have made a Coldstream Guard blush.

"I'm not showing you the footage of the incident," he said the minute Eve introduced herself. "That's under investigation."

"Which incident?" said Eve blankly — which put Banks nicely on the shiny back foot.

"Nothing," he said. "No incident."

Eve went on — all innocence — "We were just interested in the exhibition."

"What exhibition?"

"It's advertised on the flyers. An exhibition on the westbound platform. We're doing a piece on street art and artists."

"There's no exhibition," Banks insisted. "And certainly not on any platform. We've got enough to worry about just keeping the bums and the buskers and the alkies from making exhibitions of themselves on a daily basis without holding formal events."

"There are flyers advertising an exhibition," Eve insisted. "They're stuck over the large posters on the tunnel wall opposite the platform."

"Across the rails?" said Banks, immediately bristling. "That's not allowed."

"Yeah, I don't think the British Museum would be very happy about their posters being covered up."

"Not that!" said Banks. "Someone must have crossed the tracks to put them there, and that's *absolutely* not allowed."

Eve knew that — any fool would — but she was happy to let Craig Banks tell her stuff she already knew, if it smoothed her path to the answers she wanted.

"Oh dear," she said. "Really?"

"Really," he said, and sat down at a monitor and started tapping keys with vigour. "Someone should have picked up on that. Someone wasn't doing their job. As per bloody usual. When would they have been put up?"

"I only noticed them yesterday. But I have no idea how long they've been there."

"Let's take a look, shall we?" said Banks, sounding like a Bond villain. "It's all automatically recorded on the hard drive," he went on. "It used to be the case that you'd have to press Record on a video recorder like it was *Cash in the* bloody *Attic* or something. But now it's all automated, thank God. You can't trust anyone to do anything these days, can you?"

"I agree," said Eve, although she didn't. It was her business to be cynical and suspicious, but it was hard to get through life without trusting a *few* people. She trusted Joe. She trusted her brother. She trusted Mrs Solomon to look after her father, and now she supposed she trusted Mr Elias too. So far, none of them had let her down.

Banks brought up the right date and hit Reverse, then stared intently at the screen while the recording raced back through time from midnight.

It happened too fast to get details, but even so, Eve was nervous of watching Maddie Matthews' death replayed on-screen.

The platform was empty, then there were people. Only a few. Maybe that was her at the far end?

There was the train, stationary for a long time. Then the platform turned from white to black in a second as four hundred people poured backwards on to it and took up their places —

This was it.

Eve closed her eyes briefly, and when she opened them again the train was yet to emerge from the gaping tunnel, and Maddie was still alive.

If only it were that easy.

Time continued to roll backwards so fast that Eve wondered how Banks could possibly be sure he wasn't missing something. To her it was all just a blur of trains and people and empty platforms, in rhythmical rotation.

Twenty-four hours passed in less than a minute and the counter ticked back to midnight on the previous day.

"There," Banks said suddenly.

"Where?"

He tapped the screen with the point of a pen. "Right here."

The recording froze and ran forward again more slowly.

The platform was almost empty. Two figures close to the camera, and that was all.

A man emerged just under the camera and walked away from it, all the way to the far end of the platform.

Eve's heart pounded in her throat.

She knew him!

176

Immediately she dismissed the thought. It was ridiculous. She didn't know him. Maybe she'd built a picture in her mind that matched the figure on the screen.

Both indistinct.

The man was thin, and dressed in jeans and a dark hoodie. He held something in the crook of his left elbow.

Without hesitating or even glancing over his shoulder, he sat on the edge of the platform and dropped on to the tracks.

Craig Banks hit Pause and rapped the screen again. "You see! Someone should have picked up on that!" He tapped the time code and date into a box at the top right of the screen. "Whoever was on late duty."

He left the dark figure hanging in frustrating mid-step across a gleaming rail and spun across the floor on his castored chair.

"Easy to find out," he said. "I've got all the time sheets right here." He reached across another counter for a ring binder.

Eve and Joe exchanged impatient looks while Banks started flicking through the paperwork.

"Ah," he said with great satisfaction. "Here we go!"

Eve forced herself to smile at him. "Found it?" she said.

"Found it," he said. "Gary Bushman. I *knew* it would be him!" He looked up at them triumphantly, as if they knew or cared who the hell he was talking about.

"Excellent," said Eve enthusiastically, while she longed to slap Banks and hit Play.

Banks hauled his way slowly back across the room like a baby in a walker. "London Underground doesn't pay people to sit on their backsides and watch TV for the good of their health."

"Exactly," Eve said.

"Not even Mr High and Mighty Gary Bushman."

"'Specially not him," murmured Joe, and Eve had to stifle a snort.

Finally Banks made it back to the keyboard.

"Right," he said. "Might as well finish up."

It was obvious to Eve that, for Banks, the only issue was who had missed the man crossing the tracks. The man himself was irrelevant now.

He finally hit Play and the man completed his grainy, high-stepping way across the rails, then placed his flyers on the wall. Eve couldn't see how — he was too far away and the images were too poor — but the motions were unmistakeable.

"One of these days," said Banks breezily, "I'd just love to see one of these idiots get mown down by a train."

Joe gave a nervous laugh, but the glance Banks threw his way said he wasn't joking.

On the screen, the man finished his work and stepped back across the rails. He pulled himself up on to the platform with relative ease. From this angle they could see he was pale-skinned and clean-shaven. But those were the only clues to his identity.

He started to walk back towards the camera, and Eve and Joe both leaned in for the best view of his face. Then — instead of walking all the way back down the platform and leaving the way he'd come in — the man turned into the first exit he reached, and disappeared.

"Shit!" said Eve.

"Hard luck," said Banks, and pushed his chair back a little to indicate that the session was at an end. He picked up the ring binder, obviously itching to track down, and probably fire, the hapless Gary Bushman.

"Don't you have other cameras that might have tracked him elsewhere in the station?"

Banks pursed his lips and looked pointedly at his watch. When Eve didn't withdraw her request, he dropped the ring binder on to the counter top and ran rapidly through several other commands and cameras. White-tiled tunnels running to the left and the right, vaulted ceilings and archways and odd-angled corners. There were people, but they blurred past too fast for Eve to identify anyone. Only Banks had that skill, and his mind was already elsewhere. She longed to slow him down, to make him methodical, but she could only watch him go through the motions.

There were no other shots of the man. None that they could spot in the whistle-stop digital tour of the station, anyway. The screen froze once again on the last shot of the dark figure just before he ducked out of sight.

"That's all," said Banks, and picked up the binder again. This time he stood up as well.

"Could we have a copy?" Eve asked.

"Not from me," said Banks. "You would have to submit a request through the British Transport Police."

"Of course," she nodded, but needed more. "Could you do me a *huge* favour, Mr Banks, and zoom in on his face?"

Banks sighed loudly. And when that didn't put her off, he tutted petulantly and said, "I can, but it won't do any good."

He did, and it didn't.

Eve strained close to the screen, searching desperately for clues in the blurred face, the dark clothing, the shape, the walk. That vague feeling of recognition nagged at her and she was desperate for the key that might help to identify the man.

But there was nothing to see but low-resolution anonymity.

They walked to the office in the bitter cold, snow flurries hurting their faces.

"How many bodies have we covered in the last couple of weeks?"

Joe shrugged. "Five or six?"

"Maybe we should go back to each of the scenes and see if we can find any more of those flyers."

"OK then. Where first? The cinema?"

"Portman Square's closer, where they found Siobhan Mackie."

Joe nodded. "OK."

Eve was glad they had something to do. The last thing she needed was to sit around thinking about Maddie Matthews until the next job came in. She gnawed her thumbnail — a bad habit she couldn't break.

180

As they waited to cross at lights she asked neutrally, "Did you watch the bit where she was hit by the train?" "No," he said after a moment. "I closed my eyes."

CHAPTER
TWENTY-FOUR

The body of Siobhan Mackie had been found in the railed garden of Portman Square.

They looked everywhere a flyer might have been. On trees and in litter bins and on the wooden backs of park benches.

Eve was glad she'd worn her yeti boots. Here in the garden, away from the traffic of cars and people, the snow had grown to a depth of about a foot and — apart from a couple of yellow dog-pee patches around the gates — was largely undisturbed, and rather lovely.

The square itself was quiet, and the garden quieter still — as if the wrought-iron railings were a deceptively effective sound barrier. Soon the only noise was of their feet on the crunchy snow, and their breathing.

Even when they spoke, the sound was deadened. Instead of making them raise their voices, it made them aware of how loud they usually were, and they spoke only when necessary, and at librarian levels.

The garden had been cleverly designed to hide the fine Georgian buildings that surrounded it, even in winter — to give the impression of isolation where it was impossible to come by. Near the centre of the square, Eve stopped and turned a slow circle. Here and

182

there were glimpses of a roof, a window, an angle of guttering. But mostly the view was of an intricate network of gnarled black branches above waves of evergreen shrubbery, dolloped with snow.

Even though Joe was circling a waste bin just ahead of her, Eve felt alone.

They were not far from the shrubs that had hidden the body. Eve walked over there, trying to breathe less noisily so that she could enjoy the creaking, squeaking sound of her own weight compressing the crystals underfoot.

Here, she thought.

She stopped and bent.

Yes. Here was where the body had been. Naked and on its back, and so paled by death that several people had already walked their dogs before one of them had spotted Siobhan Mackie in the snow and the shadows.

She had been strangled, so Eve hadn't been sick, but she remembered feeling desperately sorry for the corpse, which had lain here for hours after discovery before being moved, with only a thin white sheet for cover.

Now there was nothing to mark the spot where the young woman had died. Or been dumped. The police hadn't decided yet.

At the opening of the inquest, Siobhan's uncle had sat silently and with a photo of his smiling niece pinned to his lapel — his face so stricken that it looked as if someone had wrung it dry of every last tear.

Eve turned. Joe was between benches.

"Anything?" she said quietly.

"No," he murmured.

He kept going — moving away from her — so she dropped to her knees and crawled into the shrubbery.

If the garden felt remote from the city of London, the cavern under the evergreen bushes was like being in outer space. Almost all light disappeared in an instant, and the silence pressed so hard about her that Eve actually touched a palm to one ear, in case it was blocked by something physical.

There was hardly any snow under here and the ground was dry, and Eve stayed on all fours while her eyes adjusted to the grey-green darkness.

Slow shapes took form on the ground and she picked each one up and held it close to her face for identification.

A cigarette packet showing diseased lungs, a Tube ticket from Ealing Broadway and a balled-up scrap of paper which she unfolded carefully, but which contained only a scribbled column of numbers and workings-out in pencil. The sum was wrong; they hadn't carried the one.

There wasn't much else. All this would have arrived since Siobhan's death, because the police had done a fingertip search of the whole square.

Eve shuffled around on her hands and knees to face the garden, but instead of crawling out of the shrubbery again, she sat down and peered through the dappled gaps in the leaf cover.

It was a dull day, with more snow in the leaden sky, but it looked unbearably white and bright out there beyond the cover of the bushes. She watched Joe checking benches and peering up trees. Moving in and out of her patchwork vision.

Although it was cold, Eve liked it here. Liked the feeling of being separated from the world and yet still able to see what was going on. It was like watching her parents through a crack in the door, or other children from a window.

Observing without being observed.

Uninvolved.

Being involved was exhausting. Involved with work, involved with her father, involved with Mr Elias and Mrs Solomon; involved with having to buy Christmas presents, which she *still* hadn't started to do, and today was the twelfth!

Eve felt a great calm come over her. She could stay here. Just stay here. Not for ever, but for a good long while. Until everything was . . . over.

Easier.

Until she felt rested and more able to cope with it all. All of life and death and everything in between.

Yes, she would just stay here.

She felt warmer. And a weight that had been on her chest lifted and allowed her to breathe the way that she used to. She hadn't felt safe for a long, long time, but being in the bushes felt safe. She was glad Joe was nearby; she didn't want to be *alone* — just uncommitted to interaction — and having him within sight was oddly comforting, even though he was in a world of his own and hadn't even *noticed* that she had disappeared.

As if he'd felt her thoughts, Joe backed out of a sprawling rhododendron, looked around the garden and called her name.

"Eve?"

The sound was short and dead. Eve didn't answer.

"Eve?" He said it more loudly.

It was silly of her not to answer him. Childish. She knew that, but still said nothing, safe in her dark-green bubble.

"EVE!" he shouted. But the snow captured the sound and sucked it out of the air so that it fell to the ground like a rock. Eve would have bet that the people in the surrounding houses would never have heard it.

Just like they wouldn't have heard Siobhan Mackie . . .

Suddenly she didn't feel safe here any more, and crawled so quickly from under the bushes that snow dumped itself in cold lumps on her head and back.

"Joe!" she called, and he turned and saw her.

Even from across the garden, she could tell he was relieved to see her, and for some reason that made her feel warm inside.

"Didn't you hear me calling you?" he said as she clumped towards him through pristine snow.

"No," she lied. "Sorry."

"What were you doing?"

Eve stopped, a little breathless from wading through the white, and waved a thumb over her shoulder at the shrubbery. "I wondered if the police had missed something around the body."

"Find anything?"

186

"No."

"Nor me."

He leaned in and brushed snow off the shoulders of her coat.

"Thanks," said Eve.

"How are those boots working out for you?"

"Embarrassing," she said, "but warm."

"I hate to say I told you so."

Eve smiled faintly. "You *love* to say I told you so."

"Oh yeah," he said. "*That*'s right."

Then they stood there for a moment, reluctant to admit defeat, and reluctant to move in the beautiful silence.

Joe finally said, "What about on the outside of the railings?"

They went back through the gate and walked slowly around the entire square, looking for a flyer — or even a place where a flyer had been ripped down. Bits of string knotted around the railings, perhaps, or a corner of paper left under sticky tape.

There was nothing.

Once Eve slipped on ice and Joe caught her.

They came back to their starting point at the phone box. It was an old-fashioned red one, like the one outside her own home, and Eve wondered whether Portman Square had its own version of Mr Elias, seeking a sense of community through a common relic, like a saint's finger in a box.

She pulled open the door and knew that if there *were* a Mr Elias on Portman Square, he was failing miserably. This phone box smelled of piss, for a start.

187

Like the damp humanity of the rush-hour Tube train, it was a smell that seemed to come from a different time — an old-fashioned doorway smell of stale urine — and Eve felt a tweak of groundless pride that *her* phone box smelled only of lavender air-freshener.

Also, the money box of this phone had been scratched and hammered and there were business cards stuck all over the dialling-information wall — cards advertising cheap Viagra and cheap blow jobs — apparently presuming the cheap Viagra worked.

But there was nothing advertising any kind of exhibition, unless you counted the countless little photos of medicine-ball tits and Kardashian arses.

"Nothing," said Eve.

Joe pointed at the cards and deadpanned, "So you don't think any of these people could be the killer?"

"No," she sighed. "And Siobhan Mackie's probably not one of our killer's victims."

"Why not?"

It started to snow again and they both shuffled into the shelter of the phone box, squashed in there, toe-to-toe. The smell of pee was even stronger now and Eve felt an unexpected surge of affection for Mr Elias. He was doing a grand job.

Still, it was not unpleasant to be crammed into a tight space with Joe. He smelled good, at least. Faintly of leather and soap.

"Why not?" he said again.

Eve remembered what she'd been talking about.

"Siobhan was killed overnight. Nobody saw it and nobody heard it. And her body was hidden. Not *well*

hidden, admittedly, but hidden anyway. It's hardly a
show, is it? I mean, if that's what our lunatic likes."

Joe nodded and absently eyed the wall of boobs and
booty over her head.

"Like some people like having sex in public," he said.

"Yeah," said Eve, and glanced at the cards. "You ever
done that?"

Joe snorted. "I've barely had sex in private."

She laughed. "I find that hard to believe."

Joe just smiled and shrugged, and Eve turned to
stare out of the dirty glass panels at the garden beyond
the railings.

"Could it have been a trial run?" she said. "Like a
warm-up murder?"

Joe nodded. "Or something unintentional that
became murder, so he wasn't really prepared for it, but
then he liked it."

"Maybe," said Eve. Then she shook her head and
looked around the square. "It just doesn't feel right that
the body was hidden."

"And there's no flyer."

Eve nodded, relieved. A flyer would have meant that
the man on the phone was almost certainly the killer. A
killer whose idea of a social overture was pushing a
thirteen-year-old girl under a train. She hoped they
never found another flyer, and not finding one here was
a start.

Using his back, Joe pushed open the phone-box
door. "Next?" he said.

"Next," said Eve.

As she left the box, she pulled one of the whores' cards off the wall and handed it to Joe.

"Don't say I never give you nothin'."

The skinny, spotty boy-manager of the Everyman Cinema, who had baulked at helping them before, was called Charlie Mazurski, and he was a lot more accommodating now he was sure that a patron being slaughtered like a pig in Screen Two was not going to reflect badly on him.

"I mean," he told them in the red-carpeted lobby, "you should see the paperwork we have to fill in for Health and Safety if someone even stubs their *toe*. When I found out someone had been *stabbed* I was like, *Oh my God this is bad!* And then when they were *dead* I was like, *Oh my GOD I am so FIRED!* But Head Office was OK about it. They said I didn't even have to inform Health and Safety, only the police, thank God."

"You ever had anything like this happen before?" Eve asked, more out of natural curiosity than any job-related interest.

"Not murder," he said. "But we once had a very large lady fall on someone when she went out to get ice cream. She broke his arm and then got stuck under the seats." He giggled, then flapped a hand in front of his face. "I shouldn't laugh, but it *was* funny. Because when the firemen finally picked her up, she had rum and raisin melted all down her front and the little wooden spoon — you know, the little ice-cream spoon? — was stuck to her face right *here*."

190

He poked a finger at his own eyebrow, then giggled and flapped again.

Eve laughed with him, then said, "So could we have a quick look around then, Mr Mazurski?"

"I suppose it can't hurt," he said a little doubtfully. "But I'll have to ask you to buy a ticket. That way you're officially customers and we're covered by insurance if something happens to you. If I just let you in for free and you slip on the toilet floor or get your hand stuck in a litter bin or something, then I'm personally responsible, you see?"

"I see," said Eve. "I had no idea going to the cinema was so fraught with danger."

"Neither did that bloke who got a knife in the neck," he said sombrely.

"Fair point," said Eve, and followed the young manager to the ticket counter and got out her purse.

"Would you like premium seats?"

Eve laughed, but he was being serious. She sighed and bought two premium tickets — £25 each — for seats they weren't going to sit in and a movie they weren't going to watch.

"Which screen did it happen in?"

"Screen Two," said Mazurski.

Regardless of the macabre circumstances of their visit, Eve couldn't help feeling a childlike excitement as they went up the escalator and into the lesser light of the area where the doors to the screens and toilets were. She hadn't been to the cinema for ages, and the dimming light and the smell of stale popcorn was like time travel.

"I haven't been to the movies since *Titanic*," she muttered.

"Nineteen-twelve?" said Joe. "That *is* a long time."

"Shut up."

This second lobby was lined with lighted posters of coming attractions — none of them sullied by a flyer advertising an exhibition.

They ventured into Screen Two. It was dark and noisy, and there was no point in stumbling about, so they just peered around the entryway for a white square on the black walls, and left again.

"No wonder he chose this movie," said Joe, pointing at his ears. "Great cover for a killing."

"They should put that on the poster," said Eve. "*Loud enough to kill by.*"

They stood for a moment, at a loss as to what to do next.

"What about the loos?" said Eve.

"Might as well get our money's worth," said Joe.

Eve went into the Ladies, her eyes raking the tiled walls. She walked down between the cubicles, looking behind every door, not expecting to find anything more than adverts for rape helplines and bladder problems. This was the ladies' loo, after all — she doubted a man would walk in here to put up a flyer when he could easily put one up in the Gents without attracting any attention.

She and Joe emerged from the toilets at the same time, like wooden folk in a Bavarian clock.

"Anything?"

"Nope." He looked down at his ticket. "Let's watch a movie."

Eve gave him a sideways look. "After this, I don't think I'll ever go to the movies again!"

He grinned. "We could always sit in the back row . . ."

Eve cocked a sceptical eyebrow at him. "Nice try." Then she said, "Hey, did you look behind the cubicle doors?"

"No," admitted Joe.

"What were you *doing* in there?" said Eve impatiently. "Come on."

She bustled him back into the men's room.

"Hey!" Joe protested. "What if someone comes in?"

"Well, hurry up and they won't." She started down the row of toilet cubicles.

"That makes no sense," said Joe, starting more slowly down the facing row.

"Yes it does," said Eve. "The — *Oh my God.*"

"What?"

But Eve couldn't speak. Suddenly she didn't have the energy. Every bit of life seemed to have drained from her in an instant, and her throat clogged with guilt.

All she could do was point to the back of the door.

There, pasted over an erectile-dysfunction poster, was a cheap flyer:

EXHIBITION
Venue: Here
Date: December 4
Time: 21.30

The same font. The same paper.
They were the same . . .

CHAPTER
TWENTY-FIVE

13 December

Under scaffolding poles and the glare of portable halogen spotlights, a team of forensics officers scraped carefully at the hoarding alongside the building where Layla Martin had died.

Bill-posters had made good use of the twenty yards of painted chipboard and there were hundreds of flyers stuck all over it, although — united in irony — they had left careful space around each stencilled warning to POST NO BILLS HERE.

The only other light now came from the shop windows and the Christmas decorations, and the street was packed with thousands of shoppers. The closer it got to Christmas, the more urgently they pushed past each other and the more panicked their expressions became. Watching from a café across the street, Eve's view of the police operation at the hoarding was like watching a flicker book.

She had told them everything. The flyers, the man calling her name at Piccadilly Underground, the phone call ... Superintendent Huw Rees had listened, expressionless.

"I should have told you sooner," Eve had admitted. "But it sounded unbelievable."

"It still does," Rees had shrugged. "But let's see what we find."

And so this painstaking search had begun.

"I got you a different cake."

Eve looked down at the cake Joe had brought her along with the coffees. It was the second cake he'd bought her since they'd sat down in the window of the café. The first was untouched, too. This fresh cake was chocolate, which was her favourite, but the thought of eating it made her mouth go dry. She shook her head. "I don't think so."

She hadn't eaten anything since yesterday. Not since they'd found the flyer in the cinema where Kevin Barr's head had been separated from his spinal column with a deft knife. Not since she'd accepted that Maddie Matthews had died because of her . . .

We're in it together now, Eve.

She thought she might never eat again. There didn't seem to be anything left inside her to nourish. She sipped the coffee, and felt it drop into a cavity so large that it grumbled at the vast emptiness.

Joe took her hand in both of his. "You going to be OK?"

"I feel like shit," she said, and he nodded. Eve liked that about Joe. He never tried to cheer her up when there was no point. There was nothing more annoying than somebody trying to jolly you out of a justifiable slump.

"You need to snap out of it," he said, and she barked a short laugh.

"What?" he said.

"Nothing."

"Seriously, Eve," he went on. "You fucked up, and nothing can change that —"

"Thanks," she said. "You're helping."

"I *am* helping," he insisted. "And so are you. You're helping by going to the police, so they can catch him before anybody else is killed. It's the right thing to do. It could save other lives. But you're the only person who's had contact with the killer, and that's critical. So you need to be thinking about what you *might* change, not what you can't, and to do that you need to be thinking objectively, so you have to snap out of self-pity mode."

"It's not *self*-pity!" she bristled. "It's just *pity*! For Maddie Matthews."

"Well, it's not helping her family. It's not helping the cops. It's not even helping *you*. So just stop it."

Eve glared at him. "You're always so bloody right," she said. "And I was enjoying a wallow."

"It doesn't suit you," he shrugged. "Can I have your cake?"

"Not the chocolate one."

He smiled and started on the lemon tart.

Eve's empty mind began to creak slowly back into action. Getting the story was no longer important. Joe was right — catching the killer was the priority now, and she needed to be sharp if she was going to be helpful — if she was going to make some small amends.

196

She cut the nose off the chocolate cake.

"What are we going to tell Ross?" said Joe with his mouth full.

"Absolutely *nothing*," said Eve firmly — and felt better already.

Her phone buzzed on the table between them and she picked it up.

"Get over here," said DS Rees. "We found it."

"My God," breathed Eve.

The three of them stood and looked at the flyer. Whatever had been pasted over it still clung to it in bitty red fragments, but there was no mistaking the remnants underneath:

EXHIBITION
Venue: Here
Date: December 1
Time: 10.00

"The day Layla Martin died," Eve said softly.

It shook her to think of how very *un*-random that murder seemed now. Not only had somebody planned it, but they had advertised it like a car-boot sale or a sideshow.

Roll up, roll up! Come see the brutal slaying!

Unexpected tears pricked her eyes. Layla Martin, who was twenty-four and would never be twenty-five. Eve wondered whether Layla had always been the target, or whether the killer simply knew how to get into the building and hoped to find somebody alone there. Maybe he had been there before — roaming the floors, riding the lifts, waiting for a victim to present herself.

And if Layla Martin *had* been the intended target, how long had he watched her? Had she been aware of being watched? Had she been concerned? Had she told her girlfriends about it over a Pinot Grigio after work? Or had she never even *noticed* the man who watched her from across the road, across the Tube, across her own *office*? Could it have been someone she knew so well that such attention might have passed entirely under her radar?

Eve wanted to slip her hand into Joe's. To feel that she was safe and anchored to somebody sane. But of course she didn't do it.

Rees turned to her and said bluntly, "We want a news blackout on the flyers."

"By lunchtime every copper in London will be looking out for them, but if we publicize them there'll be mayhem. Panic on the streets."

Eve gave him a sceptical look. "Give people credit for *some* intelligence, Huw."

Rees shook his head grimly. "I give people credit for *no* intelligence. Also, if this is the man who killed Layla Martin, I don't want to give the bastard the publicity he wants, or risk a copycat muddying the waters."

Eve thought fast. Whatever Huw Rees said, the police could only ask for, not enforce, a news blackout — and that gave her leverage.

"You're asking us to give up an exclusive, Huw."

"In the interests of public safety," he said.

Eve frowned at Joe.

"Ross will never go for it," Joe said.

"Not unless we can get guarantees," mused Eve.

"What kind of guarantees?" said Rees suspiciously.

"Even if we can't use them right now, the flyers are *our* exclusive and have to stay that way. They mustn't be leaked to any other journalist."

"Fair enough."

"And *we* get an exclusive call every time *you* find one."

"What's the point of that if you're not going to use them?" said Rees suspiciously.

"Backgrounder," said Eve. "When you catch and convict this bastard, we'll have every cough and spit on camera. We'll be miles ahead of the opposition."

Rees nodded reluctantly. "OK."

"And a credit."

"A *credit*?"

"Yes. If you get a conviction *because* of the evidence we've brought you, we want a credit. A *named* credit."

"iWitness News?" said Rees.

"No," she said. "Me and Joe. We get a public thank-you for the part we played, right there outside the court."

Rees gave her a stony look and Eve knew she was pushing her luck. The police got so little credit that it was almost cruel to ask them to share it.

"We want the same thing, Huw," she said, and shivered a little as she heard the killer's words echo from her mouth.

They didn't want the same thing exactly. But they *were* over the same barrel, and Eve knew it. If Huw Rees wanted the blackout on the flyers, he would give her this. Because otherwise, the next time the killer called her, how could Rees be sure that Eve would call *him* . . . ?

He couldn't.

"This is all assuming we catch him," he said grumpily.

"He tells you where and when he's going to strike next," said Eve. "How hard can he be to catch?"

"Ha ha," he said mirthlessly. Then he sighed and said, "All right, you've got a deal."

"*What* deal?" By horrible magic, Guy Smith appeared at Eve's elbow. "What deal?" he repeated. "How come *she* gets a deal and I don't? What's going on here? And *ohmyGod*, what the *fuck* happened to your *face*?" Then he sneezed messily three times and wiped his nose on a coffee-shop napkin.

"Fucking cold," he said, then repeated, "*What* deal?"

Eve stared blankly at Huw Rees, unable to think further than the exhibition flyer behind his left shoulder. The flyer that was right in her eyeline — right in *Guy's* eyeline. A police officer was starting to dig at its edges with a scraper.

EXHIBITIO —

"It's not a deal you'd be interested in," said Rees smoothly.

"Oh yeah?" said Guy. "Try me."

Rees sighed and Eve wanted to shout and clap a hand over his mouth —

"Royal baby," he said. "I got Alfred, she got Charles."

Eve was impressed. She'd had no idea the detective superintendent was such an accomplished liar.

"I got Samuel," Joe piped up, and Guy pulled a face at him. "*What?* Samuel's a Jewish name! They're not going to call it something *Jewish*, are they? Bloody hell, have some sense!"

"But I got a fiver on at 100–1," said Joe doubtfully.

Guy snorted. "Idiot." Then he turned back to Huw Rees. Back to the flyer . . .

"So what's all this then, Huw? Bit of a community clean-up to keep the team busy?"

Eve held her breath. The flyer was disappearing, but painfully slowly.

EXHIBI —

"There was an assault here this afternoon," lied Rees again. "Not much, but a knife was involved, so given the proximity to the crime scene we thought we'd check for DNA."

"With paint scrapers?" said Guy. "Not exactly *CSI Miami*, is it?"

"I didn't realize you were an expert," said Rees sharply.

"You want Veronica Creed on that," said Guy. "Not *60 Minute Makeover*."

"Just fuck off," snapped Rees. "I've had a long day and you bloody people don't make it any easier."

He stalked away and Guy turned to Eve. "What's up with him? You must've really wound him up before I got here."

Eve gave him a cool look. "Like Kevin Barr's father?" she said. Then she walked away too, and Joe followed her.

"Can't you take a joke?" Guy called after them. "And *what happened to your face?*"

Mention of Veronica Creed always left Huw Rees out of sorts.

She was a small, rosy-cheeked, round-faced forensics expert of indeterminate age, with glasses and bobbed grey hair, who wore fluffy cat jumpers and shapeless tartan skirts.

And she scared the *shit* out of Rees.

He had been a copper for twenty-two years and in that time he had seen things he wouldn't have wished on his worst enemy. He had arrested torturers of small children, hunted down the owners of starved and beaten sex slaves, and had once captured a cannibal — who had proudly shown him knuckles in a jar.

But Veronica Creed was the creepiest person he'd ever met.

She had all the calm detachment of a psychopath, but none of the comforting iron bars between her and the rest of the world. And although Rees had *no basis whatsoever* for any suspicions, he often lay awake at night worrying about what she might do, or might have done.

He knew it was ridiculous, so he'd never told anybody how he felt about her, but he also knew he was not alone. He'd seen grown men flinch from her near-touch and hurry from her presence. He'd watched them toss coins to determine who would have to go to her office and fetch a report. Whenever someone at work called Veronica Creed an *absolute legend*, Huw Rees always thought *like Dracula*.

If Huw Rees had had to say *why* Veronica Creed was so creepy, he would not have been able to put his finger on it, but just thinking of her pushing her glasses up her nose and fixing him with her big moony eyes made him shiver.

It had nothing to do with the snow.

CHAPTER
TWENTY-SIX

Eve went to the shop at the station on her way home. She only needed milk, but after she'd put that in her basket she wandered up and down the narrow aisles, adding random impulse buys. A pair of woolly tights, a sandalwood Yankee candle.

The few late-night shoppers averted their eyes from her bruised face.

She put a baguette in her basket. It smelled like childhood, and she thought that when she got home she would simply tear it into doughy chunks and eat it straight out of the bag. One of the good things about effectively living alone was that she didn't have to mind her table manners. Sometimes she ate beans and fish fingers right out of the frying pan and felt like a cross between a cowpoke and a caveman.

Waiting in the short line for the checkout, Eve decided that a Yankee candle was absolutely the last thing anybody in their right mind needed in their life. So what if the house smelled a bit like hamster? It wasn't as though she *entertained*.

She smiled wryly at the very idea, then took the candle out of her basket and left it on the sweet rack near the till. Instead she picked up two bars of Dairy Milk chocolate.

One for now and one for emergencies.

A weird sound confused Eve as she reached her gate.

Mr Elias was clearing her path. He straightened up and looked at her, his breath blowing clouds around his head, with a shovelful of ice. The loose, dirty snow was piled up along the edges of the path, while he had broken up the compacted ice underneath into broad, jagged plates, ready for lifting. The slab already on his shovel revealed a vague rhombus of the old path she knew so well.

Eve was oddly moved. It was the sort of thing her father would have done for her — or for a neighbour. An old-fashioned kindness unfettered by the complications of feminism.

"Oh. That's so kind of you!"

"Not at all," he said, waving her thanks away gruffly. "I should have done it sooner, really."

There was an opened sack of salt by the gate, waiting to make everything safe.

It made Eve feel warm inside, even before she went indoors to boil the kettle so she could make him a nice cup of tea.

Later, Eve sat in her mother's old easy chair, tearing bread off the baguette in chunks, and watched her father sleep.

He was curled up on his side like a child. One loose fist on the pillow; the wedding ring he never took off glimmering in the glow from the street light.

After every breath, she prayed to a God she didn't believe in not to grant him another.

This was the way to die. Warm and cosy in his own bed, and watched over by somebody who loved him.

Other futures were not so rosy.

But Duncan Singer kept breathing.

In.

And out.

And in.

Eve sighed. Either there was no God, or God just didn't care.

Her phone rang and she hurried out of the room to answer it.

Number withheld.

"Hello, Eve."

It was him.

She opened her mouth — then said nothing. Didn't know *what* to say. The man had killed three people. *At least.* What was the etiquette?

"You're wondering what to do," he mused with perfect vowels. "Should you say nothing and risk provoking me? Or say hello and play along?"

"If I ever play along, it won't be with a sick bastard like you."

He laughed. "I see you've plumped for provocation."

Eve bit her lip and thought of Mrs Crick, her form teacher in her final year at school, who used to raise her eyebrows at her across the classroom and say, "Engage brain, Evelyn. *Then* mouth."

Sometimes she forgot.

"I knew my father," he went on, "although I didn't care for him. And who's to say who's sick?"

"You cut a woman's throat. You sliced through a man's spinal cord. You murdered a *child*! That's what *normal* people call sick!"

"Who's normal?" he said dismissively. "You'd probably call yourself normal and yet here you are, talking to a killer. What normal person does that? What normal person would appreciate my work? That's why I like you, Eve — because you're *not* normal."

She didn't answer him.

"Who broke your nose?"

He spoke as if he cared and it surprised her. She hesitated. "None of your business."

"Do you think you can shock me, Eve? You forget who you're talking to. Tell me anything. I cannot be appalled."

He was right; he was a serial killer, after all. For some reason, Eve had to keep reminding herself of that.

"I am a friend," he went on, "and come not to punish."

"You're not my friend," she snapped.

"Neither is the person who hurt you," he shot back.

"Shut up!" said Eve angrily. "You don't know anything about my life and you don't care about it, so spare me your fake concern. Fake concern is *my* job! I'm the fucking *queen* of fake concern!"

He laughed hard, and with real enjoyment — only tailing off slowly with a long, amused sigh.

"You're funny, Eve," he said at last, "but you're wrong. I know you a lot better than you think I do."

She felt the skin crawl up the back of her neck.

Only the long, long silence finally told her that the killer had hung up, and that, once more, she was alone.

CHAPTER
TWENTY-SEVEN

14 December

"There's a tramp on the steps."

David Fallon looked up at the cleaning lady. Debbie Gomperts was a big, blunt woman who rarely prefaced anything she said with any kind of preamble that might tip a person off as to what was coming next, so in any conversation with her he always felt as if he were two steps behind.

"Excuse me?" he said.

"A tramp," she repeated. "On the steps." As if his failure to comprehend first time round was only because the sentence was too long, so she'd kindly broken it up into two far simpler pieces to accommodate his stupidity.

But David hadn't heard the word "tramp" for so long that it had taken a moment to register — that was all. Everybody said "homeless person" nowadays. "Tramp" was a word from his long-distant past, when idealized old men who weren't obvious alcoholics wandered the land, doing odd jobs and sleeping in haystacks.

And "steps" could be anywhere.

"Which steps?" he said.

"The steps," said Debbie Gomperts. "Out front."

Ah.

That was a problem.

David Fallon rose from his cluttered desk, padded silently through the plush red-carpeted lobby and peered through the glass doors, to see that a tramp had indeed set up home outside the front entrance of the Barnstormer Theatre, and was now curled up — apparently asleep — on the top step.

David sighed. He hated confrontation. But in two hours' time patrons would start to arrive for tonight's performance of *Romeo and Juliet*, and what theatre-goers *didn't* like was real-life drama intruding on their suspension of disbelief.

Especially if real life smelled like piss.

"Oh dear," he said to nobody, and unlocked the main door.

"Excuse me?"

The man didn't stir.

David cleared his throat and raised his voice. "Excuse me!"

The man sat up slowly and said, "What?"

"You can't sleep here," David told him.

The man looked around him as if he'd only just noticed where he was, then back at David Fallon.

"Well, I was doing all right until you woke me up."

David smiled briefly to show that he was a human being and appreciated the joke.

"I mean," he went on, "we'll be opening our doors in an hour."

The man put up a hand as if acknowledging — but rejecting — an offer.

"Oh I'm fine out here, thank you."

This was awkward. David wished there was somebody else who could deal with this, but there wasn't. All he had were half a dozen willowy drama-school ushers, Eric in the concession stand, who was almost eighty, Marge behind the bar, and Debbie Gomperts, who couldn't really be set loose on any member of the public without offence ensuing — not even a tramp.

The man settled down again in the corner he'd made shabby-chic with a floor and walls of cardboard, and a Harrods bag containing all his worldly goods in effortless style.

David Fallon was a good person. He loved his cat, Dilly, and never forgot his godson's birthday — even though he hadn't had a thank-you card since the little shit had hit his teens — and he often shopped or watered plants for elderly neighbours.

But the tramp did smell of pee.

So he locked the door and called the police.

"I'm *queuing!*" insisted the homeless man as two policemen picked up his Harrods bag and hauled him to his feet. "I want to see *Romeo and Juliet!*"

"You got a ticket, sir?" said the younger of the two officers.

"*That's* what I'm queuing for," explained the man. "For returns. Like when people sleep outside the Apple store for an iPhone. Or the new Harry Potter."

The young cop looked questioningly at David.

"He's not queuing," said David. "He's just sleeping."

"How do *you* know?" said the man. "You never even asked!"

The younger copper asked David if there were any returned tickets. Then when he was told that there were, he asked the homeless man whether he would like to buy one.

"Well," the tramp said sniffily, "not *now*."

The two coppers laughed and the younger one picked up the cardboard walls and floor and handed them to the man.

"You can sleep there," he said, pointing at the snowy pavement just a few feet away, "but not *here*."

"Sod that," the tramp grumbled. "I'm going to see *The Mousetrap*." And he stalked off.

David sighed and watched him shuffle through the snow, then turned to thank the police officers.

But they had their backs to him, and were staring down at the corner where the homeless man had been sleeping.

He stepped forward to peer over their shoulders.

Some cheeky bugger had stuck a flyer there.

For an exhibition.

CHAPTER
TWENTY-EIGHT

The Barnstormer Theatre was crawling with cops.

Eve looked around her, spotting familiar faces in unfamiliar suits, mingling with the paying customers. She saw DS Rees standing in the lobby, wearing a rather faded dinner jacket, which was only just hanging on by its single button across his broad middle. She didn't know the man alongside Rees, but he had the pinkest, shiniest, baldest head she had ever seen.

"Thank you for the call," she said, and Rees nodded curtly. Maybe he was regretting the deal they'd made. Eve would if she were him . . .

"This is DI Marr," said Rees, and she and the shiny-bald officer exchanged polite nods.

DI Marr rubbed his hands together and said, "Exciting, isn't it?"

Eve and Rees exchanged dubious glances.

"The West End," he explained. "Treading the boards."

"Oh," she said. "Yes."

Rees looked over Eve's shoulder. "Where's your colleague?"

"Joe? He'll be here in a second."

"He'd better be. I don't want anyone knowing that there's anything different about tonight's performance. And that means no coming in late, no big camera, no jeans . . ."

"He'll be here on time," she said confidently. She'd passed on the message about jeans, although Huw Rees's DJ was the most distinctive item of clothing in evidence — and not in a good way. She herself was in a simple black dress she kept for funerals.

A man in the only other tuxedo came over. A plastic badge on his silken lapel said that he was the MANAGER.

"Do you have everything you need, Detective Rees?"

"Yes thank you, Mr Fallon."

"Can we start then?"

"Just give us another ten minutes."

"Another ten minutes!" Fallon looked as if he might cry. "But we've had a freezer malfunction! If we don't start now then by the time we get to the interval the ice cream will have melted!"

"We're moving as fast as we can, Mr Fallon. This *is* a murder investigation."

"But what about the *ice cream*?" said Fallon, as if Rees had failed to identify the real issue. "It's not so much the tubs — they'll just be soft — but we have bars too and they lose their shape. I can't sell a floppy Magnum!"

"I can only do so much, sir."

Fallon flapped his arms miserably and hurried off towards the auditorium.

"So," Eve asked Rees, "where do you want us?"

214

"After everybody else is seated, you can come into the back of the auditorium with me, but you're not to film unless something happens. Don't want to raise any suspicions."

"OK, good. Where's everybody else?"

"We've got a dozen officers, mostly in the audience, with a couple in the bits on either side of the stage —"

"The wings," said DI Marr.

"Whatever," said Rees.

"Well, that's what they're called," said Marr.

"I didn't know you were a thespian," said Rees sarcastically.

"Croydon Players," said Marr. "Twenty years. We're doing *Oklahoma!* in January. I'm Curly."

Eve and Rees both glanced at Marr's shiny head, and he got all defensive.

"It's *meant* to be funny."

"Anyway," said Rees, "we've got two men up in the lights —"

"The rigging," Marr provided.

"With night-vision goggles," Rees went on, "and half a dozen more mingling with the audience."

Eve was impressed. "You moved fast."

"Hope it's enough," said Rees.

"Are you armed?"

He hesitated, then said stiffly, "We have armed officers in attendance."

Eve nodded, excited by the idea of armed cops roaming up and down the aisles of this West End theatre. She loved this feeling of being in the know, being on the inside, while others were left in ignorance.

Rees said he'd better take his seat, and joined the throng of people now streaming through the lobby.

Eve turned to see Joe standing just inside the doors, looking around for her. He was in black jeans and a black sweater.

Eve looked him up and down. "You look like a choreographer."

"Is that bad?" he said.

She squinted at him again. "Not too bad."

Joe looked great, she thought. Black suited him. He looked like James Bond with a social conscience.

"You look great," he said, and she was so flummoxed by the echo of her own unspoken compliment that she just waved it away and said, "Did you get the flyer?"

He nodded and showed her the LCD screen of a camera so small he had it in his pocket.

EXHIBITION
Venue: Here
Date: December 14
Time: Tonight

Eve nodded her approval and told him the plan, which was less a plan than a vantage point, but they agreed that it was better than not getting a call at all. And a million times better than twenty other media outlets getting the same call.

"Especially if one of them is Guy Smith," said Eve with feeling.

An announcement asked everybody to take their seats, and the last person at the concession stand paid an ancient man dressed as Buttons for a tub of melting ice cream and hurried through the double doors.

Eve and Joe joined Huw Rees just inside the doors. The two men nodded minutely at each other.

After plenty of rustling and finding of seats, the lights went down and the play began.

Romeo and Juliet was not Eve's favourite Shakespeare play. She liked *Macbeth*, with all the blood and the witches and the moveable forest. Romeo and Juliet had always seemed callow and foolish to her, a couple of infatuated kids doing over-dramatic things in the name of love. She was far more preoccupied by the audience, wondering whether a killer sat among them. If he did, she hoped that any murder attempt wouldn't involve another knife in the back of the neck, or anything else that resulted in a lot of blood.

Now and then Huw Rees murmured into a concealed radio, but otherwise she would never have guessed that there were twenty-odd people in the audience who were there solely to catch a serial killer.

She felt Rees tense beside her as Mercutio was killed, but the cast seemed unperturbed, and they got to the interval without incident.

David Fallon was sweating like a warm choc-ice.

He could barely believe what was happening, right here in the Barnstormer off Shaftesbury Avenue.

Once the police had arrived and told him what was going on, he'd wanted to cancel the performance, but Detective Superintendent Rees had assured him that they were throwing everything at the operation to catch a killer and that his cooperation would be greatly appreciated.

There'd been something in the man's manner that had made David understand that while his cooperation would be greatly appreciated, it was by no means essential.

"Well," he'd conceded at last, "I suppose the show must go on."

And it had.

And was halfway through, without incident.

The audience were doing what audiences normally did during any interval — queuing for the loo and for sweets, picking up the drinks they'd pre-ordered from the bar.

Milling about.

With any luck, *if* the man the police were seeking had come tonight, he would have caught wind of the police operation and left already, or put his plans on hold for another night. And another theatre, hopefully.

David sighed. He assumed he would look back on all this and laugh. But right now, he felt like a cigarette, and he had not felt like a cigarette for nearly fifteen years.

There was a small gaggle of people standing on the steps outside the front doors, all dressed up and smoking roll-ups like hoods. He wondered if he could cadge a smoke off one of them, like a fifteen-year-old kid outside a newsagent's.

The bell rang for the second half and he was grateful for the distraction from the growing need for a cigarette — even if that distraction was the possibility of murder.

218

Nothing was going to happen.

Eve felt herself relaxing as every familiar line of the play was delivered, and every twist twirled towards the foregone conclusion.

Joe yawned audibly next to her and she jabbed him with her elbow, then yawned herself in sympathy.

The climax of the play came with Romeo finding Juliet apparently dead on a slab, and drinking poison to join his love in the afterlife. Whereupon she would wake up and kill herself too.

Of course she would, thought Eve tetchily. It was all so contrived and predictable. Although probably not quite so much when it was written, nearly five hundred years ago, she grudgingly conceded.

But here and now she felt it was an embarrassing cliché to watch a grown man pretend to drink poison and pretend to choke and pretend to go blue.

Actually, he *was* going blue.

Even from here she could see that Romeo was quite the method actor.

But when Juliet rose from the dead and started thumping his back —

DS Rees was the first person to move. He said nothing. One moment he was standing beside her, and the next he was running full-pelt down the carpeted aisle and *flying* on to the stage like some kind of musketeer.

Eve gasped and turned to Joe, who already had his camera out of his bag.

"Hurry!" she said.

219

He did, and was filming even as he walked quickly and smoothly towards the action.

On-stage, Juliet was saying, "There's something wrong. That's not supposed to happen," while Romeo clutched at his throat and croaked and choked. Huw Rees grabbed him from behind and DI Marr's shiny head made a dramatic entrance, stage left, for a brief but dazzling moment in the West End spotlight.

The audience sat, buzzing with concern, while several people stood and craned to see what was happening. Some — the police officers, Eve imagined — scanned the audience rather than the stage for clues and threats, while others stood tensely in front of each exit.

She didn't know where to go, so she stayed put, with apprehension rising in her gut. She was used to arriving at a crime scene after the crime had taken place. This was so different, and the excitement and fear were palpable. She had a good view of the whole auditorium from this little rise at the back. Ready to see the whole drama unfold.

But instead of *unfolding*, it folded.

Huw Rees embraced Romeo and performed the Heimlich manoeuvre and something hit the scenery with a *plunk*, followed by the sound of Romeo sucking in a huge breath.

The audience sighed in loud relief and broke into warm applause, while Rees spoke quietly to the actor, and patted him on the back. Averting a crisis, even though it wasn't the crisis they'd been expecting.

Then he jumped off the stage — and made DI Marr get down too — leaving Romeo to explain to the audience that he'd been so keen to kill himself that he'd swallowed the cork.

There was a ripple of laughter and another round of applause, and people slowly took their seats again for the two minutes of anti-climax that the play had left.

Joe rolled his eyes at Eve as he approached.

Before she could say anything to him, Mr Fallon rushed past them both, muttering, "I need a cigarette," then disappeared into the lobby.

David Fallon *really* needed that cigarette now. For a moment he had truly believed he was watching a murder on-stage, and the relief that it had not been so had made him shake.

He asked old Eric for a pack, but they didn't sell cigarettes any more. Luckily Eric was a smoker himself, which was a hell of an advertisement for the vice, when you thought about it — an eighty-year-old smoker still in employment and compos mentis enough to be handling money.

"Thirty a day for sixty-five years," Eric said proudly as he handed David a Lambert & Butler and a box of Swan Vestas.

David stepped out of the glass lobby doors on to the steps of the theatre, only to find that the tramp was back.

"Bloody hell!" he snapped. "What are *you* doing here?"

He turned to call a copper to have the man removed for the second time that night.

But as he did, an arm snaked around his neck, and squeezed.

So tight and so perfectly positioned against the carotid sinuses that David Fallon never even raised his own dangling arms to try to break the hold.

In a strange, calm kind of shock, he felt the cigarette and the matches fall from his hand, and in some distant universe he even heard them hit the steps. In the brightly lit lobby through the glass doors he could see old Eric restocking the sweets, as his knees folded slowly under his body, and a man of great strength laid him down tenderly on the cardboard floor — right there on the top step of the Barnstormer Theatre.

Lips against his ear whispered, "Thank you. *Thank you.*"

Even through the cardboard, David Fallon felt the icy cold of granite and death, and he looked up dumbly — beautifully — into the face of the tramp. And finally, as his eyes rolled back, at the flyer somebody had stuck on the wall over his head.

EXHIBITION . . .

The press release went out in the early hours of the morning, too late for newspaper deadlines and so early that by the time the day shift started it was already falling down the electronic news queues.

The release itself was so parched that it would have taken a psychic to guess that anything juicy lay behind

222

the body found in an area swarming with the homeless, the addicted and the transient. Any half-decent reporter would have known at a glance that the victim was unlikely to be anyone *real* . . .

> *Metropolitan Police are investigating after a 47-year-old man was found dead outside the Barnstormer Theatre, off Shaftesbury Avenue, last night.*
> *They are appealing for witnesses.*

The police did not release a name. They did not say that the victim was the manager of the theatre. They did not say that he had been murdered under a flyer that advertised his death like a Coming Attraction. And they sure as shit did not say that the crime had been committed right under the noses of twenty-five supposedly crack murder-team officers who were in attendance *specifically because* they had been warned that someone would be murdered at the theatre that very night . . .

But had missed it.

And so the sad passing of David Fallon was barely and briefly reported, and by the morning bulletins he had been bumped out of the news completely by a cyclist under a bus in the City, and a drive-by shooting in Peckham.

Nobody fed his cat.

CHAPTER
TWENTY-NINE

David Fallon's eyes turned to heaven as he was laid down on the step. The man's hand clutching his forearm loosened, and opened like a flower.

The killer's chest thumped, and he touched his scar and smiled.

Only death made him feel alive.

And how strange that the bastard heart that had threatened for so long to kill him had finally shown him the way to live.

Selfishly.

The fire dimmed and he got up to feed it. He was always surprised by how many paintings he'd done. And all of them pointless. He took one at random from a stack and shook his head. He must have been fourteen or fifteen when he'd copied it from a book. Caravaggio's *Thomas the Doubter:* the wizened disciple with his finger in the side of Christ. Except in *his* version the wound was over Christ's heart, and Thomas's hand was in him up to the wrist . . .

At some point he must have thought it meaningful.

It was not meaningful. It was risible.

The killer gave a short, dry bark of disdain and tossed the painting on to the fire.

He had fancied himself a painter. Money didn't matter to him, of course, but he'd understood that money was how his work would be gauged by generations to come, and had craved the recognition that would let him be lauded.

Applauded.

Barely afforded.

But it hadn't happened.

At the time it had crushed him. Humiliated him. Nearly destroyed him. But now he knew that painting was a pitiful handmaiden to his real talent.

The pioneers of art had stolen corpses for their anatomy lessons. They'd risked censure, heresy, prison, to learn about the beauty within. They'd known that the law was an ass — and a philistine to boot.

And then they had flinched!

They had closed up their corpses and continued to show only the surface of their fathomless subjects.

Picasso and Da Vinci and Rembrandt had daubed a crude approximation of life.

They were mere painters: *he* was an artist!

Only *he* had ever dared to mould life into death — *and back* — in a transformation that was so fundamental that the world could not yet appreciate his genius.

No wonder he was misunderstood! The law sought to protect its own petty boundaries. It took a visionary — a seer — to discover new worlds, to open eyes to extreme possibilities. Where he led, others would follow. All a master needed was disciples to spread his word.

And Eve Singer was his disciple.

225

From their very first meeting, he had known she was special. They had a *connection*. She understood him. And, more importantly, she understood his work, and had amply demonstrated her desire and ability to share it with the world.

And that was how the generations would learn his name, and remember it long after he was gone.

His victims bought him time.

His art would bring him immortality . . .

The killer halted the recording of the death of David Fallon and turned on iWitness News.

But the midnight bulletin came and went without any mention of the performance at the Barnstormer Theatre.

CHAPTER
THIRTY

15 December

Eve stretched.

It was gone midnight and she hadn't meant to stay so late, but she'd needed some privacy before running through the theatre footage on her computer. There were at least four members of the night news team around *somewhere*, but right now the big newsroom was empty, and she worked quickly.

She could only hope that by the time he found out what was going on, Ross Tobin would be mollified by the spectacular background package she and Joe were putting together. It was so good that it could be more than just news. A chilling retrospective of a warped mind who had advertised his crimes and cut a bloody swathe through London. An hour-long documentary they could sell to Channel 4, maybe.

Her ticket off the meat beat?

Despite that sunny hope, reviewing the footage was a sad task. It seemed that Mr Fallon had lived alone and neither the police nor his colleagues at the theatre knew how to get in touch with any family he might have had. The only interview she'd got so far was from one of the ushers — a drama student who had shown off so appallingly at the sight of a TV camera that she'd had to tick him off like a mother.

This is not about you, Rafael, so take it down a notch or ten.

Even after her warning, Rafael had put on a scene-chewing performance that included everything but jazz hands.

She sighed. Poor Mr Fallon. He'd seemed so nervous about everything — the police presence, the play starting on time, the dicky ice-cream freezer . . .

Nervous about everything, in fact, except being murdered.

That was a blessing, at least. Eve thought that knowing you were about to die must be the most paralysing, terrifying thing that could happen to a person. She wondered what thoughts had exploded in Mr Fallon's head when he'd realized. Or Layla Martin's, or Maddie Matthews'. The only victim who seemed to have escaped the foreknowledge of his own death was Kevin Barr, and Stan Reddy had told her that he was an arse, which didn't seem fair.

Maddie Matthews.

Every time the name passed through Eve's mind, it left a trail of images and horror and guilt behind it like bloody bunting. Eve had to keep working, had to keep moving, to avoid thinking of Maddie, and the man who had killed her.

A man who had her phone number.

I am a friend, and come not to punish.

The words niggled at Eve. At the time she'd just snapped at the man. Tetchily. Intent on hiding the truth about her father. But the words were vaguely familiar and had stuck in her brain like a burr.

She googled them.

It was a poem. "Death and the Maiden". She must have read it at school.

Give me your hand, you beautiful and tender form!
I am a friend, and come not to punish.
Be of good cheer! I am not fierce,
Softly shall you sleep in my arms!

Softly shall you sleep in my arms. The words were a lure. It would be so nice to sleep softly in the arms of somebody who loved her.

But there were pictures too — paintings and woodcuts of grinning Death seducing the Maiden.

Eve shivered and stood up. She'd get a coffee. She'd walk down the corridor and get a coffee and think about walking and corridors and coffee, and not pink ski jackets and a hand in a glove under a splat of blood . . .

Now she was standing, Eve could see that there was somebody else in the newsroom. Way off and nearly hidden by his computer screen.

Gary Someone. He did something in Sport and Eve barely knew him.

The newsroom was creepy at night. She'd never noticed that before. Suddenly, being in a vast, near-empty office made her think of Layla Martin. Was this how her end had begun? With a lone colleague across an empty room? Someone she thought she could trust, just because they got a pay cheque from the same organization?

Eve picked up her purse and left the room.

Then she stood outside the double doors for a moment, peering back through the small porthole to see whether he was getting up to follow her.

He wasn't.

Of course he wasn't. He was Gary Someone from Sport, not an insane murderer.

"Idiot," she scolded herself, and went to get a coffee.

For some reason nobody had ever explained, the closest coffee machine was in a dim alcove, three long corridors and two sets of fire doors away from the newsroom. They used to keep kettles on their desks, but the company had called down some Health and Safety bullshit and now if they wanted a coffee at work they had to pay iWitness News 50p a time for half a paper cupful of bitterness. The tea was marginally better, but only because tea was less interesting to start with, so there was commensurately less of a gulf between expectation and disappointment.

Eve had never thought before about the distance between the newsroom and the coffee machine. Now — as she pushed through the second set of swing doors — she thought of little else.

To take her mind off it, she thought of all the stuff she had to do before Christmas.

Only everything!

She still had to do the Christmas shopping — both gifts and food. And she hadn't decorated the tree yet. The lights were in a bundle on the living-room floor where Duncan had left them, and the baubles and tinsel were still in the box in the front room, where she'd left it the other day.

The day her father had punched her in the face.

Mentally she glossed over that.

She must sort out the tree. Christmas without a pretty tree was a miserable place to be. And she would buy chicken, not turkey, because her father was less likely to choke on it.

She wondered whether she should ask Joe to Christmas lunch, but immediately discounted the idea. She wouldn't inflict her father and her tension on anyone at any time, let alone Christmas Day.

Maybe she'd buy another bottle of Advocaat to keep her company. Get pissed all by herself over the sprouts . . . *Ho, ho, ho. Merry Christmas, Nobody!*

She sighed and wished it were January, then put 50p in the machine and asked for tea.

It said it was out of tea, which was ridiculous, but she pressed "Tea" three times and got the same dumb answer. So she pressed the button for what the machine grandly called "Cappuccino", which was exactly the same as what it called "Americano with milk" except that it looked as if someone had also spat in it.

The machine rumbled like a bad day at Three Mile Island, and cappuccino sputtered angrily into the wobbly cup.

Out of nowhere Eve sneezed four times, rapidly, then stood, nose tingling, waiting for a fifth. It didn't come, but she cursed Guy Smith under her breath. All she needed was his stinking cold. She dabbed at her nose and winced at the pain. It *was* probably broken.

The machine beeped to let her know her half-cup was ready. As she picked it up, there was the smallest squeak behind her.

Unmistakeable.

Shoe on linoleum —

Eve jerked around and threw the coffee in Ross Tobin's face.

He yelped in pain.

"Don't sneak *up* on me!" yelled Eve. "What's *wrong* with you?"

"Bloody hell!" he said, dabbing his eyes with the tail of his shirt. "I think you stripped my corneas."

"Good!" she shouted. "That's fifty pence well spent!"

Then she hurled the cup at the overflowing bin and stormed back to the newsroom, where her phone was vibrating slowly towards the edge of her desk.

She snatched it up and snapped, "Yes? What?"

"I'm disappointed in you, Eve."

She flinched and looked nervously up and down the newsroom, as if the killer might appear from any dim corner.

She made an effort to breathe. Tried to calm her racing heart.

"Why didn't you review my performance tonight?"

She hesitated. "There's a news blackout. Nobody's allowed to report your *crimes*."

She held her breath.

"You don't need police permission to do your job, Eve. I don't like it when you lie to me." His voice was patient. It was the voice of a father, a teacher, a priest — and she blushed to have been caught lying.

To a murderer!

Ridiculous!

"I don't care what you like," she snapped. "Nobody gives a shit what you like when you *murder* people!"

"What I do is not murder," he said calmly. "It is *art*! In life, my models are nothing. They're nobodies. But in death, they're photographed and documented and pampered like pharaohs; teams of detectives think about them day and night; their passing is reported on TV and in newspapers; their families are venerated; the nation awaits an outcome to their story; their unknown names are on a million lips —"

"Models pose for artists," said Eve. "They don't die for them."

"You're right! They *don't* die. My art makes them immortal!" He laughed. "*That* is why the Mona Lisa smiles, Eve, because she *knows* that she will endure a hundred years, a thousand, a *million*. Would she not have been lucky to pay the Master's price? A single piffling death, when death is where all the pain and the confusion of life simply stops . . . And all that is left is the calm embrace of inevitable fate."

His voice was hypnotic.

Seductive.

Eve felt light-headed.

The calm embrace of inevitable fate.

"There's no shame in it, Eve," he said. "Where is the harm in wanting somebody dead, when dying is so beautiful?"

Eve blinked. He sounded so . . .

What?

Had she been about to think, *logical*?

"Fuck you!" she shouted in shock. "*FUCK YOU!*" Her heart pounded wildly, pumping guilt and fury. "If dying's so wonderful, why don't you kill yourself and do us all a favour? You want to murder people? Go right ahead! But don't try to make me part of your sick mission!"

She hung up.

She didn't know whether to panic or to laugh. She did a little of both.

She had just hung up on a serial killer!

She stared at the phone.

Call ended.

I did that, she thought. *I did that, and it was EASY.*

Then she shivered. He'd almost had her. He'd almost seduced her into thinking like him. It made Eve feel ill to remember that warm, dizzy feeling of surrender. Of how sane his madness had sounded to her exhausted ears.

But he *hadn't* got her. This time *she*'d won. Tonight she had stolen the killer's audience — and with it his power.

Joe would be so proud of her!

234

CHAPTER
THIRTY-ONE

The killer had no table, so he wrote on his knees, a poor painting after Caravaggio serving as a desk.

My Maiden has had a crisis of faith.
It is in her nature to question, to explore.
To doubt.

The killer was not an angry person, but he underlined *doubt*. More than once. Thickly and with increasing intent, until the paper broke open and wounded the next page, and the page after that, and the page after that . . .

So hard that his hand cramped.

He relieved the pressure with an apt accompaniment of escaping air from between his clenched teeth, then turned the pages of the A4 notebook, one by careful one. By the fifth page there was no trace of the line. On each of the preceding four pages, he drew a careful box around the inky indentation so that he would not write over it in error, which might lead to a possible future misreading of his copperplate words. Any confusion of history would be a tragedy. Like Newton's *Principia Mathematica* with a coffee ring hiding its most elegant

235

equation; the Theory of Relativity, corner-chewed by a puppy.

How perfectly she trusted me when I had come to claim her. Now she doubts like Thomas, who would not be convinced by the face or the form of the undead Christ, until he opened the Roman wound with his own finger, and touched the flesh that restored a ghost to a man.

He laid down the pen and his hand moved to his chest without conscious thought.

All was quiet there.

One nail worried the edge of the scar, but it had become a stark white ridge that wormed down his chest like the Andes. It would take more than a fingernail now to open it to reveal the truth within: the traitorous heart ticking down the systolic seconds to his own death.

He mustn't think about it. He was doing all he could.

He let his hand drop from his chest and looked across the ballroom.

He had left the washing machine on the floor, and it was still there now, arranged in a careful square, twenty feet across.

It always revived him, just as each death did.

Often, he would pad carefully among its innards, its utilitarian splendour. Now and then he'd polish a casing or adjust the alignment of a motor.

Nudge a bolt.

He flexed his long white fingers, then bent once more over the stolen notebook.

So let her worry her morals like Catholic beads.
Let her demand a finger in the side of her master.
Let her <u>doubt</u>.
I will convince her.

CHAPTER
THIRTY-TWO

16 December

Eve was woken by the bang of a kitchen cupboard. She knew what it was before her eyes even opened, and was out of bed in an instant.

She glanced at her phone. 03.33.

She crept downstairs, stepping over the creaks. There was a light in the kitchen.

She hesitated, then detoured into the front room and picked up the poker from beside the fake-flame gas fire. Munchkin stood on his hind legs, gripping the bars of his cage in the excitement of watching another inmate making a break for it, even if it wasn't him.

Eve went gingerly back through the hallway, controlling her breathing, testing the weight of the poker in her hand. Terrified that her beating heart would give her away as it thundered in the darkness.

Her father was in the kitchen, making a sandwich.

Cheese and pickle.

"Hi, Dad."

He looked up and smiled. "Hello, Evie," he said.

Eve's heart snagged on a happy nail.

He *knew* her!

He knew her *and* he knew her name!

"Dad . . ." She brushed sudden tears off her cheeks, but more came, and more, until she didn't bother wiping them away any more — just pulled up a chair and sat down and watched him through a pretty salt kaleidoscope.

Duncan Singer did everything right, knew where everything was. The bread, the butter, the cheese, the pickle. After three years of putting the milk away outside the back door and stowing bread in the sink, each element of this sandwich was fetched quickly and efficiently from its rightful place and returned there after use.

Duncan Singer even looked up now and then to smile at his daughter.

Eve didn't say a thing. Didn't want to break whatever gossamer thread was tethering him to this brief reality.

"Want one?" he said as he cut his sandwich in half, and she said *Yes, please* just to have the pleasure of watching him do it all over again. Weeping and smiling at the thrill of normality.

When he was finished, he put his sandwich in a Tupperware container and hers on a plate.

"Thank you."

"Right then," he said, "I'd better be off."

Eve's chest twitched with foreboding. "Where are you off to?"

"Work. We've got to finish Mrs Cole's wiring."

Eve hesitated.

If she pointed out that he wasn't dressed, or that he hadn't worked for years, then this bubble would burst.

239

And she didn't want it to end!

The desire to see how long she could keep her father with her inside that precious moment was so deep she felt it in her core. But she couldn't watch him walk out of the door and into the snow in his pyjamas.

"You're a bit early, Dad."

"Oh yes?" Duncan Singer looked at the watch he wasn't wearing and frowned. "What time have *you* got?"

"It's not even four in the morning," said Eve.

He looked up at the clock and frowned again. "It's not even four in the morning," he said.

He looked bemusedly at the butter. "What the hell am I doing making sandwiches?"

"The clocks went back," Eve lied smoothly. "They fooled me too. I came down for breakfast."

Her father gave a short, confused laugh. "We must be mad," he said.

"I think so," smiled Eve. "We should both go back to bed."

"Right," he said, and she got up. But he didn't move when she did. Instead he stared down into the plastic box at his cheese-and-pickle sandwich. "But the clocks only go back an hour and I get up at six thirty."

Then he looked up at her, with scared, childlike eyes.

Déjà vu.

Duncan Singer had felt this way before, but couldn't remember when.

Or why it was so frightening.

240

The sandwich was in the box and he was going to work. But he didn't work any more! Hadn't worked for years!

Why didn't he work any more?

And if he didn't work any more, why was he getting up to make a sandwich? In the middle of the night?

And why was Eve awake?

And why was she so old?

He had missed something. Duncan knew he had definitely missed something, and went back to the beginning to retrace his steps.

But where was the beginning? Was it when he'd come downstairs in the dark to make himself a sandwich? Was it when he'd woken and wondered why Maggie wasn't in the bed beside him? And had come downstairs to look for her?

But Maggie's dead.

He blinked at the sandwich as though *it* had spoken the flat, cruel words.

His wife had been dead for years.

He had forgotten.

Duncan went weak. He had forgotten his own wife was dead. How could he do that? What kind of a person forgets something so . . . *terrible*? Somebody he loved *so much*. How? *How?*

Because he was mad.

Suddenly he remembered. He remembered the doctor, Dr Gupta, touching his hand and looking at him *so kindly* as she'd delivered the news that he was losing his mind, like something down the back of the sofa.

He remembered Dr Gupta, but not the death of his own wife.

Duncan stared at the sandwich in the Tupperware box and felt a huge bubble of fear expanding in his chest, pressing out all other feelings, all other cares, all other thoughts.

He looked at Eve to see if she knew about her mother, and he saw that she did. She *did* — and hadn't told him!

Why?

"Evie?" His voice cracked. "What else have I forgotten?"

He was going. *He was going!*

Eve watched her father slipping away from reality as surely as if he were sliding off the wave-washed deck of a boat in high seas. She closed the distance between them in a flash and hugged him tightly, as if she could keep his mind with her, just by holding on to his body.

But she couldn't.

"Have you been Christmas shopping?" he said.

For a moment she couldn't speak. She just held him, her wet cheek on his warm shoulder.

Finally she said, "Yes, Dad."

"What did you get me?"

"A glass eye," she remembered.

He patted her back gently and said, "That's exactly what I wanted."

Eve helped Duncan upstairs and back into bed, and then sat slumped on the end of her own bed, with her hands twisted in her lap like a hopeless madwoman in an old painting.

Her father was still in there.

Somewhere.

For a moment he'd been back with her, perfectly normal and gentle and *present*. Then he had disappeared again — dragged back into himself by some demon that had incubated in his brain, and now had the run of the place.

And the worst thing about it was — *he had known!*

Eve had always imagined Duncan existed in blissful ignorance of his own condition. But for a few horrific, nightmarish moments, he'd known exactly who he was, and what was happening to him . . . And yet had been no more able to hold on to reality than a feather on the wind could chart its own course through the skies.

It was as if he were imprisoned, and desperate to get out, but unsure of how to find the door.

Because there *was* no door.

Her phone rang on the bedside table.

She got up on old, creaking legs, refusing to hurry, and put the phone to her ear without even looking at it, unable to care who it was or why they were calling.

"Hello, Eve."

"What do you want?"

"We had a deal."

"We didn't have a deal."

He ignored her. "You broke the terms of that deal."

"We didn't have a deal," she said flatly. "You're a killer and I'm a reporter. We're both doing our jobs, that's all."

"Well, *I'm* doing *my* job, Eve, but you'll be very sorry if you don't start doing yours."

A threat. Eve didn't have the energy to care.

"I'm tired," she said. "I don't want you calling me any more."

She hung up. This time she felt no triumph or panic. Out of habit, she hit Recent Calls.

And gazed with slow astonishment at the top of the list.

The killer hadn't withheld his number!

Adrenaline coursed through Eve like electricity. Her heart beat so fast and her hands shook so hard that it took her three attempts to call Huw Rees.

"Hello?" He sounded asleep.

"DS Rees?" she said.

"Yes."

"It's Eve Singer. He just called me again. And I've got his phone number!"

"*What?*"

"I've got it! I've got it right here on my phone! And you won't believe it — but it's a bloody landline number! You can trace it right to his home! It's 0208 —"

"Hold on."

There were sounds of mild activity — bodies moving, soft mumbles — the sounds of Huw Rees getting out of the marital bed.

Slowly.

Eve wanted to reach down the line, yank him to his feet and press a pencil into his hand so he could write the number down and have it traced and send a squad car and haul the killer out of *his* bed and put a knee in his back and twist his wrists into cuffs and end all this *now*.

"Give me the number," said Rees.

She did.

"I'll call you back," he said.

"OK."

Eve hung up. Once again, she didn't know whether to laugh or cry. She felt fear and excitement in equal measure and she didn't know which one to vent. Instead they roiled inside her, making her shake so hard that it was comical.

She sat there and tried to be calm. Her feet grew cold and she started to shiver, but she couldn't get back into bed — not while she was waiting for the police to tell her they'd traced the call and were on their way to take the bastard down.

The phone rang.

"Got it," said Huw Rees, but she could hear something was wrong. He sounded oddly deflated. "The call came from a public phone."

"Shit!" she said. "*Shitshitshit!*"

"We've got a car on the way, but no doubt he'll be long gone."

Eve was crushed. The killer could have called from anywhere — and never be there again. They had nothing. The gulf between hope and reality was gaping.

"Where *was* he?" she asked.

"Somewhere in Isleworth," he said, and Eve heard a notebook page being turned.

"College Road."

CHAPTER
THIRTY-THREE

But that's where I live.

Eve's mind slowed stupidly.

"That's *my* number," she said. "That's where *I* live. I'm sorry. I think I gave you my number by mistake."

"What?" said Huw Rees.

"*I* live in College Road."

There was a brief silence. And then he said, "But this call came from a payphone," and read the number she'd given him.

It wasn't her number.

Eve stood up. She walked to the window without using her legs.

"Eve?"

Across the road, the red phone box shone like dark blood under the street light.

"Eve? Are you there?"

"That's *my* phone box," she whispered.

And then she ran.

In her bare feet and pink pyjamas. Down the stairs and out of the front door and into the night and down the path and through the gate and between the cars and across the road to the red phone box.

She yanked open the door.

It was empty. The receiver nestled on the hook, and there was the faint smell of lavender air-freshener.

Her feet were cold.

Her feet were *freezing*.

She started to feel stupid. What had she thought she was going to do? She hadn't found the killer in the phone box, and thank God for that.

Now that her brain had caught up with her legs, she couldn't think of anything good that might have come from her mindless dash into the snow.

The payphone rang and she jumped. She stared at the big black receiver, hanging there like a club.

The phone rang again.

Let it ring. It wouldn't be for her; it wouldn't be for *anybody*. Calls to payphones were always wrong numbers — always mistakes.

The phone rang and rang and rang and rang.

And rang.

She answered it.

The killer laughed. "This is so *you*, Eve!"

"*W-what?*"

But he was gone.

She replaced the receiver with a clatter, and stood, staring at it, feeling the cold from the concrete floor seeping up her legs and making them ache.

What was so her? What did he mean? Standing in a phone box in her pyjamas in the snow was *so her*? She was confused.

"*Hello!*"

The shout was tiny. Eve realized that she still had her mobile in her other hand, and was still connected to Detective Superintendent Rees.

"I'm in the phone box," she said. "He's not here."

"Jesus Christ!" said Rees. "What the hell are you doing? Get back to your house and wait there until you see my officers!"

"He just called me on the payphone."

"What did he say?"

"*This is so you.*"

"Well, he's right!" barked Rees. "And he could be anywhere. Get back in the house and lock the doors!"

"OK," she nodded.

"And stay on the phone while you do."

"OK," she said.

Eve had run out into the night so fast that she hadn't had time to be scared.

Now she was scared. Rees wanted her to stay on the phone so that he could hear it if the killer attacked her between the phone box and her house.

She checked the street through the small, scratched panes of glass that surrounded her on three sides. Her ragged breath steamed the little glass panes, so she held her breath and rubbed them clear.

College Road was Christmas-card quiet.

The fourth wall of the call box was solid. It could hide anything. She couldn't know what might be on the other side of it, mere inches away. Waiting for her.

She would have to step out of the box and circle it to find out.

Or she could just open the door and *run*.

248

Suddenly the phone box felt like a little red trap.

Adrenaline galvanized her and, before she could change her mind, Eve shoved the door open and ran. Back across the road, past her own freezing footprints, between the cars. She tripped on the invisible kerb, fell on to her elbow and side, and was up before she'd even registered the fall. Through the gate, up the path, into the house, and *slammed* the front door.

She locked it and panted into the phone: "I'm safe!"

"OK. What number are you?"

"Four twenty-two."

"Don't open the door to anyone but the police. They will use the code word *Victory*."

"Victory," she said. "OK."

Eve hung up as she ran up the stairs, slapping on lights as she went.

On the landing she stopped and took stock. There was no point in alarming her father. He'd already had an interrupted night. She would watch the street from her bedroom window and then head the police off at the front door before they could knock. Take them into the kitchen and speak to them there. Quietly.

Eve peered round the bedroom door. Duncan wasn't there.

"Dad?"

She turned on the light.

He still wasn't there.

Shit.

She checked the other bedrooms and the bathroom and then hurried downstairs.

He wasn't there either.

She double-checked — this time calling his name. The sandwich was still in its box on the kitchen table. The back door was locked, but Duncan Singer was not in the house.

Eve stood in the hallway and thought. Hard.

A sense of unease came slowly over her.

Had she locked the front door behind her when she'd run outside?

She didn't think so . . .

Had she even *closed* it?

Prickles ran up the back of her neck. She'd thrown the door open and run out so fast, she'd wanted to catch the killer so badly.

And it was still open when she'd come back.

Oh God.

Duncan could have wandered through it without even registering that he was outside.

And gone *anywhere* . . .

Eve hurried to the front door and reached for the latch, then snatched her hand back as if burned.

Don't answer the door.

The killer could be anywhere outside. Even Huw Rees thought so. But she had to find her father! He was outside in the snow. In pyjamas!

She jogged to the kitchen and fetched the torch, then pulled on her coat and wellingtons. The boots were cold inside — colder even than her feet — but she didn't want to waste time getting socks. She dropped her phone into her coat pocket and picked up the tennis racquet that still leaned against the wall.

She put her hand on the latch, ready to twist it open.

Then she took a deep breath and —

Didn't open the door.

Instead she frowned, unseeing, at the back of her own hand. Processing something subconscious. Something important. Something *wrong*.

Her nose wrinkled as she sniffed something ... *different*.

What was it?

Where was it?

Slowly Eve turned her eyes to the right and felt her gut twist with movie-house horror.

How could it be?

There on the hall table burned a Yankee candle.

CHAPTER
THIRTY-FOUR

"It's my fault," said Eve dully.

"It's not your fault," said Joe.

"He gave me the choice," she said. "Play along or provoke him."

"And you chose . . .?"

"Take a wild guess." She blew her sore, swollen nose into a tissue.

She and Joe were on the couch, while Superintendent Rees and DI Marr were in the scuffed easy chairs either side of the fireplace.

Huw Rees had the rumpled, coffee-soaked air of an overworked man. The Layla Martin case had mushroomed from one brutal murder into something far more wide-ranging and he was at the heart of the investigation. He looked as if he hadn't slept since November.

He hadn't told Eve that it wasn't her fault, and she appreciated his honesty.

Joe reached for her hand. "I wish you'd told me about your dad," he said quietly. "I could have helped."

Eve shook her head. "Nobody can help him."

"Not *him*," said Joe. "*You*."

Eve was surprised into silence. She'd thought it unlikely that anyone would tolerate her situation; it had never occurred to her that anyone might actually want to *help*.

She squeezed Joe's hand, but it was too late now.

Now she was responsible for the murder of Maddie Matthews *and* for her father being abducted by a madman. It *was* her fault. All of it. And whatever happened next, she would have to live with that knowledge for the rest of her life.

She cupped her hands around a mug. The tea was gone but the warmth lingered. It was almost eleven a.m. and the Yankee candle had long been extinguished and dusted for non-existent prints, but the air was still thick with sandalwood.

Every so often a policeman passed the window, coming or going, in uniform or plainclothes or white paper suit and matching galoshes. They said they were keeping an open mind. They said Duncan Singer had wandered off before and might have done so again.

Eve knew they were wrong, and watching their methodical, open-minded progress was driving her crazy.

There was snow in the kitchen. Although by the time the forensics team had arrived it was no longer snow, of course — only cold, wet puddles. There were more up the stairs and down the landing and beside her father's bed, where somebody had stood over him before they'd . . .

Before they'd . . . *what?*

Led him away through the snow? Hit him? Drugged him and dragged him down the garden path that had been so well cleared by Mr Elias that it no longer showed tracks that anyone could follow?

"Let's not jump to conclusions," said DI Marr, as if to an old, stupid person. "We've got a dozen officers searching the neighbourhood."

"If he'd just wandered off, he'd have been found by now," said Eve bluntly. "Alive or dead."

"He might be asleep in a shed," said Marr. "He might have got on a bus —"

Eve hurled her mug across the living room. It exploded above the fireplace, leaving a Rorschach of dregs on the wallpaper.

"He's been watching me!" she shouted furiously. "He's been in my house! There was a fucking Yankee candle in my hall!"

In the wake of her outburst there was a sudden, crunching silence. Activity in the house stopped, and the three men exchanged nervous glances, as if they all secretly knew that a woman was made of sugar and spice and all things nitroglycerine.

DI Marr examined the remote control as if he'd never seen one before.

Huw Rees stared across the room and said, "Is that a hamster?"

Joe said, "Yes," gratefully. He got up and took Munchkin out of his cage and handed him carefully to Rees. Marr leaned forward to see, suddenly fascinated.

Slowly, the hubbub of forensic operations started again in the house, but more softly this time.

"My kids have hamsters," said Rees, and stroked Munchkin's little head with a big rough thumb.

Eve shivered. Despite the fire, she was cold to her core and wasn't sure there was anything in the world that could warm her up again.

"He knew what he was doing," she said miserably. "And what *I* would do. He knew I'd get you to trace the number. He knew I wouldn't wait. He knew I'd run out there like a bloody idiot. When he called me in the phone box he was just making sure. That's why he laughed and said it was *very me*. I didn't understand then. Now I do."

There was a pregnant silence.

This time even DI Marr didn't try to jolly her out of her guilt.

"Dad could already be dead!" Eve's voice broke and there was a sombre silence.

"I don't think so," Huw Rees said carefully. "If he wanted your father dead, he could have killed him right here in the house. It would have been a lot easier than getting a confused adult male out in the night and through the snow while you were stuck in the phone box.

Eve nodded. It made sense.

"Can I ask a big favour?" she said to Rees.

He opened his hands and said, "You can ask."

"Can you *please* not release this to the press? I know it's hypocritical, but the idea of people coming and knocking on my door — people like *me* . . ." She reddened and tailed off.

"Of course," said Rees, and she gave Joe a relieved look. "We have an ongoing security risk here anyway, so it would be counter-productive to the operation to keep you safe."

"What operation?" she said.

"He's fixated on you, Eve. And for that reason, I'm assigning a close protection officer."

"A bodyguard?" said Joe.

"I think it's wise."

Eve opened her mouth to protest, just because that was her default position, but then she closed it again. The thought of a muscular personal bodyguard — a giant wall of a man — between her and the killer was a comfort in this uncertain new world where she had found herself barefoot and stupid in the snow while a killer stole her father from his bed.

So instead she nodded her assent and said, "Did you find anything in the phone box?"

Marr shook his shiny head. "A few prints. Did you say there's a neighbour who cleans it?" He took out his notebook.

"Mr Elias," nodded Eve. She had been round earlier to tell him Duncan was missing. She hadn't said that he might have been kidnapped by a serial killer — partly because the police weren't committing themselves to that scenario and partly because Eve was too ashamed to explain it. Even though there were no fresh prints around his house, he had insisted on pulling on his boots and going to search the back garden, just in case.

"Elias, that's him," said Marr. "Right oddball."

"He's a nice man," she said defensively.

"Well, we'll take his prints for comparison. And we've got a micro-camera hidden in there now so that if the killer comes back we'll get a free mugshot."

Then Marr sighed and said, "The bad news is, he's getting bolder."

Rees gave a ghost of a smile. "But the *good* news is, he's getting bolder."

"What do you mean?" said Joe.

"If he took Mr Singer, he's escalating. Getting more reckless. We know he likes an audience so he needs to be in public, and getting reckless should make him a lot easier to catch. He's done his business in my hand."

Eve nodded, and took a blank moment to connect Rees's last few words to the fact that the hamster had shat in his hand. She quickly scooped Munchkin up and put him back in his cage, leaving Rees holding two tiny brown pellets in his cupped palm, like a wise man bearing dubious gifts.

"Sorry," said Eve, and gave him a tissue.

Rees tipped the pellets into the tissue with a grimace, and wiped his hand. "How does this man know where you live?"

"I don't —"

Eve stopped. Her mouth dropped open. In a back room in her brain, some neural minion had been slaving away, and now presented her with its findings. A flashing collage of footsteps and street lights, and the bulging front-garden hedge.

"Oh my God," she said slowly. "I *do* know how! He's the man who followed me home!"

"*What?*" said Joe. "When?"

"A couple of weeks ago," said Eve. "The night after Layla Martin was killed. It scared the hell out of me. It was about one in the morning and nobody was around and he got so close behind me ...." Eve stopped, suddenly gripped again by the fear of the footsteps behind her, of the certainty that she was never going to make it to her hedge and her home.

"Close enough to just reach out and grab the ends of my scarf ..."

They were all silent, imagining the scene. The scarf grabbed, the woman yanked backwards off her feet, the pull on the wool, the bulging eyes, the puce face, the cold, quiet death ...

"What happened?" said Joe.

"Nothing," shrugged Eve. "I asked him to walk me home and he did."

"You did *what?*"

"I asked him if he would walk me to my house, and he said OK, and then he left me at the gate."

"You asked a *killer* to walk you home?" said Marr.

"I didn't know he was a killer!" Eve flushed. "I was alone. I was scared. I thought I was going to be attacked. Robbed. Raped. Murdered. My instincts took over."

"Jesus," said Joe. "You really need to stop not telling me stuff!"

"Could you describe the man?" said Rees, and Marr opened his notebook.

"Not very well. It was dark, and he wore a hood and had a scarf around the bottom of his face. Average height," she ventured. "Slim. White. Not old, I think ...."

"What about his hair? His eyes?"

"It was dark," Eve repeated and frowned hard. "He just seemed ... *ordinary.*"

Marr wrote "ORDINARY" in big letters, then tutted and crossed it out.

Rees sighed. "This puts a different spin on things. You have a connection with him. Maybe taking your father makes him feel that he's somehow closer to you."

"We don't have a connection," said Eve sharply.

"But you *do!*" insisted Rees. "And *you* created it when you asked him to walk you home. I'm sure of it — although I'm not sure *how*. Maybe you fed his *ego*. Or maybe you unconsciously invoked the social imperative that says you *have* to help somebody, just because they ask for it. You may have appealed to some sense of decency —"

"*Decency!*" snorted Joe.

"Killers aren't crazy all the time," Rees told him with a shrug. "If they were, they'd be easy to catch."

He turned back to Eve. "Whatever it was, Eve, you made a connection with this man that swayed him from his intended path. He saw you as a person, not a victim. If you hadn't asked him to walk you home, I have no doubt he would have killed you."

Suddenly Eve had no doubt either.

I should be dead.

It was a dizzying thought. A shivery spiral of terror and lucky escape, and wonder at the fluid divide between life and death.

And then the lurching certainty . . .

If I were dead, then at least Dad would be safe.

PART THREE

CHAPTER
THIRTY-FIVE

17 December

A petite black woman carrying a holdall stood on the doorstep. "Hi," said Eve brusquely. She hoped the woman wasn't selling anything, or going to try to convert her.

"Hi," said the woman, with a brief smile, "I'm Detective Sergeant Aguda, your close protection officer."

Eve blinked and tried not to show her surprise.

Her bodyguard . . .

Was a tiny.

Little.

Elf.

"Oh," she said. "Hello. Come in."

"No," said Aguda firmly. "That's your first mistake. I'm not a police officer, I'm a hired assassin trained to kill you with my bare hands."

Eve frowned and glanced down at Aguda's hands. They were tiny too.

"Really?" she said doubtfully.

"Could be," Aguda nodded defiantly. "And you just *threw* open the door to me, didn't ask to see my ID, and invited me into your house. Doesn't that seem a bit daft for someone who's being stalked by a serial killer?"

Eve bristled a little.

"The killer's not a woman," she said. "Or black."

"And this killer couldn't have an accomplice? A girlfriend? A hired actress? Some poor stranger he's plucked off the street and threatened with death if she doesn't do *exactly* as he says?"

"Jesus!" said Eve. "That's a bit over the top, isn't it?"

Aguda shrugged. "So is severing a man's spinal cord in the middle of a Liam Neeson film."

"Touché," said Eve. "In that case, can I see some ID, please?"

Aguda smiled her approval and showed her ID. "I'm here to protect you, Miss Singer, but you can do an awful lot to protect yourself."

"Please call me Eve."

"OK," said Aguda. But she didn't say that Eve could call her anything.

Eve opened the door more widely and DS Aguda came into the hallway and glanced around with a professional eye.

"DS Rees tells me you already have good instincts, so that should make my job a lot easier."

"Good," said Eve.

"Got a cold?" said Aguda.

"Think so. I hope I don't give it to you."

"I don't get sick," said the officer proudly. "I haven't been sick for seven years. Not even a sniffle."

Eve said, "Wow," even though she thought that never being sick was probably not healthy. Then, while Aguda installed phone-recording and tracing equipment on the landline, she made them both tea.

264

They both liked builder's tea. Strong and sweet. As common ground went, it was shaky, and there was an awkward silence as they sat at the kitchen table and sipped.

"I know having a stranger in your home might be awkward," said Aguda, "but I hope it won't feel too intrusive."

You're going to be living in my HOUSE, thought Eve. *How could it not be intrusive?* But she went for a diplomatic: "I'm sure it won't be for long."

"I hope not," said Aguda.

Then Eve couldn't think of a single thing to say — although there were plenty of things she *couldn't* say.

Over the brim of her mug, she examined Sergeant Aguda's little hands and slim wrists.

Slim didn't really cover it.

"Frail" was a word that sprang more quickly to mind.

The officer got up and wandered slowly around the room.

And she's so short, too! thought Eve. She couldn't be more than five foot tall. Any serial killer confronted by Sergeant Aguda would only have to pick her up and set her to one side in order to continue his murderous rampage.

Aguda opened the back door and examined the locks. "Yale and deadbolts," she said. "That's good."

"Yes," said Eve.

"But no chain."

"No," said Eve. "Nobody comes to the back door."

"Serial killers do," said Aguda. "We'll get a chain."

The little woman carried on her circuit of inspection. As she did, she unclipped the gleaming handcuffs from the clip on the back of her jeans and toyed with them. A repeated flick of her wrist that opened them and closed them in one deft, well-practised move.

TrrrrrrT.

TrrrrrrT.

The sound was like something from a thousand prison movies and oddly hypnotic.

Eve wondered whether Aguda was trying to intimidate her, and set her jaw.

I could take her, she thought.

It sounded pretty stupid, even in her head. Eve had never had a girl-fight and could hardly believe she was thinking now of how she might fare in one. But she was so *irritated*, goddammit! If Aguda was the sum total of her so-called police protection, then Huw Rees must want her dead! Eve towered over her — and must also outweigh her by at least thirty pounds.

Sergeant Aguda made Eve feel like a giant.

Not to mention *fat* . . .

Aguda opened a window and a lump of frigid air slid into the kitchen like coal.

"No locks?" she said.

"No."

"On any of the windows?"

"No," Eve said again. It made her seem stupid, and she longed to turn the tables. OK, so she didn't have window locks. Big effing deal! She wasn't supposed to be an expert in home security and serial killers. DS *Aguda* was supposed to be the expert. *She* was the person sent to protect Eve from possible attack by a psychopathic nutcase, and here she was, examining the locks as if she were a Neighbourhood Watch volunteer and Eve were a gormless pensioner. Shouldn't Aguda be talking her through worst-case scenarios? Establishing a panic room? An escape route?

She decided Aguda was both tiny *and* shit at her job. What were her qualifications anyway? What was her experience?

She was going to ask her. What the hell! She had a right to know how many people Aguda had protected and how many she had *failed* to protect. How many had been snatched or killed while in her tiny care. She wanted percentages. She wanted stats. *She* needed to do a risk assessment. It might hurt the officer's feelings, but it was *her* life on the line. Eve decided she'd use all her journalistic skills to get the information she needed. She'd start softly and then ambush Aguda with the tough questions when she least expected it.

She cleared her throat and chose her words carefully, keeping her tone light. "How did you get into this line of work, Sergeant Aguda?"

Aguda smiled. "You mean, when I'm so small?"

"*Are* you?" Eve blushed.

"I don't want you to worry about it," said Aguda. "I have black belts in kickboxing and judo, qualifications and field experience in evasive driving, counter-terrorism, close protection, abnormal psychology, home security, surveillance and counter-surveillance, search and rescue, field medicine and resuscitation, as well as successful outcomes in hostage negotiation and conflict resolution."

"Oh I'm not worried," Eve insisted. "*At all.*"

"Good," said Aguda. "But if my size ever *does* bother you —"

"Which it absolutely *does not!*"

"Then you should also know that I do carry an *enormous* gun."

"Really?" said Eve doubtfully. "Where?"

Aguda reached behind her and her hand emerged as if by magic, holding a gun. "There."

She laid it on the table between them. It was sleek and matt black, and heavy with menace.

Eve stared at the *real* gun for *real* killing for a long, surreal, moment. Then she put her tea down with a clunk and said, "Thank *God* for that."

They both started to laugh.

When they'd finished, Aguda put the kettle on again, and told Eve her name was Emily.

Emily Aguda had taken far longer than she should have done to become a detective.

It was because she was black.

But not in a *bad* way, she always reminded herself — only *misguided*.

Although she'd been a police community service volunteer while at university, and had graduated with a first in Law from Reading, her early years in the Metropolitan Police had seen her stuck behind a station reception window like a zoo exhibit, loudly labelled with her race and sex, so that everybody could see that the Met was definitely *not* institutionally racist *or* sexist.

It was both, of course, which was why the powers-that-be had been so keen to keep Emily Aguda in that highly visible front-desk role — because it killed two birds with one stone.

God forbid they should find another stone.

While she'd enjoyed being the first point of police — public contact — and had had her share of bizarre and exciting moments — Emily Aguda had always itched to move on and move up, into a role where her intelligence could be sharpened by challenge, rather than dulled by the daily grind of only peripheral involvement with the investigative process.

Even so, she might have been doomed to sit at that window until her pension kicked in, if she hadn't been recommended for promotion by a senior officer she'd never even liked, exactly *because* of his racism, sexism and general misanthropy.

It was funny how life worked out.

So, thanks to a bastard, Emily Aguda had finally made it into plainclothes, and her intelligence and calmness under pressure had quickly seen her promoted to detective sergeant. But she'd recognized that her late start would always dog her career prospects. Why promote a thirty-year-old woman to inspector when you could promote a twenty-five-year-old man instead? And a twenty-five-year-old man who was never going to get pregnant? Not that Emily ever planned to get pregnant, but nowadays promotions were as much about the statistics as about the people. It was all about getting the biggest possible bang out of the public buck before the public had to start paying a comfy pension out of that same squeezed fund.

Ever the pragmatist, Emily Aguda had decided that, rather than battling against the numbers to make it to the top, she would carve out a niche for herself closer to the middle. She'd always been athletic and strong for her size, which was five-one and a hundred pounds soaking wet. She'd been kickboxing since she was seven and had played football since she was ten. She was good, too; she'd once been scouted by Arsenal Ladies, and had spent the summer of her fourteenth year drinking milk and lifting weights, as if her lazy little bones might be fooled into thinking they still had some growing to do.

Which they didn't.

But in her long, symbolic years at Lewisham police station, Emily had noticed that there was a dire lack of sufficiently qualified female plainclothes officers available for the close protection of witnesses, or visiting celebrities, or members of the public under threat. Even though women were so often the ones under threat.

Once she had identified a gap in the market, Emily underwent every bit of extra training the Met had to offer — and some that it did not — in order to plug it. Her fitness and martial arts experience had stood her in good stead, her driving was fast and fierce, and she'd turned out to be a crack shot too. In fact, Emily had been slightly disturbed by how much she grew to like guns, when she'd always been a vehement opponent of an armed police force.

270

But it was all part of the job now.

Luckily for gun-happy her!

Aguda had never fired a shot in the line of duty, and hoped she'd never have to, but she practised diligently because lives might depend on it, and her skill on the trigger was another string to her longbow of accomplishments.

In less than three years, Emily Aguda had stopped up that gap in the market so firmly that she'd become the go-to officer for the personal protection of vulnerable or high-profile women. Within five years, she was also helping to coordinate the recruitment of other female officers to fulfil similar roles across Britain.

But nothing gave her more job satisfaction than hands-on assignments, where her intellectual, interpersonal and physical gifts could be seamlessly coordinated to outwit and outflank any threat.

Since she'd been a close protection officer, she'd foiled a kidnap attempt on a cabinet minister, she'd taken down a man armed with a machete who was intent on beheading his estranged wife, and she'd single-handedly disarmed and arrested two assailants who had broken into the home of a controversial TV chat-show host with knives and zip ties. When backup arrived they'd discovered the more fractious of the two men under a sofa. Not a small sofa either: a huge leather three-seater with built-in footrests. Later the man had tried unsuccessfully to sue the Met. In court, Aguda — who'd had to stand on a box so that the jury had a good view of her — would admit dropping the sofa on him, but insist that it was "not from a height".

The day after foiling the kidnap attempt — before she'd even gone home after the longest shift of her life — DS Frank Sallis had escorted her into the men's toilets on the third floor at HQ to show her that someone had scrawled "*Aguda kicks ASS*" on the wall of a cubicle, and she had shed a rare tear of victory.

So Emily Aguda didn't worry about Eve Singer's evident lack of faith.

She was used to being underestimated.

It was her greatest strength.

CHAPTER
THIRTY-SIX

Duncan Singer woke in a cold, dark place that was not his bedroom. His head ached inside a soft cloth bag, and there was an odd chemical taste in his mouth. His hands were bound behind his back, which made his shoulders ache.

"Maggie?"

The cotton of the bag touched his face gently, and moved in and out against his lips with every breath. It was damp there, because of condensation. Condensation was hell to electrics. Mrs Cole had a problem with condensation. Hence the rewiring.

"*Maggie?*"

He turned from his side on to his back, but that hurt his hands, and he rolled over the other way, and bumped his nose on the skirting. The hard floor was wood; the wall was plastered and there was a deep skirting board. He felt it with his nose. It wasn't his skirting. His skirting was plain; this was fancy.

Duncan drew his head back and waited for something to happen.

He wiggled his fingers because they were going to sleep.

He was hungry.

"Maggie?" he called. "Where are you?"

She didn't hear him.

"Maggie!" he called more loudly. "Any chance of a sandwich?"

"Who's Maggie?"

"My wife," said Duncan. He hadn't heard anyone approaching, but there somebody was. A man who now put hands under his arms and lifted him into a sitting position.

He didn't know how far behind him the wall was, so didn't lean backwards. Instead he crossed his legs like a Cub Scout. It felt like years since he'd done that, and it must have been easier then. But he got there in the end.

"Got a splitting headache," said Duncan.

"Ketamine," said the man. "Vets use it."

"For headaches?"

"For dogs."

"Oh," said Duncan. "We've got a dog. Awful farts."

"I'm freeing your hands," said the man. "Don't remove your blindfold."

"All right," said Duncan.

There was a small *snip* and Duncan's hands dropped apart from each other and fell slackly against the floor on their knuckles, so numb that at first he couldn't move them at all.

"Ow," he said.

"Ow indeed," said the man, and walked away. A *long* way away. The footsteps faded while the echo grew.

The room must be very big.

"Where are you?"

The man didn't answer.

Duncan brought his hands slowly around to in front of his body, and rubbed his wrists. "Maggie?"

There was the small sound of something being moved on the wooden floor. A short scrape. And then the footsteps came back towards Duncan, but heavier this time. Slower.

Duncan felt the man walk behind him.

"OK," said the man. "You can take your blindfold off now."

Slowly Duncan lifted the bag up at the front so he could peer out from underneath it.

He was in a vast room.

Cavernous.

Dawn was breaking through towering windows, draping a soft orange glow across the dusty cherry-wood floor, and Duncan blinked in the light, and then grunted in surprise.

In the middle of the room there was a whole city.

Around a majestic modern stadium lay skyscrapers and tenements and gasworks and playgrounds and terraces, and sheets of snow and tufts of wild undergrowth — all silhouetted by the rising sun, which threw fabulous shadows down streets and across parklands, where people hurried to work and walked their dogs, or gathered in groups to chat and drink coffee.

And all in miniature.

Like the miniature villages he'd visited as a child. He and Maggie had taken Eve and Stuart to one somewhere on the south coast. Hip-high churches topped by tiny tin weathercocks; mini-farmers tending toy-sized cows. A bandstand in the park — a tuba the size of his thumb.

275

It was wonderful.

But it was impossible.

Duncan closed his eyes, then opened them again.

As they adjusted to the space and the light, he saw he had indeed been mistaken. It was not a city before him, but a jumble of disparate parts — white casings, plastic hoses, switches and relays and bundles of wires that had doubled as hedges and trees.

The giant stadium at the city's centre was a metallic cylinder with a thousand round windows . . .

"Is that —" he started, then stopped and frowned. "Is that a *washing machine*?"

The man behind him shifted his feet.

"Yes!" He sounded surprised.

The light was changing all the time and it was more obvious now, but Duncan could see how he had thought it was a city. A little city with a silver-drum stadium and copper-wire shrubbery, and nut-and-bolt people with their little screw dogs. His initial vision was fading with the sunrise, like Brigadoon, but he could see how tomorrow it might be recaptured, and the day after that, and the day after that.

"I could fix it for you," he said. "If you have all the parts." His eyes swept the components. He frowned a little, seeking something. Something obvious — to him, at least.

Something *big* . . .

Then he realized. "Where's the counterweight?"

"Here," said the man.

Duncan looked up.

The man was holding a forty-pound concrete block
. . . directly over his head.

"Ah." Duncan smiled wistfully. "Hotpoint."

CHAPTER
THIRTY-SEVEN

Eve and Aguda watched *Real Housewives of Orange County* together after a supper of fish fingers and white wine. It made Eve realize two things: first, that *How It's Made* wasn't so terrible after all, and second, that she hadn't cooked proper food for two years, and that wherever her father was, he could probably add rickets to his list of daughter-inflicted woes. When he came home she would buy fresh vegetables every day, and red meat for iron. When he came home she'd take her days off in lieu and spend quality time with him at the park or the seaside. When he came home she'd never wish him dead again . . .

When he came home.

She gulped the last of the glass of white wine and said, "Hey! Show me that thing with your cuffs."

"What thing?"

"That thing you do. That trick."

Aguda smiled and drew her cuffs from the clip on her jeans. "You mean this?"

A dextrous flick and the cuffs were open. Another and they closed with a satisfying click.

Eve frowned. "Show me again!"

She was tipsy, but Aguda was patient and within a couple of hours Eve was sober and could do the trick, albeit slowly, flicking the cuffs open, then slapping them closed over her own wrist.

It was addictive.

After a while, Aguda gave a discreet yawn and said, "I'm going to turn in."

Eve put her in Stuart's room, surrounded by old *Top Gear* crap and half a 1/24 scale model of the RMS *Titanic* that he'd started building from one of those ridiculous weekly magazines. He had only given up on it when their father had gently pointed out that, at one part a week for £5.99, it would cost Stuart almost as much to build the model in his bedroom as it had to build the original ship.

She went to bed herself, but couldn't sleep. Couldn't imagine ever sleeping again. Couldn't close her eyes on the images of her father — scared, cold, lost, confused, hurt —

Dead —

— that ran through her mind like a horror film.

If she closed her eyes on those images, it felt like leaving him to fend for himself until she could be bothered to wake and rejoin him there.

In hell.

She should call Stuart.

She *should*. But she couldn't.

The truth was, she was too ashamed to alert him. There would be plenty of time to tell him what had happened once they found Duncan.

And if they didn't find Duncan . . .

Eve's throat squeezed shut so badly that her misery could not escape except as a reedy whistle.

Please come home, Dad. I'm so sorry. It's all my fault. Pleasepleaseplease come home.

Her phone rang.

Aguda was at her door in a second, alert and dressed, as if she'd been standing sentry on the landing the whole time.

Number withheld.

Eve stared at her phone as if it might bite. What did he want? What would he say? What would *she* say?

She had no idea.

"Answer the phone," said Aguda calmly.

She answered the phone.

"Hi, Eve."

She frowned. It wasn't the killer. But the voice was familiar . . .

"Guy?"

"Hello."

She looked up at Aguda and shook her head, and her pocket bodyguard withdrew soundlessly.

"What the hell do *you* want?"

"Well, I did have something for you," said Smith haughtily. "But if that's your attitude —"

"You gave me a fright, that's all."

"Why?"

"Because it's *late*, Guy! I'm in bed!"

"It's only nine thirty. How old are you? Fifty?"

She wanted to slam down the phone on him. Playing stupid little games when her father's life hung in the balance. She had no time for this!

But he had never called her before. And there was something in his voice that made Eve hesitate. It was not the faux confidence she was used to from Guy Smith, but something new. Something smooth and smug that made her stay on the line, even though experience told her to hang up.

"Sorry, Guy," she said cautiously.

"OK then," he said, mollified. "Meet me at YO! Sushi at Paddington Station. *Alone*."

"When?"

"Now."

"I can't, Guy. I'm busy."

"You're not busy. You're in bed, remember? And I'm assuming alone."

"Shut up." Eve sneezed and winced as she dabbed her nose with a tissue.

"You got my cold?" laughed Guy.

"Yes."

"It's a stinker, isn't it?"

"Yes."

"Well, you'll be even sicker if you miss this," he said confidently. "Sick as the proverbial parrot."

"Why all the cloak-and-dagger stuff? Can't you just tell me now?"

"No," said Guy. "And *I'm* doing *you* the favour here, so you'd better be nice to me."

"What do you mean, *nice*?"

"I mean nice."

Eve pursed suspicious lips. "I'm not sleeping with you, Guy."

"Don't flatter yourself!" He laughed and she blushed.

"All right then," she said.

"All right what?"

"All right, *thank you*."

"That's better," he said, and hung up.

YO! Sushi.

Guy Smith *loved* YO! Sushi. He'd told Eve once that he always met contacts there. Eve imagined it satisfied some caveman need in him to capture his own metrosexual lunch as it wobbled past him on a conveyor belt.

Guy was eating when Eve arrived at the Paddington branch just after ten fifteen.

"You alone?" he said.

"Yes," she said. It was almost true. She was alone *here*, but Emily Aguda was waiting outside. She had refused to allow Eve to leave the house by herself, and Eve had recognized that if she had tried, Aguda would only have followed her.

So instead Aguda had dropped her off in her police-issue Range Rover, and was waiting to give her a ride home. It was quite handy sometimes, this close-protection lark.

Guy was eating teriyaki salmon and had sauce on his chin. He gestured around with his chopsticks. "You want something?"

"No thanks, Guy," she said. "You already gave me your cold."

"Bet it hurts to blow too," he said, "with that big swollen nose."

She raised a rueful eyebrow and he laughed. "What the fuck *did* happen there?"

"Somebody punched me," she said.

"Wow!" he said. "What does the other guy look like?"

"What have you got for me, Guy?"

Guy captured a plate of California rolls and popped one into his mouth. When he spoke, Eve could see it in there — tumbling around like a white wash with added spinach socks.

"Something you're going to be *very* interested in."

"Something in which I'm going to be very interested," Eve corrected him. She didn't know why; she didn't correct anyone else's grammar. Guy Smith just brought out the worst in her.

"You think you're so clever, don't you?" said Guy, washing another load. "You've always got to be so fucking clever."

Eve sighed. "I'm sorry," she said, and she almost was. "I've had a bad week."

"Well, OK then," said Guy, and gave her a patronizing smile. "I forgive you."

Eve bit back a sarcastic response and said, "Thanks, Guy. So, what have you got?"

He didn't look at her for a moment, while he chased another roll around his dish with the chopsticks. When he finally gripped one, he lifted it up and looked at her with an expression of triumph on his face.

"A flyer."

Eve's heart thudded in her chest and blood rushed past her eardrums, making the hubbub of the station fade to an undercurrent.

"A what?"

Guy popped the roll in his mouth.

"A flyer," he repeated. "For an exhibition."

Eve could barely form words with her shocked mouth. "*Where?*"

Guy tapped the front of his jacket with his chopsticks. "Riiiiight here."

"Not where on *you*! Where's the *exhibition?*"

He grinned at her in white and green. "That would be telling."

"Guy, you *have* to tell me," she said urgently.

"Oh really?" I didn't notice *you* having to tell *me* about any of the flyers *you* found."

Eve flushed. How did he know about the other flyers? Huw Rees? DI Marr? Or was the whole murder team leaking like a sieve? They had a *deal*. And now it was even more critical that *she* was the person covering these crimes! To Guy it was just a job — but to her it was a matter of life or death. Her *father's* life or death.

"There was a news blackout . . ."

"Bullshit," he said. "Listen, my job's hanging by a fucking thread, thanks to you. I've had it in the neck ever since the Layla Martin murder. Playing catch-up, missing shit. Then I find out *why*. That you've got some kind of *deal* with the cops so you get an exclusive on the flyers! Royal fucking baby *bollocks!*" He shook his head as if he could barely believe she'd behaved like a journalist.

284

"Listen, Guy, that deal was for me *not* to cover the story. *I* brought the flyers to *them*, not the other way round. I've been keeping this *out* of the news! What this prick wants is airtime. If you give it to him, you're complicit!"

"Complicit?" frowned Guy. "I'm just doing my job. Unlike you."

"Have you told the police about the flyer?"

"Don't be silly."

He lined up the final California roll and Eve snatched the bowl from under his chopsticks.

"Hey!"

"*Listen*," she started, then made a supreme effort to speak calmly. "Listen, Guy. Two nights ago this bastard kidnapped my father. I have to know where the exhibition is so the police can get there before he kills him. Now do you understand how important this is to me?"

For a second Guy Smith's mouth stopped chewing and he believed her.

Then he didn't.

"Nice try, Eve."

"It's *true*."

He smiled. "You know, all this time I thought you were a better reporter than me, but it turns out you're just a better liar. Or maybe you're fucking Huw Rees."

"I'm not fucking *anybody*!" Eve shouted furiously, to interested glances from passers-by.

Guy made a sad face and said, "Poor Mike."

Then he winked and took out his wallet. "I've got some catching up to do, Eve. Fair's fair, right? Just consider this a levelling of the playing field."

He put fifteen pounds on the counter and slid off his stool.

Eve stood in his way. "Guy, *please*. Please tell me where and when it's going to happen."

He smiled. "That's for me to know and for you to find out."

"Then tell the police! I don't care about the story, but I'm begging you. I'm *begging you*. This bastard came into my *house* and took my *dad*."

"Good," he shrugged. "Then you have your exclusive and I have mine."

Eve lunged at him, aiming for the inside of his jacket. He easily deflected her, twisting her wrist painfully as he held her hand away from the prize.

For a moment they were as close as lovers, their faces inches from each other — his breath was fishy.

"I'm in the loop now, Eve," Guy hissed at her, "and you can't keep me out."

"Please, Guy," she begged, but she knew it wouldn't help.

He let go of her hand and checked his watch. "Well," he said, "I've got places to go, people to meet, murders to witness."

He turned away and Eve felt the blood drain from her head. From her heart.

She grabbed his arm.

"You mean *now*? The exhibition is *now*?"

Guy fixed her with a grey-eyed smile. "Not so tetchy now, are we?" he said. "I like you a lot better this way."

Then he shook his arm free of her grip and walked away.

286

★ ★ ★

Eve watched Guy Smith walk briskly across the concourse. He glanced back at her twice, then turned up the ramp to Praed Street.

She couldn't go after him. She couldn't move. She felt weak and woozy, as if she might faint. A swirling nightmare was unfolding while all around her people bought books and burgers and checked train times on the big boards. She wanted them all to *just stop*. She wanted the whole world to *just stop*, so she had time to think, time to plan better than she had done, time to do everything differently. Not just everything today or this week, but everything in her whole *life* that had led her to that ghastly moment where she had wished her father dead, and now it was going to happen and she had no way of taking anything back.

Somebody took her arm and she almost screamed.

It was Aguda.

"Walk fast," she said calmly, and propelled Eve along beside her.

"He's got a flyer," said Eve desperately. "He's going there now!"

"I know," said Aguda, turning over Eve's jacket lapel and showing her a microphone the size of a pea. "Walk fast."

"But we need a car!" They had parked at the other end of the station.

"I know. Walk fast."

They walked fast to the bottom of the ramp.

"There!" Eve pointed at the News 24/7 crew car pulling away, its indicator flickering left.

Aguda opened the door of a car and Eve baulked, before realizing it was the Range Rover, magicked here. Somehow.

"Get in," said Aguda.

Eve got in.

Aguda had said *something* about driving qualifications, Eve was sure. What she *hadn't* said was that they'd apparently been acquired at the Hollywood School of Speed, Stunts and Abject Terror.

Eve wanted to get out, and she wouldn't really have cared whether Aguda stopped to let her do that. Or even slowed down. But staying in the lurching, sliding, gunning Range Rover through the congenitally congested heart of London was the only way to catch up with Guy Smith and save her father's life.

It was like having a tiger by the tail. She just had to hold on tight and hope for the best.

With her free hand she called Joe and told him what was going on.

"Where are you?" he said.

"Going north on — *Jesus!*" Eve squeezed her eyes shut so she couldn't see her life flash before her as Aguda steered straight at a red light.

She opened them fractionally to discover they were still alive, and still with the News 24/7 crew car in view, a block ahead. She glared furiously at Aguda, but the woman looked as calm as a mum on the school run.

Only half the size.

Her tiny hands, her size-three feet, all moved on pedals and wheel and gear-stick in perfect harmony to propel the two-tonne 4x4 at breakneck speed through lines of traffic that seemed to be stationary by comparison. Sometimes they *were* stationary! And when they were, Aguda's uncanny anticipation always chose the lane that moved the fastest and cleared the quickest once the lights had gone green.

"Can you put a siren on?" Eve managed to say between gasps.

"I don't want to alert them to being followed," said Aguda. "We don't want them to stop. We want them to lead us right to the killer."

Without taking her eyes off the road, Aguda called Superintendent Rees, while Eve peered at the side streets to relay their position and direction. They were right behind them now. There was no way they could lose it.

They swung around a shallow bend and headed down a hill under a railway bridge.

Something fell out of the sky.

"*Shit!*"

Aguda hit the brakes. The Range Rover swerved to avoid a collision and they would have been OK, except that the crew car fish-tailed then flipped on to its side, carrying them both into the oncoming traffic with a horrible blackboard squeal.

Eve braced her hands on the dash and closed her eyes.

CHAPTER
THIRTY-EIGHT

"Stay in the car!"

The door slammed and Eve slowly opened her eyes.

There was a great ringing in her ears, as if someone had rapped her on the head with a tuning fork. Somebody was shouting from somewhere a long, long way away.

She looked across to Aguda for answers, but Aguda had gone.

The bonnet of the Range Rover was pressed against the dark Victorian brick of the bridge, and there was steam coming out of the front as if it were an old jalopy in a hillbilly film.

Then the steam cleared and — like a bad dream — graffiti on the brick swam into focus:

EXHIBITION . . .

Eve gasped as if she'd been slapped, and opened the door.

She couldn't get out.

She tried again and again and finally realized that the seatbelt was what was stopping her. She jabbed the catch half a dozen times before hitting it right and getting free. But her legs gave way the minute her feet hit the road, and she fell on to her knees on the rough tarmac.

She struggled to her feet, holding on to the car, not so much remembering how to walk as making it up as she went along.

A hand on her arm. "Stay here."

"I have to get there."

"Just stay here," the woman said again. "You're in shock."

It was a middle-aged woman in a bright-blue coat.

"Yes," Eve nodded, "I'm in shock."

She looked around her. The traffic was stopped. A crowd was gathering. Police sirens were already approaching.

Aguda was at the crew car. *On* the crew car, pulling the door open like a submarine hatch . . . She reached in and Eve held her breath.

Guy Smith clambered out, battered and bloody, and lowered himself gingerly to the road.

Emily Aguda didn't need her extensive field-medicine qualifications to know that the driver of the crew car was dead.

He had no head.

A chunk of concrete the size of a microwave oven had smashed through the windscreen and hit him in the face. His shoulders were still there, and his arms. One slack hand still held the wheel. But his head had been pulped, and had coated the inside of the Volvo with lumpy blood and jagged white shards.

She stood up on the side of the car and called Huw Rees.

"This is Aguda, sir. There's been an RTA. One dead, one walking wounded. Eve Singer's OK."

"Is it connected?"

"Could be, sir. Those involved got a flyer supposedly from the perp —"

She glanced up at the bridge. A man's head drew back quickly from the parapet.

"*Shit!*" Aguda was away from the car and running before she'd even processed the thought. If she moved *fast*, there was a chance she might catch the man and stop this nightmare right here, right now.

"Sir, I see a suspect! I'm after him! Do I have permission to leave the job?"

There was a cavernous pause and her eyes darted all around for the most direct route up the steep embankment to the tracks. On either side of the bridge, her way was barred by brick walls topped by wrought-iron railings that guarded the line and trapped the litter of decades.

"Is Eve Singer safe?"

"People are with her and backup is on its way."

"Then go!"

She went.

There was no way up from the street. Her swift mind changed direction in an instant and she burst into Lou's Fish Bar alongside the bridge, scattering a gaggle of alarmed customers who were pressed against the door and windows to gawp at the accident outside without losing their place in the queue.

"Police! Can I get on to the railway line through the back of the shop?"

A middle-aged man in whites — presumably Lou — peered over the stainless-steel counter and looked her up and down.

"Police?" he squinted.

"Sir," said Aguda, holding up her ID, "I need to get up on the railway line. *Fast.*"

"You're too small to be police," said Lou.

"Sir!" Aguda put away her ID and held up her gun.

Lou dropped below the counter and croaked, "Out the back."

Out the back was a small yard cluttered with pallets and white plastic boxes, and lethal with spilled ice. The back wall was brick, and bowed from years of keeping the embankment at bay.

Aguda tucked the pistol into its holster at the small of her back. She leapt nimbly on to the boxes and from there on to the wall, and started up the steep slope. Brambles didn't want her there, and clutched at her sleeves like beggars. She fought them off, tearing her coat and her hands, spraying fresh snow as she pulled and punched her way to the top.

Finally she made it to the tracks.

Nobody was there.

Aguda switched on her torch and ran to the middle of the bridge — where she could see snow scraped off the parapet.

The spot from where the block had been dropped.

She stopped short, so as not to cover any footprints, and looked down at the road. She had a clear view of traffic coming down the hill. Flashing blue lights were her backup, wending their way slowly through the logjam of cars. The killer had tipped off Guy Smith — no doubt with a nearby location — then just waited for the TV crew car to come along.

It spoke of daring and meticulous planning.

It spoke of cold blood.

Aguda ran her torch across the ground. The snow here was patchy and dirty from the grime of passing trains, but the footprints were clear, leading to and from the parapet. She angled the beam against the best of them and quickly took a photo with her phone, just in case it started snowing again.

Then she crossed the tracks so as not to ruin the scene, and ran alongside them — her eyes scanning the shallow, dirty snow and the gravel rail-bed beneath for anything that might be a clue. Both were littered with plastic bottles, fast-food wrappers, old newspapers and disposable nappies.

Who the hell changed a baby on a train and tossed the dirty nappy from the window?

Everyone, apparently.

She pressed herself into the brick as a train clattered past, feeling the wind of it sucking her in.

When it had gone, she ran on.

Aguda followed the killer's tracks a hundred yards to the point where she could see them veer off down the embankment. She slithered down the bank behind them. There were fewer brambles on this side of the bridge, and the fence at the bottom had stopped being railings and started being chain-link just beyond the stanchions.

She shinned up the fence, turned a neat tumble at the top, and dropped softly into a quiet street with cars parked solidly all along the kerb.

Her torch found the killer's tracks again easily. And when it did, a shock ran through her.

They weren't leading away from the scene of the crash.

They were leading straight back towards it.

CHAPTER
THIRTY-NINE

Eve watched Guy Smith with dull sympathy as he threw up into the gutter.

The darkness made everything more confusing. There were street lights and headlights and shop-window lights — but they only made the spaces in between the lights that much darker.

In the distance she could hear sirens, and hoped they were coming this way. In the absence of anyone to stop them, cars continued to crunch slowly around the debris.

Her mind slowly pieced things together. Something had fallen or been thrown off the bridge and had hit the News 24/7 car. She didn't know what it was, and she didn't care. Ricky the cameraman was dead. He must be, because otherwise Emily Aguda would not have left the scene and Guy would not be throwing up.

The woman in the blue coat was still with her. Still touching Eve's arm now and then in a proprietorial way.

"Are you all right? Can I get you something to drink? Are you injured? What's your name?"

Eve answered, but couldn't hear her own voice so didn't know what she was saying.

Guy Smith sat on the kerb beside the Range Rover's front wheel — his elbows on his knees, his head and his tie dangling between them, staring down at his personal puddle of recycled YO! Sushi.

Eve looked around at the gawpers gathering on the pavement. It was strange to be the object of interest, to be at the centre of that circle, instead of on the outside, trying to get in. She scanned the blur of faces, seeking Joe, but finding only strangers — most with their phones out, so not looking at her at all but at their little screens, so that later they could appal their friends with the carnage they'd stumbled upon on their way to McDonald's or coming back from the pub.

One man was covered in blood and the woman was just standing there, like, Oh My God! . . .

A man stepped off the kerb and crossed the road towards her.

Not Joe.

An ordinary man.

He walked past the crew car without looking inside it, then he went up to Guy Smith and hit him once — *hard* — over the back of the head with something long and thin and black. Eve jerked with shock. There were gasps and stifled squeaks from onlookers, and the woman in the blue coat shrieked and clapped her hand over her mouth.

As Guy pitched forward soundlessly, the man hit him again in a vicious chopping arc, as if he were killing a snake with a golf club.

Guy's dead face hit the road in a black splash.

The man dropped the bar with a casual iron clang and smiled at Eve. "You know what to do," he said. Then he walked away, under the railway bridge, and was swallowed by the dark between the dazzle of headlights.

In her mind, Eve ran. In her head she raced after him and grasped the back of his jacket and swung him around until he overbalanced on to the ground, and put her knee on his throat and gripped his hair and banged his head to pulp as she screamed in his face: *Where is he? Where IS he, you fucking bastard? Where! Is! My! Father?*

In reality, she took a single step and then buckled, and dropped clumsily to one knee.

"Stop him!" she croaked. "Stop him!"

Nobody stopped him. Although several people kept him in frame on their camera phones until he disappeared.

"Oh my God!" said the woman in the blue coat. "*Oh my God!*"

The killer was gone. He'd been *here*, but now he was gone. And so was her chance of catching him, holding him, making him *tell* . . .

Eve stumbled to her feet again, using the Range Rover for support.

She stared at Guy Smith's lifeless body, and felt the brittle wings of madness fold slowly around her.

You know what to do.

She did.

She walked over to the body on unsteady legs.

She took out her phone and started to film.

She filmed the broken back of Guy's blond head, his slack face against the tarmac, the bloody iron bar discarded nearby.

She squeezed her hand under his still-warm chest and pulled out the flyer from inside his jacket, and unfolded it flat on the road.

EXHIBITION
Venue: Westbourne Green
Date: December 17
Time: 23.00

She filmed it.

Then the graffiti.

Then a close-up of the crew car. She remembered a wide shot. Joe would have done a wide shot . . .

A police siren whooped half-heartedly and the last few cars in the jam started slowly to manoeuvre aside to let the law through.

Eve handed her phone to the woman in the blue coat, who was slumped against the Range Rover.

"Here," she said. "Film me."

"What?" The woman's eyes were cloudy with trauma, although her forehead was smooth and untroubled.

"It's already recording," said Eve. "You just have to hold it."

"But," said the woman. "But —"

"*Just hold the fucking phone!*"

The woman held the phone.

"Good," said Eve more calmly. "The police are here now and this will all be over soon. I am going to stand over there and all you have to do is hold the phone up and make sure I'm in that picture and so is the body, OK?"

"Yes."

"Don't worry about anything else."

"OK."

"Can you see me?"

"Yes."

"Can you see the body?"

"Yes."

"Good," said Eve.

She smoothed her rumpled jacket, brushed the hair off her face with a bloody hand — then held up the flyer and did her piece to camera.

The killer could not have done a better job himself.

Everything was there. *Everything.* The mayhem of the car crash, the close-up of the concrete block in the smashed windscreen, the body behind the wheel covered with a blanket that failed to hide the fact that *there was no head*!

iWitness News had even bought or stolen a jerky iPhone clip of *him*, walking over to the reporter on the kerb and hitting him with the bar — although of course it was very dark and the moment of truth was deliberately blurred out, so that people had to go to YouTube to hunt for the good bit.

But the best part of the whole review was Eve Singer.

She looked like shit. Her hair was all over the place and there were dark rings around her eyes. There was blood on her cheek and her jacket, and a wobble on her lower lip which made her seem so affected by his work that it brought tears even to *his* eyes.

Her review wasn't of her usual professional standard.

It was far, *far* better than that.

It was raw and immediate. A companion piece to a *danse macabre* that captured the wonderful essence of unscheduled death.

Unscheduled for those who had died, at least . . .

He smiled at the TV.

Eve Singer spoke in disjointed fragments that built a perfect crazy-paving picture of mayhem, shock and horror.

". . . we got a tip-off . . . smashed into the car from the bridge you can see. If you look, you can see . . . we thought we were safe . . ."

That made the killer laugh! People who thought they were safe! They made his life easier, certainly — but that was all that could be said for their foolishness.

Nobody was safe.

Immortality was a privilege, not a right — and alien to the billions who were just making up the numbers. It required great talent and had to be meticulously planned and perfectly executed.

And then, at the end of the report, Eve Singer held up the flyer he had sent to Guy Smith. Unfolded, and with blood staining its creases like the Shroud of Turin.

". . . a decoy," said Eve. ". . . deliberately misleading . . ."

He giggled. It *had* been a decoy. And it *had* misled!

And a perfect cut to the graffiti on the brick of the bridge:

EXHIBITION
Venue: Here
Date: December 17
Time: 23.00

Then Eve moved close to the camera. Too close, so that the auto-focus hastily adjusted.

It was all so *real!*

Better than real! It was like being there all over again, but with time to savour the moment.

Eve shook the flyer at the camera — peering around its edge, looking desperate and deranged and devastated.

"Please look for a flyer like this. *Exhibition.* You could save the next life. If you find one or have any other information, please call the police so you can help to *stop* this ******* *lunatic!*"

The killer laughed again. *Fucking* had been beeped out, but everybody knew what it had been.

Only *he* understood the subtext of Eve Singer's message. The bit that was only for him.

The bit that told him:

We're in it together now.

CHAPTER
FORTY

18 December

Huw Rees had been right about one thing. About two minutes after Eve Singer's report had gone out, all hell had broken loose.

The Metropolitan Police social media team scrambled to catch up with the game started by Eve's close-up of the bloody flyer, but as soon as their own photo of the Layla Martin flyer had gone up on the Met's Facebook page, the internet wobbled under the weight of spurious comments and suggestions and photos of possible matches. A few were well meaning, some mischievous, many complaining, most self-serving.

None helpful.

First and foremost, there was outrage that nobody had warned the ten million inhabitants of London that there was a killer among them. Then, quickly afterwards — alerted to a guaranteed audience of fifty-five thousand curious Facebook friends on the Metropolitan Police page — anyone with anything to sell or to publicize rushed to leap aboard the bandwagon.

EXHIBITION
SQUARE ROOT
Tonite Rose and Crown Southwark
Admission £5 Be there or be SQUARED

EXHIBITION!
Local Arts and Crafts!
Trinkets and Gifts!
Buy Cheap for Christmas!
Hackney Community Centre!
Admission FREE!

EXHIBITION
Bengal Cat
Answers to the name of
JOANIE
Lost on Brompton Rd
REWARD and NO QUESTIONS ASKED

Eventually the police admins had had to delete the posts and request that anyone finding a genuine flyer simply call the police incident room.

By the next morning, calls were flooding in about what quickly became known as "flyer incidents". Anyone trying to post a flyer was an immediate suspect. Police had to be called to a near-riot which started with a newsagent refusing to allow a woman to put up a notice in his window for an exhibition of cross-stitch in aid of Age Concern. A scuffle broke out at an arts centre in Golders Green when two amateur sleuths pulled down every notice on the community wall in an effort to find an exhibition poster. And in Regent Street, a student was chased and roughed up after tying a flyer for a Tinie Tempah gig to railings near the Apple Store. He was finally brought down by a mob, and when police arrived there was a Santa sitting on him with a sign reading GOLF SALE.

Huw Rees monitored the situation grimly and hoped that letting the cat out of the bag would somehow be good for the investigation. That they'd find the next flyer more quickly and be there in time to apprehend the killer, rather than hours — *days* — too late.

By the time the lunchtime news aired, the exhibition flyers were the talk of the town.

But soon that talk had turned to why the police couldn't catch the killer, even when his last murder had now been witnessed by millions of people.

And even though he'd told them where and when he was going to strike next.

TrrrrrrT.

Eve Singer had gone mad.

Not permanently or showily. She wasn't running round the house with her knickers on her head, being Nefertiti, but Detective Sergeant Aguda knew she was no longer completely sane.

No sane person could have done what she'd done, even if it *was* in an attempt to save her father.

They'd tried keeping her in at the hospital, but she'd insisted on coming home. Insisted, not in a normal way, but in a low, cold, scary way so that even the rather arrogant young doctor had faltered.

Now she was slumped on the sofa beside her cameraman, Joe, pale and bruised and playing with Aguda's handcuffs.

TrrrrrrT.

She'd been doing it ever since they'd got back from the hospital. Although "playing" was no real description of the hours that Eve had spent, trance-like, obsessively snapping the steel cuffs over her own wrists — first left, then right. She was so fixated on the activity that it made Aguda's own considerable cuff skills look like the fumblings of a thumbless child.

TrrrrrrT.

TrrrrrrT.

TrrrrrrT.

Huw Rees said, "Can you stop that?" but Eve didn't. She jerked Aguda's cuffs open with a twist, then slapped them closed on her reddened wrist again with the harsh rattle of a metal snake.

TrrrrrrT.

TrrrrrrT.

Aguda deeply regretted leaving the cuffs on the coffee table. She sighed and glanced up through the front-room window as Mr Elias from next door walked carefully down his path with a bucket of steaming water and assorted sprays and cloths. Heading for the phone box, no doubt. While all this was happening, next door life went on.

Rees said firmly, "I'm getting you to a safe house."

Eve shook her head. "You can't make me."

"You're a target here."

"If he kills people in public, then I'm a target anywhere *but* here."

DS Rees started to say something, then had to stop while a plane passed low overhead. Instead he swapped a meaningful look with Emily Aguda.

Aguda had no desire to scare Eve Singer any more than she had already been scared. In fact, she wasn't sure that that would be possible. But logic and experience dictated that Eve was a sitting duck in her own home.

Now she spoke gently but firmly. "We think it would be best if we moved you out of London entirely, Eve."

"I'm not leaving," said Eve. "My dad was born in this house. He knows it. What if he escapes? I have to be here when he comes home."

TrrrrrrT.

Aguda swapped another look with DS Rees. They knew that Eve wasn't thinking rationally. It wasn't her fault, of course, but it made everything more difficult.

And more dangerous.

"Eve," Aguda said gently, "if you stay here, it makes it much harder for me to protect you. Do you understand that?"

Eve nodded.

TrrrrrrT.

"All I want is for you to be safe," said Aguda.

"I know," said Eve.

"Then let us get you out of here."

"No."

TrrrrrrT.

Rees gave an audible sigh of exasperation.

Aguda tried again. "Eve. Until now, he's led and we've followed. Now we *have* to try to get ahead of *him*. We have to be proactive, not reactive. And the only way to do that is by understanding what he wants. To work out what he's going to do next. To catch a killer, *we* have to think like a killer."

Eve Singer fixed her with a cold stare. "That's exactly what I'm trying to do."

Eve *was* trying to think like the killer.

It wasn't a good place to be.

She had long pushed the envelope of her work and her resilience, but she had never before pushed the envelope of her own imagination.

Now she lay in bed and stared at the dark ceiling, and started to explore. Once she did, it was disturbing what horrors lurked in the soft folds of her own grey brain. What tortures and cruelties might be inflicted. What fears might be imposed. What a killer's cold, empty heart felt when it looked at a scared and vulnerable person in its care.

Which was . . . nothing.

CHAPTER
FORTY-ONE

19 December

"Eve!"

Eve woke in the dark with no memory of having fallen asleep.

"What?"

Emily Aguda was in the doorway, holding her phone.

"They've ID'd the killer," she said. "They're on their way to an address right now."

On a bitter and foggy winter's dawn, outside a cream-coloured Georgian terrace in west London, Detective Superintendent Huw Rees looked at his watch and said a short prayer for the first time since his daughter was born.

Holly had come out with the cord wrapped around her neck. Silent and blue in the face. Maureen had been exhausted, but desperate to hold her.

But Huw had seen that the frantic efforts going on in the corner of the labour room were not so that the baby could be presented neatly to her mother, but to save her life.

So Huw Rees had prayed — *Please, please, please* . . . Reminding the Lord — and himself — that he was only one generation away from God-fearing folk.

And all the time he had prayed, he had lied to his wife.

She's beautiful.

Yes, all of her fingers and toes.

She'll cry any minute. Then likely won't stop!

Any minute now.

Here it comes.

Any minute . . .

And Holly had cried, and *he* had cried, and he had never told his wife — or anybody else — of the terror of those long, lonely moments . . .

The forty-pound chunk of concrete that had been dropped from the bridge and decapitated the driver of the News 24/7 crew car had turned out to be the counterweight of a front-loading washing machine.

A Hotpoint, to be exact, according to the serial number.

Huw Rees hadn't known it was a counterweight. And if he had, he would never have known that a washing-machine counterweight *had* a serial number.

But Veronica Creed knew both those things.

Turned out Veronica Creed had quite the passion for concrete counterweights. Turned out she had a *collection*. "Not *many*, of course," she'd told him with a spine-chilling blink as she handed him her report. "Just the more interesting ones."

Who the *fuck* thought that concrete counterweights were in *any way* interesting? What kind of friend-free lunatic? Seriously!

Huw Rees shivered.

"Fucking frigid, innit?" murmured Hamilton beside him, without taking his eye from the sights of his semi-automatic rifle.

The counterweight had broken into several pieces and been ghastly with blood. Concrete was notoriously difficult to work with. Concrete covered with blood was impossible. The chances of getting a fingerprint off it had been zero. Nobody could do it.

But Veronica Creed had done it.

And that print belonged to thirty-two-year-old William Stafford Vandenberg, who'd had a single caution nearly three years earlier for nicking four notebooks and a Bic ballpoint pen from WHSmith at King's Cross station.

It seemed a puny rehearsal for serial murder.

Rees took out his phone and looked again at the mugshot of Vandenberg. He had to keep doing it. It was so *bland* that he couldn't fix the man's face in his head. It was a face the eyes would slide easily over, in a crowd or a line-up. Regular without being good-looking, dull brown hair. He looked like someone who worked in an office, at a job his wife didn't understand and couldn't be bothered to ask about, for money that would never make a difference.

So dull. So *ordinary*.

It was hard to imagine the man in this photo doing anything as risky as buying a scratch card, let alone committing murder.

"*Three, two, one —*"

Huw Rees was jerked back to the now.

Beside him Hamilton gave the *GO* signal and suddenly a dozen heavily armed men were rushing at the front door.

And as he followed them, Huw Rees prayed in time to his footsteps.

Please . . . please . . . please . . .

Because the fingerprint had been the good news.

The *bad* news was the blood that Veronica Creed had analysed swiftly but thoroughly. Most of it had belonged to the News 24/7 driver, Richard Short.

But some of it was Duncan Singer's.

Please . . . please . . . please . . .

Rees didn't like his life being dictated by prayers and miracles, but in a case like this, he would take help anywhere he could find it.

While they waited, Eve and Emily Aguda watched *How It's Made*.

Aguda was fascinated, but not in a good way. It reminded her of the Open University programmes her mother had watched when they were growing up. Men with sideburns and tank-tops drawing squeakily on blackboards and tipping liquids into test tubes to elicit repeatable results.

It was just as hypnotically dull.

Rollerblades and frying pans and sticky tape. A pinsticker's guide to mass production. It went on for ever and the music was *awful*.

Halfway through sticky tape, Eve Singer said, "Why haven't they called?"

"I can't tell you that," said Aguda honestly. "The whole operation could be over but confused, or been delayed and not even started. Anything I told you would be a guess."

"Are they armed?" Eve said dully.

"DS Rees was calling in a firearms unit."

"What if they shoot Dad by accident?"

"They're highly trained not to make that kind of mistake."

"It happens all the time!"

Not all the time, thought Aguda. *Only now and then*. But she knew that was unlikely to comfort anyone who had a loved one anywhere remotely near the line of fire. So instead she told her, "It'll all be over soon. Nobody's going to take any stupid risks."

Aguda wasn't in the lying business, but she was all for empty reassurances.

So she reassured Eve until Joe knocked on the front door.

Then she let *him* reassure Eve, while she made them all tea.

With the first blow of the battering ram, Superintendent Rees knew they had made a terrible mistake.

The house was Georgian, and the front door was three-inch oak. None of this modern MDF plywood-balsa bullshit.

The Specialist Firearms Command wasn't equipped to batter down posh doors.

Another mighty blow, and another violent recoil that made one man stagger and tumble backwards down the steps. Somebody laughed and Hamilton barked furiously to *Shut the fuck up!* and there was a moment of panting silence.

The glossy black door was barely dented.

The element of surprise, however, was beyond repair.

Then they had to mill around like drunks outside a Portaloo, with their Armalites and Glocks and stab vests and riot helmets, while one of the squad took for ever to pick the lock and let them in.

The first thing that hit Huw Rees was the smell. Woodsmoke and oil, and something underneath that made his nose twitch with primitive caution.

Hamilton pointed skywards and six armed men stormed the elegant winding stairs, the beams of their helmet torches criss-crossing the air ahead of them like Fox searchlights.

Rees flicked on a light switch, but nothing happened.

Even in the semi-dark of dawn, he could tell that the house was enormous, and made more so by being free of furniture. The ceilings were high and the floors wooden, and the space in between them echoed with emptiness.

Everything was covered by a fine layer of dust that woke under the invading boots and rose to make the men cough.

Rees stood in the cavernous hallway and listened to Hamilton's team move through the house. The only sound was of heavy footsteps, and shouts of "Clear!" as they checked each room.

He was so tense he shook. Only when they had their man would the knot in his gut start to unravel. For now it was just about holding his breath and getting through to the other side.

The other side of *what*, he wasn't sure. A madman was an unpredictable foe. He'd once seen a lunatic leap out of an Aga, still murderous, regardless of being on fire.

"Sir. Over here . . ."

Rees joined Hamilton at a doorway off the hall and followed his pointing finger.

"What the fuck is *that*?"

The room was huge, and in the middle of the floor was a square made up of small things. Small, misshapen things.

Hamilton ran a quick eye around the doorway for booby traps, then they stepped into the room.

Rees walked thirty feet before he reached the edge of the perfect square.

He walked slowly along its edges.

It was made of machine components. Nuts, bolts, plastic piping, elbows, washers, motor casings and — in the middle, like a prayer wheel — a large stainless-steel cylinder.

Perforated.

"You think it's a bomb?" said Rees cautiously.

"I don't know," said Hamilton. "Careful where you step."

The two men split at the corner of the array and walked cautiously away from each other along the perpendicular edges.

Hamilton stopped. "I think it's a bloody washing machine."

"I think you're right," laughed Rees.

"Beautiful, isn't it?" said Hamilton.

His words surprised Rees.

And then they didn't.

Because it *was* beautiful.

Removed from their place in the machine and laid out precisely within the strict parameters of the square, the utilitarian components had taken on a new — more romantic — existence.

Every part had been mined from the machine and exposed, like a diamond dug out of the dirt. Each could now be appreciated in its own right, laid out in its own space — no longer a cog, but a gem.

There was an overwhelming sense of the parts having been freed from their dark and cramped confines and finally allowed to *breathe*.

As Rees carried on walking quietly around the square, the light from his torch threw long shadows beyond each piece, which pivoted away from him as he moved, each shadow rippling protectively over its neighbours as if they were all still somehow joined together, and all turning together warily to watch him circle them.

Huw Rees felt oddly emotional. Strangely *connected*.

Stupid, he told himself, *stupid*. But that didn't stop a lump coming to his throat.

He would never look at a washing machine the same way again.

At one corner of the perfect square was something shiny. A single chrome-plastic word.

Rees touched it cautiously with the toe of his boot, then picked it up and held it out to show Hamilton, with a boyish smile on his face that spoke of gold and pirate treasure.

"Hotpoint!"

"Sir, we've got a body!"

The shout from somewhere above him jolted Rees out of his reverie and he felt his gut go heavy with prescience.

Shit.

Duncan Singer. Dead. Murdered. Eve Singer's face as he broke the news and her heart . . .

He hated this part of his job.

With a deep sigh, he placed the Hotpoint badge back where he'd found it, then followed Hamilton up the stairs, sweating itchily under his unfamiliar helmet, even though the house was barely warmer inside than out.

"Got a body, sir," said an officer on the third-floor landing, pointing through a doorway.

That was the smell. Rees recognized it now, although it was faint, and different from the usual decay of a corpse.

More distant.

He went through a room where the ashes of a fire still glowed. Vaguely he registered a yellow chair and a television and a box and a cup and a saucer.

Notebooks piled high.

Into the next room, where half a dozen men had gathered at a bedside, like mourners paying their last respects. A magnesium lantern cast the only real light — a ghostly white glow — on the faces of the black-clad men.

Shit. Here we go.

The body was on the bed.

And *in* the bed.

"What the shit . . .?" said Hamilton.

Rees frowned and bent over to understand it more clearly.

It wasn't Duncan Singer.

Thank you thank you thank you.

Whoever it was had died here, and stayed here, and had swollen with gas and then deflated here. And then had soaked right into the mattress, so that the body and the bed had become one homogenous mass — both mummified and pocket-sprung.

It was dry now, and dessicating, which was why the smell was so changed and old, and soaked up by the innards of the bed, the wadding of kapok.

It was the body of a woman, he thought, from the size of it. A denture fixed with silver wire in the corner of the grim grimace glimmered like a diamond in a coalmine.

Gingerly, Rees lifted the lacy counterpane. In places it stuck to the bed and to the rancid corpse; someone behind him gave a grunt of disgust, and then a short laugh of embarrassment.

It was impossible to say how the woman had died.

"Sir, the house is clear, sir," said a man from the doorway.

Hamilton looked at Rees, and Rees stepped back and away from the bed.

"Check again," he said. "The fire in the next room is still warm. He must be here. Check again."

PC Dougie Trewell was having a shitty day.

He had been knocked down the stone steps with the recoil of the battering ram and as punishment Hamilton had left him outside to guard the door, instead of allowing him to storm the building with his unit and his gun.

Now he was standing on the doorstep like a fucking spare part.

This was only his second raid with SCO19 and on the first one he'd got his foot stuck in a drain. If he didn't shine soon he'd be back in crap uniform and without a gun.

Early commuters were starting to pass, so Dougie straightened up and tried to look as if he meant business, and not as if he had been left outside the door like a kid wearing a dunce's cap.

"What's going on here?"

A man peered around the door of the neighbouring house.

"Police, sir," said Dougie gruffly.

"You're making a hell of a noise."

"Sorry, sir," said Dougie. "Bloke who lives here is a suspect in a murder case. Can't go in light." He jerked his semi-automatic carbine to show just how light you couldn't go in.

"Murder?" The man gave him a suspicious look. "*Him?*"

"Yes, sir," said Dougie. "Do you know him?"

"Not really," said the man. "He's an artist."

"Yeah?" said Dougie, without interest. He reckoned art was just a trick played on people with more money than sense.

The man came out. He was dressed beyond his years in old-man slacks and a Pringle jumper. Pink-and-yellow argyle. Pale-cream loafers with little tassles.

He probably liked art, thought Dougie with an inner snort.

They stood for another moment, staring up at the cream house together, listening to the muffled shouts and the thumping of boots coming from within.

"They'll be making a terrible mess of those floors," said the man. "They're all cherry wood, you know. All these homes have cherry-wood floors."

"Yeah?" said Dougie again. He'd never lived in a house where the floors were anything but carpet or lino. Cherry wood meant nothing to him. "Well," he said, "I'm sure they'll put right any damage." That was a lie. Especially if they arrested a killer inside. Then Dougie was pretty sure they *wouldn't*.

"I hope so," said the man, then he turned and wheeled a box on a sack trolley from the house and started to tilt and tip it down the steps. The box was big and it was a precarious process. Dougie's instinct was to help, but he had already screwed up once today and dared not abandon his post, even for a second, so he turned his back and pretended not to see how the man was struggling.

His ears burned a little at the grunts and the clunks, and he scowled up and down the street, hoping he looked harder than he felt.

"You like art?" said the man.

Dougie jumped a little. The man had left the box at the bottom of the steps. But instead of going back inside, he was standing out here making small talk.

About art.

"Never really thought about it," Dougie said with a shrug.

The man smiled. "You're not even one of those people who say, *I know what I like?*"

"Nope," said Dougie.

He wished the man would go back inside. He should, because it was really cold and he was only in indoor clothes and silly shoes, as if he'd been interrupted while eating kippers for breakfast. Plus he was as bald as a coot.

He must be chilly as fuck.

"I *do* know what I like, though." Dougie surprised himself with the afterthought. "Cars."

"Mm," said the man with a sniff. "Cars." As if he thought Dougie was a moron.

Dougie flushed and hurried to explain himself. He wasn't sure why he felt the need; he just *did*.

"Not just cars," he said, "but all the little *bits* in cars."

"Little bits?" frowned the man.

"Yeah," said Dougie dreamily. "All the little bits. I like to take an engine apart — every single jet and spring and washer — and see how it all went together to make the car run. Spreading it all out so that I understand it. It's not, like, *art* — but that's what I like."

The man said nothing, and Dougie suddenly felt very self-conscious. Somehow he felt he'd said too much, and to the wrong person. Some rich bloke in a snobby jumper and a ten-million-quid house. What would he know about the beauty of an engine? What would he care about clip-springs and washers? It made him feel exposed and a bit angry, the way he had when he was a kid. Made him feel like stupid little Dougie, brother of Skew Ronnie the car thief, instead of PC Doug Trewell, Guardian of the Galaxy, which was how he liked to think of himself nowadays, in the privacy of his own head.

Embarrassed and a little cross, he abruptly turned his back on the man, hoping he'd get the message and go back indoors. But he didn't. Dougie could feel him, just standing there behind him. It made his neck itch . . .

So he stepped up to the threshold and pretended that he'd heard something inside the house. It was good timing, because just as he reached the door, he *did* hear a shout of excitement from inside.

Fuck!

Adrenaline shot through his body as he waited for gunfire. His finger tightened on his trigger and his heart pounded, because if the killer made a run for it now, he

322

was the last line of defence, and wouldn't *that* be fucking ace? If the killer gave everybody the slip but Dougie the Dunce standing guard outside the house?

But nothing happened.

There was some more shouting, but not of alarm. Whatever they had found, it wasn't making a run for it.

Shit.

Dougie relaxed a little. Not too much though. SCO19 was an elite unit, and relaxing could get you killed. And Dougie had worked too hard and come too far to get himself killed now.

A rattling noise made him turn around.

The man had gone down the stone steps, and was now pushing the big box briskly away through the snow, in his indoor shoes.

The shout of discovery had come from an officer called Rollins, who'd found a trapdoor to the attic inside a built-in cupboard in the smallest bedroom in the house.

The operation came to a halt while they checked for booby traps. Rees was impatient — and then chastened when they actually found one just inside the attic. It was a small device contained in an old Quality Street tin. The tin took him back. It was huge! He remembered his father having a tin like that one Christmas, and it had seemed a bottomless treasure chest of chocolate jewels. Quality Street tins were tiny now. No value. This one even had a *Half Price!* sticker on it.

Bargain!

A small, blond officer with a pair of needle-nose pliers declared the device safe. "Wire's come loose," he said, holding up a spike of glimmering copper. "Otherwise you'd have got a hundred three-inch nails right in the fucking face, Rollins, you muppet."

Finally in the attic, they cautiously followed a cable stuffed with stolen electricity through the man-sized hole that had been knocked in the brick wall between the two properties.

Then they dropped through another hatch into the house next door.

There were lights in this house, and warmth, and the décor was sumptuous. There were ornate vases and French-polished tables and Japanese lacquered cabinets.

There was also a broken mirror on the landing, a single pile of dirty clothing on the floor of the master bedroom, and — oblivious in the en-suite shower — an elderly man crooning "Love Me Tender".

CHAPTER
FORTY-TWO

20 December

When Aguda first told her that the killer had escaped and that they hadn't found her father, Eve had the sickening sensation that she was falling, out of control, backwards through time, spinning and breathless and seven years old again, skinny and chilly, with the smell of fresh-mown grass in her nose and panic-stricken over the bean-bag race.

Those same frantic tears welled inside her once more, like a geyser about to blow.

Only her father wasn't around any more to push her hair aside and dry her tears, and tell her to *just keep going*.

And never would be again.

So why the hell do you keep waiting for it to happen?

The voice in her head surprised Eve so much that she straightened in her chair.

She wasn't a child any more.

Her father's kind advice to get her through the bean-bag race had become a motto, a mantra, and — finally — a way of life that was all about moving on and leaving difficult things behind.

But there were some things that couldn't be left behind.

Some things you just had to turn and face . . .

And with that simple clarity, the crazed carapace that had enfolded Eve as she'd stood over Guy Smith's battered body released her like a dove.

While Emily Aguda told her what had happened during the raid, and what would happen next, her mind was off somewhere else, seeing things clearly, and making other plans.

Eve had handed over all her control — first to the killer and then to the police.

But the police couldn't keep her safe.

And they couldn't catch the killer.

And they couldn't find her father.

For the first time in her life, Eve realized that *nobody* was going to ride into town on a white horse and end this nightmare.

She would just have to do it herself.

CHAPTER
FORTY-THREE

Three days after Guy Smith was beaten to death in front of her, Eve Singer announced that she was going back to work.

"Are you sure you want to do this?" Aguda said warily, over breakfast of toast and Marmite.

"I have to be busy," Eve said. "If I sit and wait I'll go mad."

"Are you sure you want to do this?" Joe said when she called him and told him her plan.

"Yes," she said simply. "Will you help me?"

There was a long pause at the other end of the line and fear flared in Eve's heart. In that moment she realized that Joe was the only person she trusted in the whole wide world, and that if he said he would not help her then she truly *was* alone.

So when he said *yes*, her throat tightened with an overload of emotion.

Even so, leaving the house was harder than she thought it would be. Joe had offered to pick her up, but she knew she needed to get back into a normal rhythm if she was to maintain her tenuous grip on some appearance of normality — even if she did now have her own personal bodyguard in tow.

At least Aguda didn't *look* like a bodyguard.

Eve stood behind the front door for an age, trying to remember how to breathe in a rhythm, while she grew hotter and hotter in her hat and gloves and scarf.

Then she opened the door to find Mr Elias standing there with a spadeful of salt.

"Are you going to work?" he said in surprise.

"Yes," said Eve. "I need to keep busy."

Mr Elias scattered the salt on the icy pathway, then leaned on his shovel.

"I saw your . . . *report* on the news, Eve. Are you sure you're all right?"

Eve's smile faltered a little. "I'll be fine," she said. "And thank you for all your kindness and help. It means a lot to me."

Mr Elias waved it away. "Any news of Duncan?"

Eve shook her head and pointed at Aguda. "This is Detective Sergeant Aguda," she said. "She's part of the search team."

Eve thought she'd keep things simple. She didn't want to worry Mr Elias with kidnapping and killings.

Mr Elias nodded and shook Aguda's hand. "Good luck," he said.

By the time they closed the little wooden gate behind them, he had bent to his task once again.

"*Shit*," said Eve as they headed for the station. "I still have to buy him a Christmas present. I still have to buy *everyone* a Christmas present!"

Eve took a deep breath and opened the newsroom door.

"Fuck yes!" Ross Tobin shouted. "That's what I *call* a fucking reporter!"

Everybody looked at Eve and she reddened. It felt like for ever since she had been here. She felt like a stranger — and people treated her that way.

Because she was.

Stranger than she had been the last time they'd seen her.

They had all reported crimes and tragedies and shocking events — but none of them had straightened their hair and done a piece to camera as a murdered colleague bled out behind them.

After a few wan smiles, people sidled past her nervously, or pretended not to see her sitting at her desk.

Eve had planned to introduce Aguda as a contact, but nobody asked who she was.

Joe arrived and gave Eve a quick, reassuring hug and Katie Merino came over to say a rather stiff *Welcome back*, but Ross dismissed her with a flap of his hand. "Not half the journalist you are," he told Eve as Katie disappeared. "I'm not even sure she's a natural blonde."

Eve turned to Ross Tobin, all business. "So what have you got for us?"

"Take your pick," said Tobin. "Man's decapitated body found in Camden Lock; woman eaten by two dachshunds in Belsize Park; and what looks like a double suicide in a car park off Edgware Road."

Eve and Joe exchanged glances. Any one of the deaths might turn out to be the work of their killer —

329

or none — but they both knew which was guaranteed to make the evening news.

"We'll take the dogs," said Eve.

The guilty dachshunds had been taken away by the time they got to the upmarket address in Belsize Park, and the police on the scene weren't saying where. Aguda wasn't sorry — she wasn't crazy about dogs at the best of times, and thought that two dogs who had eaten their owner — even post-mortem — would be particularly creepy.

Eve and Joe were inexplicably gutted.

"Why?" Aguda asked. "People know what dachshunds look like."

"Not *these* dachshunds," Eve said. "Not dachshunds that have eaten their wealthy owner in Belsize Park."

But Aguda was confused. Police had already said that Katinka Nasarenko had apparently fallen downstairs and died at least a week before her body was discovered. The dogs had only chewed on her thighs a bit, not brought her down in a pack.

"It's not Watergate, is it?" she said.

Eve shrugged. "Maybe not," she said. "But it's the best story of the day and guaranteed airtime."

Aguda still didn't see the point. She didn't say so, but to her the whole job of TV crime reporter seemed faintly ridiculous — a foolish retelling of life and death in the midst of the real thing. She was all in favour of a free press, but couldn't be doing with all this petty prurience.

She stood on the corner of the street, stamping her feet to keep warm, while Eve and Joe wandered about looking at angles and stepping backwards into the road between cars to stare up at the relevant address. It had been a grand row of old houses; some had already been made into flats, others were still undergoing the change. Aguda was starting to wonder whether there was a street anywhere in London that was unsullied by scaffolding and eight-foot hoardings smothered in peeling flyers.

Eve and Joe rejoined her at the end of their discussion. "We need the dogs," Joe said ruefully. "Otherwise it's never going to make the news."

He gave Eve a meaningful look and there was a brief silence. Aguda knew something was afoot.

"You couldn't help us out, could you?" Eve said.

"In what way?" said Aguda suspiciously.

"Find out where the dogs are and put in a good word for us? Ask if we could get a quick shot of them? Then we could do a piece here and go straight to the kennels or wherever and get a shot of the killer dogs, and then we're done."

Aguda smiled at *killer dogs*, then realized that Eve was deadly serious.

She hesitated. It wasn't her job. Her job was to keep Eve Singer from being killed, no more, no less. But she liked Eve, and Joe seemed like a nice enough bloke, and it wouldn't be hard to help them so she would have felt churlish saying no.

"OK," she said, "I'll ask for you, but I'm not begging. Not for dogs."

"Thanks," said Eve. "We'll do a few shots here and then go wherever, if you manage to find out."

Aguda detached herself from them and spoke to the officer at the scene, who gave her a number. She pulled out her phone and called it, while Joe and Eve messed about with light meters and microphones. They kept looking over to see how she was getting on, so she moved a little distance from them so that they couldn't hear her appeal on their behalf. Emily Aguda was used to getting what she wanted because she'd worked hard enough to deserve it, and hated asking for favours.

But it wasn't a big favour and the officer who was the last line of resistance said he had no problem if Aguda wanted to send someone along to take a picture of the dogs.

"Lovely little things, they are," he told her. "If the family don't want you I'll have you myself, won't I, sweetheart?"

Aguda realized he was talking to the killer dogs, not being a sexist pig, so she thanked him and hung up and walked back towards the hoardings where Eve was finishing her report.

". . . Eve Singer in Belsize Park for iWitness News." She continued to look into the camera with a bright-yet-sympathetic look on her face.

Only when Joe said, "OK," did Eve's face crimp again into real concern.

Aguda had to hand it to her — she must be sick with worry, but on camera she was a complete professional.

"Did you get it?" Eve said grimly.

"I got it," said Joe.

They both turned to look at Aguda and she couldn't help a triumphant little smile. "I got it too."

They ate leftovers. That's what the label on the packet in the freezer said in Eve's hasty scrawl. Leftover *what* it didn't say.

It had turned out to be some kind of chicken risotto, which was bland to the point of tastelessness.

Emily Aguda glanced at the kitchen clock. "Are we going to watch the news?"

"Why?"

"Your report on the dogs."

Eve waved it away with a little smile. "It's not Watergate, is it?"

Aguda reckoned she probably deserved that — but she'd done her bit for the story, and couldn't help feeling a little disappointed.

CHAPTER
FORTY-FOUR

Humanity enjoys only two states of truth and beauty: the new-born and the corpse . . .

Huw Rees put down the book and rubbed his red eyes.

It was two a.m. He had been at this for hours now. This notebook was one of sixty-six. He'd had them transported to his office, and from there to his home, in the hope that they would give him some insight into the killer's current state of mind, but so far it had been little other than ramblings — some esoteric, some religious, all egotistical. All nutty as hell.

He picked up another book and opened it at random.

Immortality must be the artist's goal.

A true artist must seek to reveal everything EVERYTHING about his subject — not only the outer shell but the inner workings.

The Cubists tried but failed. They reveal their subjects from multiple perspectives but all is exterior. If I want to see every angle of the Nude Descending, can I not simply walk around her?

And from every angle she is still only two-dimensional. He shows me her backside, but it is very like her frontside! To understand her we must show her INSIDE!!!

Art was not Huw Rees's strong point. He knew what he liked — which was paintings of Spitfires and Messerschmitts duelling in the summery skies over Kent — but he would never have called himself a *lover* of art.

He didn't know *Nude Descending a Staircase*, so he didn't get the killer's joke — although he recognized that a joke must have been made by the thick and repeated exclamation points at the end of the sentence.

They had gone through three pages.

DI Marr was cultural. *He* might get the *Nude* joke. Huw Rees made a mental note to ask him if it had any relevance, then flicked forward a few pages.

Jack the Ripper had some insight, although he lacked control. He sensed that truth was to be found within, and should be exposed and shared with others . . .

Sick prick. He turned the pages, reading in snatches, his tired eyes seeking trigger words like "kill" and "blood".

How perfectly she trusted me when I had come to claim her. Now she doubts like Thomas, who would not be convinced by the face or the form of the undead Christ, until he opened the Roman wound with his own finger, and touched the flesh that restored a ghost to a man.

Now *that* Rees recognized. Vague memories of school religious instruction, and an illustration in the little Bible his grandmother had given him on his tenth birthday: a watercolour plate of a confused old man sticking his finger into Jesus's ribs. Thank God his father had bought him a Wales rugby shirt on the same day or his birthday would have been a right downer. He had never read the Bible, but he'd looked at the pictures, because they'd been as gory as hell. Beheadings and beatings and the bloody crucifixion . . . Happy birthday, little boy! Hip-hip-hooray!

Rees sighed and dropped the notebook on to his desk. He rubbed his eyes. He hadn't slept. He couldn't recall the last time he'd slept without waking at least once — his brain was working too hard to give itself over to slumber.

After they'd linked the first three murders, he'd moved to the spare room so that he could switch on the light and go over the files without waking Maureen. It hadn't really worked. Often he would look up from photos of Layla Martin's drained body, or the bloody cab of the Piccadilly Line Tube, to find his wife at the door, offering coffee or a sandwich.

At three in the morning.

Thinking about it now, Huw Rees almost cried at her kindness. Actually got a lump in his throat! He snorted. He was emotional only because he was exhausted. He had pinned all of his hopes on the raid, without realizing that they were the last hopes he had. And when that effort had failed to yield a killer *or* a hostage, Huw Rees had felt his mental and physical resources implode with a weedy *pfff*. Since then he'd been running on empty, propping up his mind and his body with false hope and Jelly Babies. Someone had once told him you could ride the Tour de France on nothing but water and Jelly Babies, and so far, so good. But he'd be a toothless diabetic if they didn't catch this bastard soon.

It made him feel doomed.

He had been getting heat from the Commissioner's office *before* Eve Singer had gone rogue with her iPhone and flyer. Now he felt like a man being force-fed face-first into a furnace. He didn't blame Eve for publicizing the flyer. She was desperate to find her father, and desperation did strange things to people. But it had made everything a lot more complicated.

Rees picked up Vandenberg's mugshot. For two days now, it had stared off the front of every newspaper and from TV screens, but nobody had seen him. At least, nobody *remembered* seeing him. Maybe it was just that nobody had noticed him in the first place.

The man had a Teflon face; there was nowhere for the eyes to stick and fix the image in the memory.

The incident room had had a hundred calls a day about flyers that turned out to be for carpet sales and doll's-house fairs, fifty calls a day reporting men sticking flyers on bus shelters and lamp posts — every one of which had to be checked out — but not one

337

single call claiming a sighting of William Stafford Vandenberg.

The system wasn't working.

Everything was shit.

All Rees knew was that he was desperate for a break he couldn't take and a sleep that wouldn't come. He worried not only that Vandenberg would carry on with his festive killing spree, but that his own capacity to hunt him down was diminishing exponentially with every day that passed. He dreaded every new dawn while the threat of another public murder hung over his head like a sword.

Huw Rees finally went to bed, but not to sleep.

The phone vibrated silently under Eve's pillow and she answered it before the second buzz.

Number withheld.

"I got your message, Eve. Very clever."

She got up and gently clicked the bedroom door shut, then walked silently to the window — missing the creaking floorboards without even thinking about it. The cool air seeping through the glass caressed her bare legs.

The street outside had been softened by fresh snow. Under the lamp post the phone box was blood red with a thick marshmallow cap.

Was the killer in there?

He could be calling from anywhere; the interior of the phone box was dark. Impenetrable.

"What do you want?" he said.

"My father," she said. "Alive."

"Are you *sure*?" he teased. "The monkey's paw?"

Her gut lurched. She knew the ghost story. Everyone knew it. A bad bargain, and a dead son returned to his parents — but still horribly mangled by the accident that had killed him.

For a moment Eve was angry that he would joke about it, but she let it go. She drew a deep breath. She had to play along, not provoke him. If she took it personally then she wouldn't be able to *think like a killer*.

"And what do *you* want?" She did not stammer — and wondered fleetingly whether that was a good thing.

Or very, very bad.

In the phone box: a movement. Eve flinched as a single pale palm pressed against the glass.

Splayed.

"Death wants his Maiden."

Eve went liquid with horror. She put her own hand on the window to steady herself, and it was a long, long time before she could find enough breath to make any sound.

Then she whispered, "We have a deal."

She hung up, and stepped unsteadily away from the window and back into the shadows.

He's going to kill me, she thought numbly.

And I probably deserve it.

CHAPTER
FORTY-FIVE

22 December

Mr Elias never swore, but when he found that the phone box had been defaced, he said *something*, very forcefully, under cover of an Air France jet, and then strode briskly back to the house to fetch a bucket of hot water and a scrubbing brush.

He was angry, but he was also hurt.

More hurt than he'd ever have believed possible.

Surprising tears welled in his eyes. First Phoebe, then Jennifer, and now *this*.

He knew in his head that the first two things were unconnected to the third, but in his heart they were still open wounds, and this felt like salt.

He blew his nose into his handkerchief as the water beat noisily into the bucket.

Who could have done it? He hoped it was a stranger. If it were a stranger it wouldn't feel so *bloody personal!*

He trudged back out to the phone box and started to scrub the flyer off the wall.

He'd almost removed the bottom left corner before the red mist cleared and he actually read what it said.

EXHIBITION
nue: Madame Tussaud's
Date: Christmas Eve
e: 14.00

Mr Elias dropped his bucket, hurried back across the snowy road and banged hard on Eve Singer's door.

It was night. The door of the phone box opened, showing a brief flash of greenish night-vision snow. A dark figure entered, hood up, face wrapped in a scarf.

Only the eyes glittered, like a fox in headlights.

There was a brief glimpse of the flyer being unfurled, and then gloved hands raised it and pasted it over the lens . . .

"You think it's real?" said Joe.

"I think we have to take this one seriously," said Huw Rees. "There's no way we can ID Vandenberg from this footage, but his prints are all over the door." He held up a copy of the flyer. "At least now we know where and when to find him."

"You knew where and when to find him last time, too," said Eve.

"Trust me," said Rees grimly, "this time we'll have everything covered." He paused and glanced at Aguda. "We just need to swing the odds in our favour . . ."

They both looked at Eve. There was a pregnant silence.

TrrrrrrT.

Then Joe said with dawning anger, "They want to use you as bait!"

Rees winced. "Not *bait*," he said. "As a distraction."
He spoke to Eve. "Vandenberg is obsessed with you.
Obsessed with you showing the world his work. You're
the person he most wants to impress —"

"Or murder!" said Joe.

Rees ignored him. "This is different from the raid on
his house. This time we know exactly where he's going
to be and when. We've got forty-eight clear hours to
secure that scene. We can get in there and *control* it,
Eve. For the first time we'll have the upper hand. You'll
be surrounded by police. Emily will be right there and
we'll have a team of twenty armed undercover officers,
who can be so tight on you that, trust me, this maniac
will never get within ten feet of you. The moment we
spot him, we'll take him down."

Eve held the handcuffs still for a moment.

Aguda glanced at her and said carefully, "It seems
like a good plan."

"But it's *not* a good plan," Joe snapped. "It's a
fucking *terrible* plan. What if you *don't* spot him? What
if you spot him, but you screw up somehow? Like you
screwed up at the Barnstormer Theatre? What if this
nut doesn't *need* to get within ten feet of Eve? What if
he's in the rafters with a fucking rifle? What *then*?"

"Joe . . ." Eve put a hand on his arm. They all looked
at her. She spoke carefully. "I know you're only trying
to protect me. But I just want this to be over. I'm the
one who screwed up. I made a connection with the
killer; I showed the Kevin Barr clip; I went to his
fucking exhibition at Piccadilly Circus; I let this bastard
into this house and he stole my *dad*! —"

She stopped before she could cry. A plane passed, giving her the moment she needed to go on. "And if this is the only way to get him back, I have to try it. I just *have* to."

Rees said, "So you'll do it?"

Eve gave a half-shrug. "The killer wants me," she said. "We have to give him what he wants."

"This is *bullshit!*" said Joe, and stood up and stormed out.

Eve went after him. She caught him at the gate, shrugging on his jacket. "Joe . . ."

He turned to face her, but didn't return her smile. "These bastards don't give a shit about you *or* your dad. All they want is to take down a serial killer."

"Isn't that what *we* want too?" said Eve. "Whatever they're planning, it makes no difference to *us*."

"It's the principle."

"It's their job. And it's the obvious move. You can't blame them."

"Yeah I can," he said angrily. "Fuck 'em. And fuck their job."

He looked close to tears.

Eve put her hand over his on top of the gate. "What's really wrong?"

Joe looked around him as if the answer were to be found hanging on a snowy hedge. "I just want you to be *safe*."

"Everything will be OK."

"You don't know that."

She nodded. "You're right. But none of us knows that. Every day we get out of bed and assume we'll climb into it again that night. Some of us are wrong. But Joe — most of us are *right*."

"Most of us aren't trying to outwit a serial killer."

Eve smiled. "How can I fail? I'll have you there to protect me."

Joe didn't smile. "This is not a game, Eve. This is serious shit."

"You think I don't *know* that? You think I *want* to take this kind of risk? I'm shaking in my boots here, Joe, but there's no other option. Whatever Huw Rees says, if the killer makes one wrong move, they're going in with all guns blazing. And if he dies I'll never find my dad. And *that's* all I care about. That's all that matters."

Joe squinted at the snow and shook his head.

"I want to do this with you," she said. "But I *will* do it alone."

He slid his hand from under hers and opened the gate. "I know you will."

He got into the crew car and revved the nuts off it before pulling into the road, narrowly missing a UPS delivery van.

Eve walked slowly back inside.

CHAPTER
FORTY-SIX

Mr Elias opened the door to a UPS driver.

"Mr Elias?"

"Yes."

"Parcel for you. Sign here, please."

"For what?"

The man stepped aside so Mr Elias could see a large box on a trolley. On the side it said *Hotpoint*.

"I didn't order a washing machine."

"Surprise," said the man with a shrug.

That was true, thought Mr Elias. It *was* Christmas, after all. But he checked that the box was properly addressed to him before signing a poor approximation of his name on a screen with a stylus.

The box was big — nearly waist-high — and looked heavy.

"Is it heavy?" he asked.

"Yes, pretty heavy."

"In that case, would you mind bringing it in for me?"

"Not really my job," said the driver, and looked at his watch. Then he sighed and manoeuvred the trolley around, and tilted and pulled and levered it up the doorstep and over the threshold with a grunt of effort that made Mr Elias glad he'd asked for help.

He peered into the front room but realized there wouldn't be enough space to open the box without disrupting his own neat life, so he led the driver towards the second room at the back of the house, with Jennifer's piano and all the bits and bobs he'd packed up after she'd died, but *still* hadn't taken to the charity shop.

"In here will be fine, thanks," he said.

Then he thought he'd better tip the man, so he dug about in his pocket for a pound. He knew a pound wasn't a lot, but he had no idea of how much one tipped a deliveryman these days, if at all.

"Thank you," he said. "And this is for you."

He looked up from his palmful of change, too late to see what hit him.

The UPS driver's name was Tyson Reid. He had been named for his father's boxer dog. For a short while they had overlapped, he and the dog, but then the first Tyson had been hit by a delivery van outside the flats one summer evening, and after that their household was a lot less confusing.

It wasn't a UPS van.

Young Tyson had been destined for great things. That's what his mother always told him, anyway. And for a while it seemed that that might actually be the case. At school he was as smart as his friends would allow him to be while still remaining friends, and he had a knack for football that might have become a gift if he'd kept working at it. He played for the school and for a local youth-club team — Hackney Hunters — and was once invited to a training camp at West Ham. It came to nothing though, and after a while he'd started to lose interest in hard work without tangible reward.

His mother gave him her stock lecture on instant gratification, but she wasn't the one who had to run three miles in the rain four times a week for fuck all. So he'd stopped playing football, apart from against the wall by the garages where all the kids hung out, and by the time he was sixteen, Tyson wasn't smart any more.

He had dribbled out of school, rather than graduated, and had a brief brush with the law when he'd attempted to make money by selling a little dope. Nothing much — just baggies to friends and acquaintances — but you'd have thought he was Breaking Bad, the way his mother raged and ranted at him as the police slowly piled everything he'd ever owned in a jumble on the landing outside his bedroom door.

One of them had trodden on his Millennium Falcon.

He'd said, "Oops, sorry," — but with a dead look that had made Tyson realize that he wasn't sorry at all, and that Tyson could expect more of the same if he chose to go down the path of more of the same.

It was that, rather than his mother's fury, that had saved him. Reminded him of how much easier his life had been when he'd been smart.

It wasn't too late for Tyson. Football and university were no longer on the table, but — because the police had decided on a warning and a broken *Star Wars* toy rather than an arrest — an honest job was still an option, and Tyson took it.

He'd got a crappy nightshift in a petrol station, but it had paid for driving lessons, and then he'd started at UPS. Sorting and labelling for the first two years, then finally on the vans. He liked being out on the road all day long, with people always happy to see him, and only his ugly brown uniform to remind him that he wasn't his own boss.

It wasn't the life Tyson had imagined for himself, but it wasn't bad. He started playing football again — just a Sunday-morning league, but he'd forgotten how much he loved it, and had retained enough skill to shine.

He had a girlfriend, Rose, and a baby on the way. They were going to call her Brady or Fern. They were on a list for a flat, and *must* be getting near the top. Tyson's mother was knitting up a stocking-stitch storm, and his father had popped up from God knows where to put £50 in an account for the baby. He made a great show of it and said he was going to put in £50 a month to pay for her education, and then they never saw him again. But it was something to laugh about, and — because he'd opened the account and given them the book — Tyson figured it was a good idea anyway, and so, whenever he could, *he* put £50 a month into it instead. Brady or Fern had £300 to her name already, and she wasn't even born!

Plus Christmas was only a few days away and he'd be getting a good bonus because work was crazy busy from all the people buying stuff online instead of getting off their arses to go shopping.

Tyson was grateful for their sloth.

Happy with his lot.

348

He sang under his breath as he drove. Mashed-up snatches of childhood songs and raps, about bare necessities and drunken sailors and bitch-slapping hoes.

"*Ear-lie in the morning . . .*"

On December the nineteenth, Tyson was despatched to pick up a parcel in west London. It was a big heavy box, but luckily the guy had it on the kerb for him already on a sack trolley. He even helped Tyson to manoeuvre it on to the hydraulic ramp of his van, even though he was dressed in loafers and a golf jumper.

Tyson got him to sign the paperwork, then raised the ramp and closed the door and jumped into his cab.

The guy was in the passenger seat.

"Hey, man," said Tyson. "Get out!"

But the guy wouldn't get out.

The guy had a knife and a cold look in his little black eyes.

He made Tyson drive to somewhere out near Heathrow — a broad flat field where hungry gypsy ponies were tethered by long blue ropes in the snow.

He made him take off his ugly brown uniform.

Tyson stood shivering and embarrassed in his underwear, watching the man put on his clothes and wondering whether he would still get his Christmas bonus.

He knew he was being robbed.

But it wasn't until it happened that he knew he was being murdered.

Mr Elias opened the big box cautiously while the UPS driver sat on the sofa, oozing anticipation in a repulsive parody of Christmas.

They were in the front room, but the room had been so vandalized that opening the box would no longer make any difference one way or another. Mr Elias imagined that the rest of the house must be in a similar state, and was almost grateful that he hadn't seen it. He had come round, tied and gagged on the sofa, listening to the sound of his home being destroyed around him.

UPS would be hearing from *him*.

He had been scared. He was *still* scared, but that was fading to a fatalistic numbness, coupled with discomfort and growing irritation.

The driver seemed to have no interest in him whatsoever. He hadn't hit him since that first time, or even looked at him, until he had pulled him into a sitting position, pushed the box in front of him, laughed and said, "Open it."

He hadn't untied Mr Elias's hands, but after he finally got a fingernail under the brown tape on one side, the whole thing opened quite easily to reveal those little foam peanuts that protect the contents.

"Take them out," said the deliveryman.

Mr Elias scooped up a double handful and looked for somewhere to place them, but the deliveryman slapped his hands from underneath, knocking the whole lot into the air and scattering them all over the carpet and the coffee table.

He laughed like a schoolyard bully.

Mr Elias would have had something to say about *that*, but the gag wouldn't allow it. It was one of his own pillowcases, stuffed hard into his mouth and taped around the back of his head with the same brown tape as was on the box.

He scooped handfuls of peanuts on to the floor until, a few inches down, he touched something *weird* and recoiled with a little *nnngg* of surprise.

The UPS man laughed and shouted, "Happy Christmas!" and reached into the box, scooping the peanuts into the air in great showers of indoor snow, then ran out of the room, giggling.

Mr Elias leaned forward gingerly, then grunted in shock.

There was a head in the box.

CHAPTER
FORTY-SEVEN

23 December

The killer batted around the poky little house in a caged frenzy of anticipation.

Everywhere he sought enlightenment. He stuck his fingers into every curious crevice. Every cupboard was spilled, every cabinet bared.

He walked on jam and lettuce.

He laughed at the UPS driver shivering on the phone in his pocket. *At least give me some shoes, mate! How am I gonna walk home?*

"You're not!" he shouted gleefully in time to his own voice. "You're not walking anywhere!"

Now and then he pressed his ear against the adjoining wall, closing his eyes to hear better, silently muttering in time to the plans he heard in his ear or his head.

There had been a piano; now it filled the back room with splinters and spun hoops of golden wire, and in the front room every ship and sepia portrait had been ripped from the wall to show much cleaner paper and paint underneath.

Squares of loss and pain.

352

No more. No more!

He had eviscerated the house and now was so full of life that he thought he might burst! He tore off the brown uniform, and felt his skin straining to contain all the life he'd collected; all the blood and the guts and the eyes and the hair and the teeth and the meat and the bones filled him up to the *brim*! He was replete with life! His legs were all muscle, his cock like a rock. His once-numb heart was a great booming chamber pumping ox blood and fire!

And his scar held tight. Not even a squeak.

"Look at me!" He spun on the rug, with arms like sparklers. "*Look at me!*"

The sofa said nothing, exploded and torn.

The chairs said nothing, piled like Jenga.

The man said nothing, bound and gagged.

Detective Superintendent Rees walked past the window, and the killer dropped to his haunches beside the big box.

The policeman went down Eve Singer's path, and then the faint sound of the rusty latch on the gate took the killer back to that very first fateful night.

Right back to the beginning, in a wonderful circle.

"The end is nigh," he hissed in the ear of Mr Elias.

Then he ran up the stairs.

Ten at a time!

To the attic.

CHAPTER
FORTY-EIGHT

Christmas Eve

Christmas Eve never really dawned. London became marginally paler around the edges, but otherwise day was almost indistinguishable from night, as lights stayed on, and a sky the colour of a winter sea gave fair warning of foul weather. The top news on the *Today* programme was that the bookies were whining about the white Christmas to come that was going to put them all out of business.

Emily Aguda rolled over and turned the radio off.

TrrrrrrT.

She sighed and went downstairs.

Eve Singer was already up and dressed, drinking coffee and playing with the handcuffs.

TrrrrrrT.

Aguda poured herself a mug and sat down.

"Nervous?" she said. There was no point in beating about the elephant in the room.

Eve nodded. "Feel sick."

She slapped the cuffs over her left wrist, then disengaged and did the right — all in the glittering blink of an eye.

Aguda looked at the clock. 09.30. They were due at Madame Tussaud's at noon, and she was allowing two hours to get there because of the snow.

"Once we're moving, you'll feel better."

"Sure," said Eve. "You're probably right."

"Great." Aguda drained her mug and stood up. "I'll grab a quick shower and my *enormous gun* and we'll go kick some serial-killer ass."

Eve smiled.

But when Emily Aguda came downstairs twenty minutes later, Eve had gone.

Shit shit shit.

Aguda called Eve repeatedly while she searched the house. She even peered into the attic with a torch but found only a rocking horse, ghostly with a thick layer of dust. Then she called Huw Rees to let him know they had a problem.

"Has she gone or been taken?" he demanded.

Aguda hesitated. She'd only been in the shower for ten minutes, but a shower was an effective sound barrier.

"I'd say she's gone, sir. There's no sign of forced entry or a struggle, and I think she's the type who would give him a run for his money."

"So she's chickened out."

Aguda hesitated, then said, "Yes, sir." She didn't like the term "chickened out" because she didn't blame Eve Singer for not wanting to be bait for a serial killer. But what other explanation could there be?

She stood at the kitchen table, awaiting further instructions.

But before Rees could give them, she said, "*Shit!* Sir — I think she's taken my cuffs!"

The silence on the line told her that Superintendent Rees grasped just as well as she did that if Eve Singer had bolted simply because she'd chickened out, that was one thing.

But if she'd deliberately taken Aguda's handcuffs with her, that might be a whole *other* thing . . .

"Right," said Rees. "We'll proceed early to the scene. We'll look out for her there in case she's thinking about going freelance. You stay there and see if you can speak to her, or come up with any ideas about where she might have gone or what she might be doing."

"Yes, sir."

"Stay in touch."

"Yes, sir."

"This is *all* we bloody need," sighed Rees.

"Yes, sir," Aguda agreed, with feeling.

She hung up and immediately started to ring Eve again. As she did, she jogged up the stairs and started her search again — this time looking for clues in the form of items she was pretty sure had disappeared along with Eve. She couldn't find her bank cards. There was a phone in the drawer next to the bed, but it was an old model and didn't switch on and had a grubby sticker on the screen that said BUY ONE GET ONE FREE!

So Eve had her phone with her, she just wasn't responding. Hopefully out of choice — however irritating that might be.

356

Emily Aguda tried to think like Eve Singer. Her father had been kidnapped, her life was at risk, the killer was still at large. And the police weren't helping.

She felt a jab of shame. If she were Eve Singer, she'd have lost faith in the Met's ability to rescue her father. In fact, if *she* were Eve Singer . . .

She'd be opening hostage negotiations on her own.

A sudden fluttering in Emily Aguda's gut told her that she was on the right track. She hurried downstairs. The clock in the hallway showed ten thirty.

Already?

She stood in the front room, trying to think *faster*, as the hamster ambled along in his squeaky wheel behind her.

Could Eve Singer have put something in her diary? Feeling a little stupid, Aguda did a quick circuit of the house looking for one. There was a calendar over the fridge with two Border terriers on it, but it was from two years ago. She checked today's date anyway.

It said *Do Christmas Shopping*.

She laughed at Eve. And then laughed again at herself. What had she expected? *10a.m. Yoga, 1p.m. Serial Killer?*

Even if Eve *had* needed a reminder, nobody under the age of seventy put that stuff in a real calendar any more. It would be on her phone.

Which she had with her.

But which *might* just be synced with her computer . . .

In the front room on the coffee table was the trailing power cable for Eve's laptop. If she had taken her laptop, then surely she'd have taken the cable too?

Aguda started at one end of the room and searched it. She found the slim silver MacBook hidden under the sofa cushion, and plugged it in and opened it up. She had a little pang about the invasion of privacy, but her priority was to keep Eve alive, and that end could be justified by almost any means.

The browser was already open, but it looked as if all Eve Singer had been doing online was her Christmas shopping.

As far as Aguda could tell, everybody was getting a charity goat.

Emily Aguda explored the Mac, seeking familiar programs and menus to guide her. There was a calendar, but there was no event or reminder listed for today. She found the Search program and typed in trigger words like "killer" and "murder", but got so many results that she had to refine it to "Christmas Eve" and "December 24", but still found nothing relevant.

There was a drop-down menu called Recent Items. Twenty file names appeared in a new window, and she ran her eye down them for clues.

She didn't need to be Sherlock Holmes . . .

EXHIBITION.pdf

Aguda opened the file.

EXHIBITION
Venue: Madame Tussaud's
Date: Christmas Eve
Time: 14.00

It was a copy of the flyer that the neighbour had found in the phone box. Maybe Eve would be using it at some point in her background report on the case.

Aguda thought that felt possible. But it didn't feel *right*.

She dug about and found the properties for the file. The new window listed the type of file, its size and location, and the date it was created — December the twentieth.

She stared at the screen.

That couldn't be.

She counted back in her head. The flyer in the phone box had been found on the twenty-second, Mr Elias had been sure that it hadn't been there even the day before. So how could Eve have seen it before the twentieth? She couldn't. It was impossible.

Unless she was the one who'd *made* it!

That thought stopped Aguda in her tracks. *That* was possible. Confusing and disturbing, but definitely possible. And if Eve had created the flyer on the twentieth, had *she* put it in the phone box?

Aguda thought of the brief night-vision glimpse of muffled face and glittering eyes before the flyer had been pasted over the lens of the hidden camera. They had assumed it was Vandenberg but it could have been anyone. It could have been Eve Singer.

But why would she do that? Aguda struggled to follow the logic. If Eve wanted to contact the killer, why would she make a flyer and put it somewhere she knew it would be so easily found? Giving away their plans to the police?

Aguda gasped as the answer hit her like iced water — a shock and then a chill.

The flyer was a decoy!

What had she told Eve? *To catch a killer, you have to think like a killer.*

And Eve had replied: *That's exactly what I'm trying to do.*

The killer had sent Guy Smith a fake flyer — a decoy to misdirect him. If she was thinking like a killer, Eve's flyer would have been created not to connect with Vandenberg, but to misdirect the police.

And they had been duly misdirected, thought Aguda grimly. Like a fool having his pockets picked while gawping at something shiny.

And if there was a fake flyer, then there must be a real one!

But *where*?

Aguda didn't know.

She only knew two things with sickening certainty.

That the firearms unit was lying in wait at Madame Tussaud's for a killer who would never arrive.

And that — *somewhere* — Eve Singer was going to try to save her father from a serial killer.

Alone.

CHAPTER
FORTY-NINE

TrrrrrrT.

Joe drove east, towards central London. The roads were clear of snow, and none was yet falling, despite the lowering sky.

"Do you have the camera?" said Eve. "He'll want to see a camera."

TrrrrrrT.

Joe only nodded, and glanced nervously at the cuffs. They were at Hyde Park Corner.

But instead of turning north towards Madame Tussaud's, Joe took a right and they curved south, and headed for the river.

Joe stared at the back of a bus. "I just hope you know what you're doing."

"I'm going to a showdown with a serial killer, Joe," said Eve grimly. "How the *fuck* would I know what I'm doing?"

Aguda left a message on Eve's phone.

"Eve, it's Emily Aguda. I know what you're planning. Please don't do this alone. Please call me and tell me where you are so I can come and help you. It's not too late."

Aguda hoped desperately that was true.

She called Huw Rees at Madame Tussaud's and told him her theory.

"You may well be right," he said. "But I can't move on a hunch."

"But sir —"

"Emily," he cut her off. "I trust you, but you have no viable alternative for me. You bring me any shred of evidence of where this bastard is going to be at two o'clock today and I'll move to wherever the hell that is. But until then, this location is all we've got."

"Yes, sir." Aguda hung up. She stared at her reflection in the living-room mirror. Rees was right. She knew that. But she also knew he was wrong. She would just have to prove it to him, or a few hours from now they'd get a call from *somewhere* in London, and go and pick up the pieces.

Of Eve Singer, most likely.

Or her poor father.

The clock over the mantel read 11.17.

There was irregular banging through the walls from next door, and a plane passed low overhead. She barely registered them now. It was amazing how the senses just excised what was unnecessary. Made things invisible, inaudible.

But it didn't mean they weren't there. She just had to work harder to find them. She just had to *think* harder.

She opened the file again. *Exhibition.pdf*

She looked at the properties of the file again.

She ran her eye down Recent Items again, opening files at random, scanning them for relevance, closing them and moving on.

Then her eye was caught by a file name at the bottom of the list.

Watergate.avi

She opened the file. It was the iWitness news report about the killer dogs.

Aguda recalled her sarcastic comment: *It's not Watergate.*

And it wasn't Watergate, but the report was still pretty good. Serious yet ghoulish. Aguda supposed that was the skill of TV crime reporting, even when the alleged criminals were eight inches high. She let it run while her subconscious rumbled on in the background. Eve did her piece to camera outside the building, talking about the dogs by name — Boris and Bubba — while standing in front of the hoarding covered with —

Flyers.

Aguda gasped. She looked at the screen without seeing it as her memory went into overdrive.

Eve Singer had not let her watch the TV report. At the time she'd thought Eve was just being churlish because of her Watergate comment.

Maybe there was another reason . . .

She hit Replay and watched the shot again. Not looking at Eve this time, but at the hoarding behind her.

And there it was.

She hit Pause and studied the image. You'd have to be looking for it. Or studying the report very closely. Or watching it repeatedly.

You'd have to be obsessed . . .

Off to one side of the bottom of the hoarding, freshly pasted over the other flyers:

EXHIBITION
Venue: Tate Modern
Date: December 24
Time: 14.00

The Tate Modern gallery.
What better place for an exhibition?

CHAPTER
FIFTY

The Tate Modern squatted darkly on the South Bank of the Thames.

The former power station's utilitarian bulk was a brooding presence that could not be improved by the shimmering Millennium Bridge, the Eye to the west, or even the saintly gaze of St Paul's Cathedral directly across the water.

It was what it was. Sullen and squat and ugly and with a single giant tower its only remarkable feature. For thirty years it had powered south London, along with its more elegant, more popular sibling at Battersea, until oil prices drove it out of business. Even the knowledge that it was now home to the world's most treasured modern art could not change its brutal post-war façade.

But inside, the power station was changed beyond recognition. It had been disembowelled. The turbines and pipes and pumps had been removed and in their place were airy galleries filled with light and beauty.

Joe and Eve descended the broad ramp from the early winter dusk into the hall, and stopped at the bottom, jostling with other amazed visitors whose first glimpse of the Turbine Hall itself might well be the most breathtaking moment of their entire visit. Five storeys high and running almost the whole length of the building, the hall was as impressive as any art contained in the gallery.

Eve and Joe stared up, open-mouthed, at the giant iron tree that almost filled the cavernous space. Its thick, wintry black branches stretched out between the balconies above, and dwarfed the tiny people below, who milled about its trunk like ants.

"That's *big*," said Joe, momentarily distracted from the whole serial-killer thing.

Eve smiled. "You like it? I can cancel the goat . . ."

"Hmm," he mused. "But where would I put it?"

They both laughed and then looked around, sobering up quickly as they remembered why they were here.

"Where are we going?" said Joe.

"I don't know," Eve confessed, and looked around a little nervously. "But if I don't find him, I'm sure he'll find me."

"There's still time to change your mind."

"Maybe for you," she said, then looked at him seriously. "I wouldn't blame you if you wanted no part of this, Joe."

He shrugged. "I couldn't just leave you to it," he said. "But I still think it's a bad plan."

"It *is* a bad plan," she said. "But it's the only plan we've got."

"It's the only plan *you've* got. *My* plan is, we go to the airport right now and fly to Jamaica. Sun, sea and sand while somebody else sorts all this murder shit out. That sounds like a *better* plan, don't you think?"

"And what about my dad?"

Joe reddened. "Sorry," he said. "I was only thinking of you."

"I know you were." She kissed him hard on the cheek, and he looked at her suspiciously.

"You're not going somewhere, are you?" He was only half joking.

"Of course not!"

She looked away from him. She hated lying to Joe.

Eve started up the stairs to the galleries. As she walked away from Joe, she felt as if she were stepping into quicksand. Suddenly shaky underfoot, and with no safe anchor, she felt she was stepping off the edge of the world.

She took out her phone to remind herself one last time of the slip-slidey face of William Stafford Vandenberg.

She had never thought Death would look so *ordinary*.

After the Turbine Hall, the white-walled galleries at first felt boxy and nightmarish. She hurried through three rooms without seeing a thing before she remembered that she was supposed to be looking for the killer — and that she was supposed to breathe. She slowed down and tried to focus on faces, but it was crowded and everybody looked like him — and nobody did. His face kept dropping out of her mind, so unremarkable that it couldn't take root. She kept second-guessing herself. So scared she'd miss him that she kept turning for a second look, and missing someone else . . .

She felt dizzy. She was in a panic. She stood still and breathed and breathed and breathed until she felt that air was actually entering her lungs.

Her head cleared a little and she looked round for Joe. He was there — across the busy gallery, frowning in concern. She looked away from him, so as not to give him away. He was using the hidden camera he'd had at the Barnstormer Theatre, so as to stay under the radar of staff.

Eve took another deep breath and prepared to move on. She turned and almost bumped into Elvis Presley.

He was nine feet tall, and silver and black. All quiff and narrow hips, angled for danger and sex. No hint of the drugs or the fried peanut-butter-and-banana sandwiches to come. Only his youth and beauty were captured here on this canvas, and standing in front of the painting made her feel somehow *connected* to Elvis. She smiled and turned so that Joe could share the feeling with her, but there were too many people passing between them and she couldn't see him.

She looked around her — half for Joe, half for Vandenberg. She kept expecting to lock eyes with the killer and feel the lurch of recognition and fear.

But all eyes were on the walls, and even hers could not be dragged away for long.

Elvis had opened the door, and Eve floated through the galleries like a child turning the pages of the world's most amazing pop-up book — with every wonder seen through new eyes, and revealed between the shoulders of strangers. After viewing each masterpiece Eve looked around her, but in seeking a killer, she found only more magnetic beauty. The milling crowds would thin and suddenly part to surprise her with *Whaam!* or refresh her with *Splash*. There was a Freud nude, all pallid fat and cold light; buxom girls baking on a Matisse beach; a shimmering waterfall of Klimt.

The crowd split to reveal a surprising Van Gogh. Surely too early for this collection — and even Eve could tell it was not a *good* Van Gogh. Not sunflowers, or a self-portrait. Only dull, windy cypresses and pinkish skies and a brown ploughed field. And . . .

Eve leaned in and felt the breath sucked from her lungs.

And a thumbprint.

A single accidental print in the thick paint.

The realization struck her like lightning.

She was standing where the artist had stood. Vincent Van Gogh had stood right here — *right here* — and watched these creamy-pink clouds roll in, watched these cypresses sway in the breeze, travelled every muddy inch of these furrows — first with his boots and then with his brush.

And then he had reached out and touched the sky.

Maybe while lifting the canvas off the easel, or holding it as he tilted his uneven head for another view. Or had a bug landed on a cloud? A tiny French aphid, squashed by a quick thumb?

That left its mark there.

For ever.

Had he decided he liked it that way?

Had he intended to correct it but run out of time?

Had he even *noticed*?

Or had his feverish mind already moved on from the dull field and the trees? Had it already left this staid, unromantic day for a starry, starry night?

Eve was overwhelmed.

The whorl of thumb in a swirl of sky was like time travel — connecting her not only to the artist himself but to every other person and animal and tree and rock that ever was, or ever would be.

This was immortality. Eve knew it in her very core.

This was what the beautiful dead left behind when they moved out of the corporeal and into the hearts and minds of all humankind. This connection, this sense of sharing something wonderful, something beyond mere life, something that had endured and *would* endure. The painting was worth millions, but the thumbprint was priceless — a mark made on history, a trilobite, a hieroglyph, a footprint on the Moon. Eve's heart broke for anyone who had not experienced such beauty. Her throat ached so hard that she thought she would weep.

If she only lifted her arm, she could place *her* thumb where *his* thumb had been . . .

She raised her trembling thumb to the canvas.

"Hello, Eve."

Eve flinched from the painting.

The killer stood beside her.

He looked anything but ordinary.

His head was newly shaven, red-nicked in places, and unnaturally small. His brows were shaven too, making his pale forehead lumpy and alien. His eyes were as black as the photo had promised, but in life, oddly jittery. Although he was looking at her, Eve found it hard to maintain eye contact.

Strapped to his chest was his phone, the camera lens pointing at her. She thought of Kevin Barr.

Now she was the star.

And she knew how this movie ended.

"This is perfect, Eve. Trust you to get it right." He smiled. His teeth were short and white — like a child's teeth.

"Where's my father?"

"Have you seen the Bacon exhibition?"

"No."

"We could see it together," he said. Then added, almost shyly, "If you like?"

"Where's my father?" said Eve. "We had a deal."

He looked disappointed. "Straight down to business?"

The business of her murder. She kept breathing. Kept going. "Yes."

The killer sighed. Then he took his phone from the clip on his chest.

Eve glanced at it; she knew what was coming and got angry. "Not on your phone! I want to see him *here*. For *real*."

He ignored her and tapped at the phone.

Eve watched his wrist. His left wrist. The one that wasn't moving so much. She'd practised so often. It would be easy. The cuffs were snug on her right wrist. It would be so easy to flick one open and snap it closed . . .

She did a quick mental rehearsal. Her thumb releasing the catch. The flick of the wrist. The *TrrrrrrT* of the ratchet clicking home . . .

And then he couldn't escape. Couldn't get away. Let him murder her right here beside the Van Gogh. He'd be cuffed to her corpse and Joe and the police would arrest him and make him reveal Duncan's whereabouts, and her father would be safe.

She twisted her hand and gripped the free cuff.

Slid the catch open soundlessly . . .

"Here."

He held out the phone and all thoughts of the cuffs left her mind.

Duncan Singer was sitting in the dark. Just his head, shoulders and chest were visible, but Eve could see enough to recognize her own father.

Alive.

"Dad! Are you OK?"

There was only white noise for a long moment, while Duncan Singer looked around him, seeking the source of the words. Then his irritable voice came out of the darkness, "Who's Dad?"

Eve nearly cried with relief. "Where *are* you?"

But the killer snatched the phone away. "No cheating!"

"You said you'd let him go. We had a *deal*."

"And I'll stick to it. As long as you do."

She pointed at Duncan's chest, where a line of green numbers flickered. "What's that?"

"Oh," said the killer, "that's the timer for the bomb."

"W-what?"

He grinned and Eve stared at his little white teeth in shock, while a deep, dark pain began to spread just under her ribs, as if every organ inside her were being squeezed dry by a giant fist.

"I like your father, Eve. But if I don't get what I want . . . if something happened to me, if I were *denied* . . ." he paused meaningfully and then shrugged.

She felt numb. But she couldn't be numb. She had to think.

Engage brain, Eve!

She stopped looking dumbly at the killer and focused once more on the phone, searching desperately for clues — seeking more than the dim picture had to offer. The only light was the ghostly green glow of the numbers running down.

01:58:29 . . . 28 . . . 27 . . .

Her father had less than two hours to live.

But there was *something else*. Something more important. Her gut told her that, and her gut was rarely wrong, but *what was it?*

The killer slid the phone back to the harness on his chest.

"Can I speak to him again?"

"No."

Shit.

Desperately, she reran their brief exchange in her head. She was missing something critical. About her father? Or the room? Or the numbers, or the sound of his voice . . . *something*! Eve was desperate to speak to him again — to see him again — just one more time! If only she could work out where he was, she wouldn't have to honour this horrific bargain. She could just turn and run away, leave this nightmare behind her and find her father and live happily ever after. If only she knew where he was.

If only.

"How do I know you won't kill him anyway? Afterwards?"

The killer looked at her intently. "Nobody has ever trusted me like you did that first night we met, Eve — and you can trust me now. We have a deal, and I plan to honour it."

He looked beyond her to the galleries and the crowds that filled them. "Sharing your death with the public is the most . . ." he searched for the right word, "*perfect* thing you'll ever do. Beyond art. Beyond *life*."

His eyes jittered and glittered, but only his little teeth smiled.

"And afterwards I will halt the countdown and release your father, unharmed. We have a special connection, Eve, and it cannot be broken by mere death."

His uncertain eyes shone with emotion and Eve felt sick. She wanted to hurt him. She wanted to kill him. She was ashamed by the savagery of her hatred.

But, however crazy, this was *his* truth — and it was the only truth that counted here.

She could only trust him.

So when he said, "Follow me," she did.

Out of the high white galleries and on to the fourth-floor balcony. There were fewer people here —

just a half-dozen or so, leaning over, looking down, waving at friends far below, or gazing out into the dark branches of the huge tree.

She saw Joe. He was keeping pace, maybe thirty yards behind them. She met his eyes briefly and saw growing concern there. She looked away, before she could waver, and focused on the killer's back. He reached the end of the balcony but didn't stop. Instead, in one smooth movement, he put his hands on the rail and vaulted lightly off the edge and on to the tree.

Then he turned and held out his hand to her.

"Come."

She hesitated. His hand. His wrist. The cuffs. *Do it now! Do it now!*

"*Eve!*"

She looked over her shoulder. It was Joe, breaking into a run. Trying to stop her. Trying to save her!

But if she were saved, her father would die.

So Eve Singer took the killer's outstretched hand and climbed over the railing and on to the broad branch of the great iron tree.

Now they really *were* in it together.

CHAPTER
FIFTY-ONE

For a horrible, dizzying moment Eve was on her knees, looking down through the gnarled branches to the floor of the Turbine Hall a hundred feet below. She was frozen by terror, unable to move.

The killer helped her to her unsteady feet beside him. "Don't look down," he told her. "Look at me."

"OK," she said.

He started to lead her along the branch. It widened as it approached the thick trunk, but wasn't wholly flat, and Eve gripped the killer with one hand while the other reached gingerly from twig to wrought-iron twig to maintain her balance, while all the time she tried to *think*.

Her brain raced, still rerunning the video clip. There was *something* . . . Something in the dark room. In the vague shape of Duncan. In her father's words or his voice or . . .

Something.

But what?

While her feet found safe passage, her head hurt. Her whole life was about hourly deadlines, but never had she been more conscious of time ticking past her —

away from her. Running out. She had to suppress panic.

She had to think fast. *Faster!*

With every sway and wobble, the crowd below gasped, as if they were watching a high-wire act. But the killer was sure-footed, and held her hand tight.

"Scared yet?" he teased.

"No," she lied.

He laughed and said, "Always so bold, Eve. That's why I love you."

"If you love me, why kill me?"

"Is there any better love than this? That I would kill you, and you would die for me. What are songs and roses compared to that?"

"I think I'm getting the thin end of the stick."

He laughed again.

They reached the massive black trunk of the tree, and he turned and looked down, holding her hand so that they both faced the crowd. "We have our audience, Eve."

Far below, growing hundreds of pink faces turned up to them in anticipation. Eyes wide, hands over mouths.

Phones at the ready to capture the thrill of death.

Eve felt sharp shame. It was exactly the audience she deserved.

The killer reached into his pocket and drew out a small coil of gleaming gold wire. He knelt and knotted it around the thick branch they stood on.

Piano wire.

Eve recognized it from her childhood, when she'd taken lessons. "Chopsticks" and "Für Elise".

"Do you play?" she said stupidly.

The killer said nothing as he rose beside her. And before Eve understood what was happening, he'd looped the other end of the wire over her head.

The crowd gasped and Eve froze.

Suddenly everything felt very real. Up until now it had been too mad to be real — too crazy to be true. And now it was not. Now it was mad and crazy *and* true. Eve swayed on the branch and gripped the killer's arm for support.

This was how she was going to die. She would jump, or he would push, and the wire would slice through her neck like soft cheese.

And her head would come off.

It was *real* — and the terror was so extreme she couldn't move. Couldn't breathe. Couldn't hear. Couldn't *think*. There was a roaring in her ears that blocked all sound, like a 747 making its final approach —

And the answer to everything exploded in her head like a wonderful firework.

The killer said something, but under the thunderous beat of her own blood, his lips moved without sound. She stared at him, and he asked again.

"Are you. Scared. Yet?"

He wasn't teasing. Not this time.

"No," said Eve.

And she wasn't lying.

Not this time.

Because she knew where her father was!

Her gut had been right. The clue was right there in the clip. She'd sought answers with her eyes, but the solution was in her ears! That white noise that had faded before Duncan had spoken — she'd known it all her life . . .

It was a plane passing over their house.

Duncan Singer was in his own home! His own fucking *home*!

"Give me your hand, you beautiful and tender form." The killer started to recite the poem in a gentle, sing-song voice.

Eve almost laughed. A mere second ago, she had been prepared to die.

But now she was only prepared to kill.

"I am a friend, and come not to punish."

He was trying to lull her to eternal sleep.

But Eve Singer wasn't sleeping. Eve Singer was *thinking like a killer*.

And feeling like one too. Cool. Confident. Calculating.

"Be of good cheer!" he said. *"I am not fierce."*

I am, thought Eve with cold murder in her belly. *I'm FUCKING fierce!*

Slowly, she sank to her knees, as if in prayer. He nodded down at her in satisfaction.

"Softly shall you sleep —"

In one swift move, Eve grabbed his ankles and yanked his feet from under him.

The audience roared.

The killer twisted awkwardly and dropped on to his side with a grunt. He half rose; he flailed at her, and overbalanced; he grabbed wildly at a metal twig.

Then at her leg.

And then they *both* fell.

CHAPTER
FIFTY-TWO

If Eve hadn't been thinking like a killer, she would have been dead. As she was dragged off the tree, she flicked out the handcuffs.

The crowd screamed —

TrrrrrrT.

The cuff locked on a slender metal limb and Eve screamed in pain as she jolted to a cruel halt.

The killer still clung to her legs.

They dangled together like baubles from the tree, high above the ground. He clutched at her thighs like a terrified monkey, squealing in terror, his own legs kicking the air below them, weighing her down. Eve looked up and prayed that Aguda's cuffs and the artist's welding and her own flesh and bone would hold. The first two looked solid enough, but already her skin was starting to stretch and tear, while her palm folded unnaturally, painfully, in on itself — seeking away through the sharp metal loop . . .

She slid half an inch, and the fine golden wire bit into her neck.

"Help me!" the killer gasped. "I can't hold on!"

"Then let go!"

He didn't, but slipped a few more inches down her in a relentless drag. Eve shouted in pain and looked up to see the skin slowly start to peel up her hand in its effort to fit through the shackle. She twisted and pulled and kicked one desperate leg free of his grasp.

He shouted furiously, "If I fall, he'll die! You'll never find him!"

"I already *found him*, you prick! I already *know* where he is! And as soon as I've kicked you off me I'm going home and we'll all have a good laugh about you over Christmas fucking *lunch!*"

"Whore!" he roared. "*Whore!*" He tried to climb her. Strengthened by fury, his fingers squeezed and bruised her thighs, his nails scraping deep gouges in her hip. His hand grabbed for hers . . . Eve shrieked and snatched it away, then groped above her head and found the cuffs with her left hand; she gripped the short chain — a little relief for her right wrist — and started to twist and strain against him. She felt *something* start to trickle down her neck, under her right ear. She hoped it was sweat; she knew it was blood. How much flesh and tendon was left between the wire and her jugular vein? Half an inch? Half a *millimetre*?

She needed him *off her!*

Eve ignored everything but her own survival. Kicked madly at him. Felt his grip loosening —

His contorted face was flecked with blood that Eve knew must be hers. And beyond him, below him, the crowd — the audience they'd both craved. The faceless, amorphous mass of stupid humanity staring up expectantly, like sea lions waiting for fish.

Except for one small space where the masses had parted to give room and respect to . . .

. . . a tiny black woman pointing a gun.

Even from here, the gun looked enormous.

The killer saw it — and then looked up at Eve with such raw terror that she laughed.

"Now it's *your* turn to die!" she cried.

And then kicked him in the face. And again. And again. Even as he clutched and jerked beneath her, and even as her own hand funnelled agonizingly through the metal cuff.

"Not me!" he shrieked. "Not me!"

"Isn't it beautiful?" she laughed at him. "Don't you feel *lucky?*"

"We had a deal!" he screamed. "This is *my* exhibition!"

"Well, everyone's watching you now," she said. "You fucking show-off!"

And she kicked him one last time.

The crowd scattered as the killer fell, but Eve never saw him hit the ground.

With an inhuman howl, her thumb finally gave way and her hand slipped right through the shackle of Emily Aguda's best handcuffs.

But she didn't fall.

Why didn't she fall?

For a moment Eve was disorientated. She swayed drunkenly in the air — still waiting for the dizzying drop to her death.

She looked up into Joe's face — sweat on his brow, and teeth gritted with the effort of holding on to her slick, bloody wrists.

Slowly he hauled her up to the precarious safety of the broad iron branch.

He loosened the golden wire from around her bloody throat while she cradled her swelling hand and shook like a leaf on a great iron tree.

"We have to go," she croaked.

He nodded. "I've called an ambulance."

"No!" she said. "We have to go *home!*"

Joe didn't argue. He led her shakily back to the balcony, while far below them, the last audience Eve would ever have barked their approval and clapped their flippers and jostled to film the exploded corpse on the gallery floor.

CHAPTER
FIFTY-THREE

"Eve! Wait for the bomb squad! *WAIT!*"

But Eve Singer didn't wait. She had opened the door and was out of the Range Rover before Aguda had brought it to a halt. She disappeared through the garden gate.

"Shit!" Aguda slammed on the brakes in exasperation and threw open her own door. "Is she always like this?"

"Always," said Joe as he followed both of them.

Aguda thought he made it sound like a good thing.

"Dad! *Dad!*"

Eve ran through the house.

Duncan wasn't downstairs. She ran upstairs. His room. *Her* room. The box room.

"*DAD!*"

Joe and Aguda came after her.

"He's not here," cried Eve, with panic rising within her. "He's *not here!*"

She'd been so sure that he *would* be. So sure, that she hadn't cared any more if the killer died. Kicked him to his death! She didn't need him to find Duncan! She *knew* where he was! All she had to do was go home and he'd be *right there*! She *knew* it. Her gut had told her so.

Her gut had been wrong.

How stupid she'd been. How arrogant! To equate random white noise with the ambient soundtrack of her own life! Even if what she'd heard on the video *was* a plane — and even if that plane was landing or taking off from Heathrow — there must be a hundred thousand buildings under the flight path. A hundred thousand places Duncan could be!

And if this wasn't the right place, then how would they find him?

The ghastly truth was that they wouldn't. Not in time to save his life.

Eve checked her watch. Fifteen minutes to go.

It was too late. Her father was going to die.

Somewhere.

And it would be her fault.

"I smell cat's pee."

Eve and Joe both looked at Aguda. Her nose was wrinkled in disgust.

"I don't have a cat," said Eve.

"Then it could be gas," said Aguda.

"I don't have gas either." Then she frowned. "Mr Elias has gas . . ."

Joe banged hard on Mr Elias's front door, but there was no answer.

No lights were on, even though it was already dark outside.

Eve peered through the letter box and shouted his name, but heard nothing in return. A shiver ran up the back of her skull as she spotted loops of golden piano wire spilling from a pile of splintered wood in a doorway off the hall.

"Stand clear," said Aguda, and pulled out her gun.

Eve quickly put her good finger in her ear, but Aguda didn't fire. Instead she smashed the front window.

The stench of gas spilled out.

"Stay here," said Aguda, and switched on her torch. "No sparks!" Then she cleared the frame with a few swift swipes of the barrel of her gun, and dived head-first into the house.

The room looked as if a bomb had already gone off in it. Mr Elias was lying on his side on the destroyed sofa, unconscious. With a grunt, Aguda heaved him on to her shoulders and then tipped him through the window to safety.

"Get him away from the house!"

She didn't wait to make sure she was obeyed. She checked her watch. Twelve minutes to go.

The beam of her torch was narrow and the house was torn up, so it was hard to see what was what. If there was a bomb, she wasn't going to find it unless it was very big, and labelled BOMB. So instead of searching for it, Aguda started to throw open doors and windows, running from room to room, trying desperately to empty the house of gas so that the explosion, when it came, might not be so great.

Ten minutes.

The gas got her in the back of the throat and made her cough, but it wasn't at killing levels. That was good. It meant Mr Elias was probably still alive when she'd thrown him through the window — she hadn't stopped to check.

She had a coughing fit, as she dashed up the stairs to check the bedrooms for Duncan Singer. Or anyone.

There was nobody there.

Eight minutes.

Aguda had done all she could. She yanked open the front door and ran up the garden path.

"He'll be OK," said Joe.

They were kneeling in the snow outside the gate. Joe had peeled the tape from around Mr Elias's head, and once the gag had been removed from his mouth, his colour had started to come back.

They could hear approaching sirens.

"We need to get away from the houses," said Aguda, skidding to a breathless halt beside them. "Over the road!"

"But what about Dad?"

"He's not in there, Eve. I checked. I'm sorry."

Aguda and Joe got Mr Elias to his feet and supported him as they crossed the road to the red phone box.

Eve looked at her watch.

Seven minutes to go.

"Shit!" she said. "*Munchkin!*"

Before anyone could stop her, she turned and dashed back inside. Munchkin was waiting for her, up on his hind legs accusingly.

"Did you think I'd forgotten you?" she said. "Well, I *had!*"

And she leaned and scooped him up in her good hand and popped him in her pocket.

"There were birds in the sky . . ."

Eve froze. Then slowly turned her head towards the song.

"But I never saw them winging . . ."

"Dad?"

It was her father's voice. That old song he used to sing to her mother in the car. So clear and yet so far that it was like a magical memory, buried deep inside her own head.

"There were bells on a hill . . ."

A heart-ache of a tune and timeless words. And a simple acoustic guitar —

"Oh my God!" she shouted. "He's in the attic!"

Eve took the stairs two at a time, so fast that it was more like flying. In the box room she looked up, panting, and felt the blood drain from her heart.

It was there — on the hatch.

EXHIBITION
Venue: Here
Date: Today
Time: 16.00

Eve looked at her watch.
She had four minutes.

CHAPTER
FIFTY-FOUR

Only one of Eve's hands was useful and it was the wrong one.

The hook on the end of the long wooden pole wouldn't go through the eye in the hatch for what felt like *days*! Eve's eyes were so blurred by desperate tears and her hand so shaky that she couldn't keep the bloody thing still!

Finally it hit home, and she yanked the ladder down, threw aside the pole and clambered awkwardly up the rickety wooden steps.

The stink of gas was much worse up here.

"Dad!"

Duncan Singer looked at her in surprise. He was sat on a box in the dark, with his guitar on his knees and a phone on his chest that counted down the last minutes of his life in glowing green numbers:

00:03:17 . . . 16 . . . 15 . . .

Eve scrambled across the rough planking and hugged him, and a single great sob of relief escaped her.

Old relief, new panic.

"Dad, we have to get out of here." She took his hand and tried to pull him to his feet, but he didn't budge.

"Who's Dad?" he said blankly.

That was why he hadn't answered her earlier. Of course! He never knew he was Dad.

"Da — Duncan," she said. "We have to go! Hurry!"

"I'm busy," he said, tapping the guitar. "I'm doing important work for the government."

"But there's a bomb in the house!"

"I know," he said, looking at his own chest. "Three minutes to go!"

"Duncan, you have to come with me or we're both going to *die*!"

She grabbed his hand again, but he shook her off.

"You go on ahead," he said. "And your mother and I will catch you up."

"Don't —"

Eve almost cried. She almost gave up. She almost did. She almost just left him and ran.

00:02:22 . . . 21 . . . 20 . . .

Eve looked around desperately for inspiration. The attic was just as she'd last seen it, except for a pile of rubble that had been part of the wall between their attic and Mr Elias's. Her mother's books were newly covered in brick-dust.

Seeing those books made her ache for the people they used to be. No wonder Duncan's mind had taken refuge in the past. Everything was easier there.

Not everything, she thought suddenly.

"Duncan," she said firmly. "Mrs Cole's electrics have gone."

"Oh no!" he said, and put down the guitar. "I only just rewired that house!"

"I know!" she said. "Hell of a job!"

He stood up a little shakily and walked towards her in the darkness. All she could see were those glowing green numbers: 00:01:55 . . . 54 . . . 53 . . .

She went down the ladder so fast she nearly fell, wincing every time her injured hand touched anything.

"Where are we going?"

She looked up. Duncan had stopped near the top of the ladder.

"Mrs Cole's. The wiring. Hurry!"

"Who's Mrs Cole?"

Eve looked up at her father in horror. He'd *never* forgotten Mrs Cole. Not once! Mrs Cole had been a constant in their lives for three long years — a touchstone she could always rely on to connect her to Duncan. And now, just when she needed her most, Mrs Cole had dropped from the crumbling edifice of her father's brain like a chunk of falling masonry.

Eve reached up and grabbed his trouser cuff and tried to drag him down the ladder, but he tried to pull away and climb back into the attic.

"Daddy! Duncan! *Please!* I don't want to die and I don't want you to die, so we *have to get out of here!*"

But her father looked down at her without recognition or understanding in his eyes, and Eve saw the numbers on the timer turn red.

One minute to go.

She yanked him off the ladder. He landed on top of her and she shoved him off her. He was dazed and winded. She didn't care. She didn't care if he'd broken every bone in his body. She gripped her father's arm and dragged him down the landing to the top of the stairs.

"Joe!"

Joe grabbed Duncan and slung him over his shoulder like a pig off to market.

"Get out!" he yelled. "Get *out!*"

And she did. They all did. They went downstairs and out of the house and into the Christmas-card street, where fairytale decorations were joined by the flashing blue lights of two fire engines coming slowly down College Road.

Joe put Duncan down at the garden gate and between them they led him off the kerb and between cars, towards the blood-red phone box where Mr Elias was standing and breathing and alive, beside Emily Aguda.

So what if the house blew up? It wasn't important. They'd got out! They'd made it by the skin of their teeth, but they were all alive and that was all that mattered —

"Eve! *EVE!*"

Suddenly Aguda was running and shouting, "Get down! *GET DOWN!*" And pointing.

But not at *her.*

At her *father.*

Eve turned to look at Duncan.

And it was only then — under the silver puddle of street light — that she saw he was *wearing* the bomb.

CHAPTER
FIFTY-FIVE

"Eve! *RUN!*"

It was the only thing to do.

But Eve didn't do it.

The red numbers ran down.

13 . . . 12 . . . 11 . . .

Joe had her arm, but Eve didn't move at all. Not even her heart. It stopped, and she actually felt the absence of beats.

Instead she stood and looked stupidly at the bomb that was strapped around her father's waist with brown packing tape. Wires and switches and connectors and a grey block of what she assumed was plastic explosive. Hidden first by the guitar, and then by the dark, and then by her own mad panic.

She couldn't outrun it.

Facing it wouldn't help.

8 . . . 7 . . . 6 . . .

"Eve!" Joe pleaded. But he didn't let go of her.

Eve lived a thousand lifetimes in the eternity between second six and second five, and replayed her decision a million more —

5 . . . 4 . . . 3 . . .

— and always came up with the same answer.

"I love you!" she said fiercely, and hugged her father as hard as she could.

He put his arms around her and said, "No seconds to go."

Eve never heard the bomb go off.

CHAPTER
FIFTY-SIX

Slowly, slowly, Eve Singer opened her eyes.

They were still in the snow in the middle of College Road. She looked down at the timer between them.

00:00:00

"It didn't go off," she said.

"I know," said Duncan as he stepped away from her. "I made it safe."

He held up two loose wires. Next to one was a little yellow sticker off a banana.

Fairtrade, it said.

"He made it safe?" said Joe, as he slowly opened his eyes. "He could have told us!"

Eve started to laugh.

Duncan smiled at them both. "Sometimes I just wish I could die too," he said, and Eve's laugh died on her lips.

"But not today," he said cheerfully. "Not today."

CHAPTER
FIFTY-SEVEN

Christmas Day

By order of Detective Sergeant Emily Aguda, Eve Singer saw in Christmas Day in an A&E department that was a lino purgatory of drunks, blood and vomit.

Her thumb was dislocated, and putting it back into its socket now that her adrenaline had worn off was even more painful than popping it out had been, but for some weird reason the NHS saw no need for a painkilling injection to complete the operation.

Finally, in the face of Eve's howls of pain, Aguda shouldered aside the tight-lipped nurse, opened a cupboard, found a syringe and a bottle and gave Eve a shot of morphine, right in front of the furious, frazzled junior doctor.

"I'm reporting you to your commanding officer," he yelled.

"And I'm reporting you to Hippocrates," she said calmly as she depressed the plunger. "So I win."

While Emily Aguda was being underestimated by the National Health Service, Huw Rees was sitting at his

396

desk in a near-empty office, watching the video footage found on the killer's cracked but functional iPhone.

Rees had had no compunction whatsoever in using the man's bloody thumbprint to unlock the phone before the corpse was zipped into a black bag. However, they had been unable to get it to a tech specialist before the timer ran out on the bomb that would have blown both houses sky high — if Eve Singer's crazy old father hadn't made it safe.

Thank goodness for Health and Safety training, thought Huw Rees for the first time *ever*.

He had come back to his office before exploring the phone any further, for the sake of privacy.

Thank God he had.

There were videos of all the victims.

They were too gruelling to watch, but he had to watch them anyway — sometimes sick, sometimes angry, sometimes jaw-achingly sad at the terror, the heart-rending pleas, and the casual theft of life.

They were all here, including the Tate footage of Eve Singer. He was appalled and impressed in equal measure.

Then there were two more victims he did not recognize. A girl throttled by her own scarf in a dark place; a young man shivering in his underwear, knee-deep in show and ignorance. Neither was poor Siobhan Mackie, but still, that was two more cases they would be able to clear — two more families who would have closure. There was a grim satisfaction in that, but Rees was in no mood to celebrate.

There were other videos. Not many. He ran through them in chronological order. Most were of the killer's mother — dead in her bed, at various stages of decay. Others showed nothing but dusty curtains in sunlight, or the exploded washing machine on the cherry-wood floor.

Hotpoint.

It was five in the morning before Huw Rees opened the last few videos.

They were all of Duncan Singer.

Rees shifted uncomfortably, dreading what was to come. What cruelties? What torture?

The first showed Duncan Singer walking slowly around the Hotpoint. Every now and then he would ask a question, or make an encouraging comment.

"The motor is quite lovely, isn't it?"

"My goodness, it's a crime to hide that drum away, don't you think?"

"They don't make them like this any more."

And after every comment, an answer from the killer, close to the microphone. Too loud. Distorted.

"It took ages to take it apart. I had to find all the right sockets."

"The drum's my favourite bit too. It's so shiny!"

"They're all plastic now."

Rees had never heard the killer's voice, but here, he sounded . . . *happy.* Like a boy being praised by a favourite teacher, he fairly *wriggled* with pleasure every time Mr Singer made a positive comment.

And that was all.

Rees played the next one.

The two of them sitting on the floor, cross-legged and opposite each other — the phone obviously propped somewhere nearby. Duncan was building something small and with wires.

Their heads almost touched.

It was harder to catch what they were saying this time, but again, the tones were of kindly master and humble pupil. Duncan using a screwdriver to point out something in his hand; Duncan asking for something; the killer going out of shot and coming back with a jar of nails —

It was the nail bomb that would have killed the first man in the attic on the day of the raid.

Duncan Singer had made it.

And doubtless disabled it, marking it with his trademark sticker.

Had he understood why? Had he known what he was doing — whom he was saving? Or did his safety-first instinct simply trump everything else?

The final video featuring Duncan showed him wearing the Christmas Day bomb, and explaining to Vandenberg some aspect of its operation.

Then Duncan climbed into a large cardboard box and the killer's hand came into shot as he closed the thick flaps over his head.

Then opened them again.

"*Helloo!*" said Duncan Singer, and waved, and the killer laughed the delighted laugh of a small boy who feels *special*.

Huw Rees remembered that same feeling vividly, and discovered a well of tears so deep that he had to blow them out of his nose.

"What's so sad?"

His heart nearly stopped.

Veronica Creed.

He hadn't heard her open the door. Hadn't heard her walk across the office. Didn't know how long she'd been standing there, watching.

And watching him watching.

"I've got a cold," he said brusquely.

Creed stared at him, unsmiling. Her jumper had a kitten on it, with a pom-pom of wool in high relief, like a purple tumour on her ribs.

"Is this the Vandenberg material?"

"Yes."

"I look forward to seeing it," she said.

That was exactly what Huw Rees was afraid of. He got up and took his jacket from the back of his chair. "Better be off," he said, hoping he sounded more confident than he felt. "Got to get home for the great unwrapping."

"Unwrapping?" she said, with her head on one side like a goblin.

"Christmas gifts," he said.

"Of course," she said.

Rees put the phone in his pocket. He noticed that she watched it all the way from the desk to its destination.

He reached the door and felt he ought to turn.

"Happy Christmas then, Mrs Creed."

"It's Ms," she said.

Huw Rees walked out of New Scotland Yard and into a Christmas Day so white that the bookies might never recover.

He looked at his watch. Seven a.m. Holly and Bronwyn would be up already, desperate to start on the gifts. Maureen would make them wait for him, so he'd better hurry up.

He walked to his car and got in and put the key in the ignition — and then fell asleep so fast and so hard that he didn't wake up until Christmas was over for another year.

CHAPTER
FIFTY-EIGHT

They had just finished Christmas dinner. They would have had leftover lasagne if it had been in the gift of Eve's freezer, but luckily Mr Elias insisted he had far too much food for one and, because the killer had emptied his freezer all over the kitchen floor, the turkey was even defrosted.

So they cooked Mr Elias's turkey and all his trimmings, and they pulled his crackers and drank his wine and ate his Christmas pudding. Eve felt a bit cheeky, but Mr Elias didn't seem to mind at all.

Then they opened the gifts they'd bought each other. Mr Elias gave Eve a little pot of white hyacinths that smelled of spring, while Joe gave her a hedge-trimmer.

"I don't know how to use it," she said archly.

"I do," he said.

Eve had got all her gifts from the one-stop shop at the station, which was open even on Christmas Day, thank goodness. It was surprising what you could find there, if you looked with the right eyes.

For Mr Elias, a calendar called Your Gardening Year; for Joe, a snow-globe bauble with a yeti inside it. She'd even found gobstoppers that looked like eyeballs, and had slipped one into her father's Christmas cracker.

"It's exactly what I wanted!" he shouted as it rolled across the tablecloth.

When it got late, Joe helped Eve to make up the bed in the box room for Mr Elias. Tomorrow she and Joe would go round and help him start clearing up the mess that the killer had left behind.

She thought she might owe him a piano.

And it hit her.

All of it.

Eve sat on the spare bed and cried and cried and cried.

Mr Elias made a tactful withdrawal to the bathroom, while Joe rocked Eve gently, until she was empty of tears.

"I really didn't expect to be alive today," she said on a final shuddering sigh.

"I'm really glad you are though," he said, pushing the damp, tear-stained hair out of her eyes.

"Me too," nodded Eve.

"And your dad, too."

"Me too," she nodded again. "I mean, I know he's not going to get any better . . . I know it'll be hard, and he's going to die *some time*, but losing him now . . ." she tailed off.

Joe nodded sombrely. Then he said, "Nobody dies who leaves beauty behind."

Eve blushed, and smiled at her hands in her lap. "That's lovely," she said. "Who said that?"

"I did," he grinned. "Just now." And he kissed her lightly on the lips.

"You're too young for me," she said, without conviction.

"No I'm not," he told her, and kissed her again. "See?"

"Oh yes," she nodded. "My mistake."

They said goodnight to Mr Elias and went back downstairs, where Duncan was still watching TV.

They sat on the sofa, touching all the way down from their shoulders to their knees, and with their hands newly intertwined.

There was no respite from *How It's Made*. In an anti-Christmas spectacular it was doing drinking straws, clogs and bicycle tyres.

"Have you seen this, Dad?" said Eve.

Duncan frowned. "Of course I have!" he said. "About fifty times!"

Red wine seemed to have resurrected his former self and made him more jovial, more grounded. Parts of his mind had gone on ahead, for sure, but there was so much of her father that was still *here*, and could be held and touched and cared for.

And Eve was grateful. She watched him watch TV — the gobstopper scrunched between his eyebrow and his cheekbone, which amused the hell out of him. Every now and then, he took it out and looked at it.

And it looked at him.

Then he licked it and put it back.

"Don't do that, Dad."

"Who's Dad?"

Eve rolled her eyes at Joe. "If he were immortal, I'd kill him!"

Finally Duncan began to snore.

Another episode of *How It's Made* began.

"*Jaws* is on BBC1," whispered Joe.

"*Perfect* Christmas film," Eve whispered back.

The remote control was still in Duncan's slack hand and Eve reached for it carefully, not wanting to wake him. He stirred and the sticky eyeball popped out and rolled down his jumper.

Joe giggled and Eve froze.

But then Duncan snored again, and she removed the remote with a surgical flourish. She pressed a button but nothing happened. She held the remote at a different angle but still nothing happened. She opened the battery compartment but the batteries were gone — in their place was a sticker that said *Buy One Get One Free!*

"Oh, what the hell!" laughed Eve. "Let's go to bed!"

And they did.

But first they had to push Duncan Singer up the stairs.

It was a lot easier with two of them.

Acknowledgements

Heartfelt gratitude to my agent Jane Gregory and editors, Frankie Gray, Sarah Adams, Stephanie Glencross and Amy Hundley for their patience, skill and good humour.

Thanks also to heart-transplant survivor and marathon man John Fisher at ttab.co.uk for his generous insight into the psychology and symptoms post-op and beyond. Keep on running . . .

Huw Rees won the right to be a named character in this book by means of a generous bid in an auction run by the charity Clic Sargent, who care for children affected by cancer and their families. Many thanks to him and to the underbidders who pushed the price up!